The Gamekeeper

BARRY HINES

With an introduction by
John Berger

SHEFFIELD – LONDON – NEW YORK

This edition published in 2022 by And Other Stories
Sheffield – London – New York
www.andotherstories.org

The Gamekeeper and quoted letter copyright © Barry Hines, 1975

The Gamekeeper first published in 1975 by Michael Joseph

Introduction ('The Storyteller's Position') and quoted letter
copyright © John Berger, 1975, and John Berger Estate

1 3 5 7 9 8 6 4 2

ISBN: 9781913505301
eBook ISBN: 9781913505318

Proofreader: Alex Middleton; Cover Design: Tom Etherington, from the print 'Midwinter,
North Yorkshire' by Norman Ackroyd, used with permission. Typeset in Albertan Pro and
Syntax by Tetragon, London. Printed and bound on acid-free, age-resistant Munken Premium
by CPI Limited, Croydon, UK. And Other Stories would like to thank Tom Overton for
sending us his transcriptions of 'The Storyteller's Position' and the letters between John
Berger and Barry Hines, as well as to thank Sue Vice and David Forrest, authors of *Barry
Hines: Kes, Threads and Beyond*, for their book and their research in the Hines Papers.

And Other Stories gratefully acknowledge that our work is supported
using public funding by Arts Council England.

Supported using public funding by
**ARTS COUNCIL
ENGLAND**

MIX
Paper from
responsible sources
FSC® C171272

THE
GAMEKEEPER

CONTENTS

The Storyteller's Position – Introduction by John Berger   7

THE GAMEKEEPER   13

Acknowledgements   301

The Storyteller's Position

> He stood on the doorstep and banged the boots together, and segments of dried earth fell from the tread of their soles like typeset from a tray. The noise woke up the dogs in their pen, and they appeared from their kennel in slow procession, the springer spaniel, the black labrador and the cross-bred terrier, stretching and snuffling, and yawning clouds into the cold morning air.

Most published novels are a more intimate form of soap opera. Hines's *The Gamekeeper* is more like a handbook, a manual.

The text, undivided by chapters, covers a year of a gamekeeper's life or, rather, of the work which determines his life. Because this work follows the seasons, when we reach the end we are back at the beginning.

The gamekeeper, aged about 40, is married with two sons. Previously he was a steelworker. (The setting is probably Yorkshire.) Long before the book begins, he has left the steelworks to become one of the Duke's half dozen gamekeepers. He is independent-minded; he feels good out of doors; he likes dogs and is fascinated by wildlife. His choice was towards a relatively larger freedom.

But the purpose of his life's work now, with no holidays and less leisure than before, is absurd. He breeds and protects pheasants so that the Duke and six or seven of his associates can shoot 300 birds in a couple of days. Shoot and do nothing else. They do not carry or load their own guns; they do not walk; they do not train their dogs. They aim and pull the triggers. And they are not anachronisms: they are men of very considerable modern power.

To ensure these powerful men their few hours of amusement, the gamekeeper daily throughout the year – and sometimes at night – pursues poachers; intimidates kids bird-nesting or picking flowers; lays traps; ferrets rabbits; kills crows and magpies; shoots foxes; hatches the pheasants in incubators or under broody hens; feeds them absolutely regularly; administers medicine to them; releases them and watches over them so that on the prescribed day they can be driven by men with sticks towards the little line of trigger pullers.

Such is the absurdity of his chosen life. He recognizes the absurdity. Yet he accepts it and in no way allows it to undermine his singlemindedness and efficiency as a gamekeeper. He gives himself over – just as the writing gives itself over – to all the practical tasks at hand:

> The gamekeeper removed the spade and placed the ferret at the entrance to the hole. He did not rush around to relieve his confinement, or dash straight down the burrow. He just stood there for a moment, extended his head, snake like, to confirm the judgement of the dog, then calmly walked into the dark. There was nothing extravagant about his movement. Yet he was all the more dangerous for his calm.

Marginally, in the vitality of some of the wild birds or animals around him the gamekeeper deposits his minimal belief that life has another dimension.

> While the gamekeeper was on his rounds, and the boys were raking the rearing field, the pheasants inside the first incubator were starting to hatch. Cushioned in their sacs of water, protected by their shells, they had been growing for twenty-three days, and now they filled their shells. They stirred, they had to peck their way out, through the membrane, through the shell.

This is a book that borders on despair. No emotions or feelings are described in it. The near-despair resides in the contrast between the practicality of everything described and the unproductivity of the final outcome. A near-despair with a profoundly proletarian origin.

To assess the book, one must interrogate its meanings. The meaning of its method: in place of the endlessly exchanged opinions and constantly fluctuating feelings of the middle-class novel, it substitutes jobs, causes and effects. Its social meaning: without explicit judgement it shows the difference between the lives of privileged and underprivileged. Its philosophical meaning: it describes a 'world' in which the ruling class has succeeded in recycling nature, the game of the woods and moors has been proletarianized, it is fed and housed so as to produce the maximum surplus value – which, in this case, is the number of brace 'in the bag'.

The book also invents its own meaning which is stronger than any other and which Hines probably calculated less. This is the meaning of the gamekeeper's solitude and the relation of this solitude to the will-to-live of animals. Here, I suspect, is where Hines's heart and obsession as a writer reside. His earlier novel *A Kestrel for a Knave* was also about such a relationship. It is very rare to know and write about animals as well as he does in narrative form. To do so may well require a deep experience of solitude. The only modern writer I would compare Hines with, in this respect, is Louis Pergaud, who was killed in the First World War.

Applying the highest standards and bearing these meanings in mind how should his new book be assessed? The thirty-page description of the grouse shoot on 12 August is unforgettable. So are other shorter passages. But the whole may be flawed. The signs of the flaw are very few: they all imply an uncertainty about the storyteller's exact position in relation to the story he is telling:

'What's up with you this time, John?'

John looked at his stomach, then marked its position with his hand.

'I've got a stomach-ache.'

The gamekeeper levelled a forkful of egg at him. The portion of white, hanging over the prongs, looked as languid as a Dalí watch.

'Stomach-ache my arse. You're telling lies again, John . . .'

The reference to Dalí shatters the integrity of the scene. It belongs neither to narrator nor narrated.

Occasionally he allows an animal a time-sense which is sentimental: 'The grouse were accustomed to mists, and for them, this was a day just like any other day.' The comparison with any other day is false. Throughout the book there are maybe a dozen slips like this. Apparently unimportant except that the book concerns extreme technical rigour. But even so unimportant in themselves. Important only as signs of why a strength which should one day be there in a book by this writer is not yet there.

These slips suggest that Hines is not sure of his story. Yet he evidently is master of its content. So if he is not sure, it is probably because he is *using* the story, treating it as a means, not accepting it as an end. Occasionally he appeals over the edge of the story he is telling.

I can only guess why. I think Hines sees no way out. He lives with a sense of historical hopelessness. 'Ar, well, there's nowt we can do about that, George.' In the animal world situations of 'hopelessness' are redeemed by the animals' unawareness and instinctive and ferocious struggle to survive. In return for his empathy, Hines borrows this redemption from the animal world and it consoles him. But the consolation risks turning the story into a means. Hence his unsureness.

Finally animals lead any close observer into metaphysics.

One day Hines will have to write about why women and men need hope. Whether he then sees that need with full despair or with support, nobody but Barry Hines can decide. But when he writes with complete conviction about his position as story-teller – because the story is sufficient to the truth which he must write – he may well produce a great book. Meanwhile this is an outstanding one, which I read with admiration.

—*John Berger*, 1975

11

EDITOR'S NOTE ON
'THE STORYTELLER'S POSITION' BY JOHN BERGER

Never before published, the text above by John Berger, here published in full, is in the Hines Papers at the University of Sheffield's Special Collections, where it is accompanied by a letter dated 6 November 1975 from John Berger to Barry Hines, in which Berger says:

> I read *The Gamekeeper* with excitement and much admiration. I asked to review it for *New Society* – and then wrote the enclosed. They cut it in an imbecile way – pruning out all the reasoning, drawing only an *opinion*. (The reduction of intellectuals to opinion-taps is one of the small ways in which the system ensures its continuity.) So I refused to let them publish it. But I thought you might like to see it – so I enclose it.

Whatever Hines' thoughts about the review not being published may have been, he replied on 27 November 1975, in a letter now in the John Berger Archive at the British Library: 'What was warming for me was that at last somebody knew what I was on about. You actually talked in details about the politics of the book.'

THE
GAMEKEEPER

The countryside is the stronghold of most myths about free enterprise, independence, self-reliance, but it may be, in the end, that the wheel will turn full circle – that the common land which was grabbed and enclosed by the landlords in the eighteenth century will be given back to the public, and that the whole land of Britain will come to seem so precious that the public will insist on having it for themselves.

ANTHONY SAMPSON
The New Anatomy of Britain

February. It was time to catch up the pheasants.

George Purse bent down and picked up his boots from a news-paper which his wife had put down to keep the mud off the kitchen floor. Holding the boots in one hand he unlocked the kitchen door and stepped outside to put them on.

He stood on the doorstep and banged the boots together, and segments of dried earth fell from the tread of their soles like typeset from a tray. The noise woke up the dogs in their pen, and they appeared from their kennel in slow procession, the springer spaniel, the black labrador and the cross-bred terrier, stretching and snuffling, and yawning clouds into the cold morning air. The terrier was awake first. He rolled over and rubbed his back hard against the concrete floor, simultaneously kicking his back legs into the air as though trying to brace them against something solid. Growling with pleasure, he practised a few bites at nothing in particular, then he jumped up and shook himself so vigorously that he went stiff-legged and his pads kept vibrating from the floor.

George Purse sat down on the bench underneath the kitchen window to fasten up his boots. Overnight, the leather laces had dried stiff, and although this made them easy to thread, it made them difficult to knot when he reached the top. Cursing the laces softly and passionately, he tugged hard and managed to tie a double bow in each one. But the knots had not jelled, there were spaces between them, and when he stood up, his head aching from bending over, his fingertips sore and already feeling the cold, it looked as though he had finally solved the problem with a couple of Chinese puzzles.

He looked up at the sky; it was a habit, a reflex action. What happened in the sky was important to gamekeepers. The weather and the birds which occupied the sky above their territories were important factors in their work. There was only one bird up there, a lapwing flying upwind, its broad supple wings carrying it easily through the north-east wind. George Purse saw it, identified it and forgot it. He was not interested in lapwings. They did not interfere with his work. Lapwings were not enemies of game.

He walked across the yard to let the dogs out for a run while he collected grain and water to feed the pheasants. The dogs were waiting for him at the door of the pen. He did not have to open it. As soon as he removed the lock they pushed their noses into the crack by the jamb and sent the door crashing back on its hinges. George Purse cursed them as they rushed past his legs. They came out in this way every morning, and he cursed them for it every morning. He inspected the hinges. They were still firm, but the jamb was splitting vertically above the top one.

The dogs sniffed and cocked their legs at familiar corners, then the springer and the labrador got their noses down and worked over the whole of the yard. The terrier just ran about wildly with his hackles up, barking. He kept running at the other dogs, jumping at them and growling at their throats. The labrador ignored him. He just stood still, lifted his head out of the way and looked about him until the irritant went away.

But the spaniel was less patient. He would tolerate two or three of these mock attacks then retaliate, snapping and snarling the terrier into yelping submission on his back, pink belly exposed, front paws together at his chin. Dominance reasserted, the springer continued to quarter the yard. The terrier just jumped up and started all over again. This was what he was bred for, fighting. He was just as obdurate when put down a fox's earth. Sometimes he would come tumbling out yelping with pain, an ear torn, his face gashed, or a patch of hair ripped from his back; but after a quick examination by the gamekeeper to check that the wounds were only superficial, he was always willing to run back to the blind fight down the stinking burrow.

The labrador and the spaniel having systematically worked the ground between the outhouses and the cottage, left the yard and started to work in amongst the trees at the edge of the wood. The gamekeeper let the hens out into the yard, then unlocked the stable door of the adjoining outhouse, where he kept his feed and all the tools of his profession except for his guns.

He pulled open both doors to let the light in, and the clean whitewashed walls of the interior reflected the light, held it, and made it bright enough to use. The room was immaculate. Every object had its place.

Sacks of dog meal, hen meal and grain for the pheasants were stacked beneath the bench along the back wall. On the bench there was a box trap and two folded ferret bags, and on a shelf above the bench stood cans of vermin poison, and other cans and bottles containing medicine for pheasants.

Through the years, a succession of gamekeepers had hammered nails and hooks into the walls on which to hang their equipment. Some of these pegs had worked loose and were fragile through corrosion, and during his ten years at the job George Purse had knocked in several six-inch nails of his own. From one nail hung a selection of leather collars, leashes and rabbit skin dummies used in the training of gun dogs. From another, a dozen wire snares. A bunch of Fenn traps, suspended tautly by their chains, threatened their hook with extraction, and next to them, carefully coiled and tied, a long net, used for rabbiting. The gamekeeper's waterproofs were hung directly above his wellington boots. On another nail hung a keep net and a fishing rod in its canvas sheath; and on the flagstones, beneath these nails, stood three buckets, two oil lamps, and in one corner, a rabbiting spade with a sharp worn blade.

The gamekeeper pulled open the mouth of a sack of grain, then fetched a bucket and started to ladle grain into it with an old enamelled jug. Load after load of teeming grain until the bucket was almost full. Then, there was such a squawk from outside that it made him jump, he jerked the jug, and grain spilled on to the floor. Furious, he hurried to the door.

The sight of the hens had been too much for the terrier. He had approached one, it had shied away, therefore he had been forced to chase it. When the gamekeeper reached the door of the outhouse the hen was still winning, just. Neck out, squawking, it strained forward with flailing wings. But its weight was unevenly distributed, the bulk of it was too far back for serious sprinting, and its action was merely a preliminary to taking off; which it did, every time the terrier snapped at its tail.

Each flight lasted two or three flaps, then it plumped down in a brown flurry and strode on again before the terrier could force it down and get its jaws across its back.

The gamekeeper let out such a roar after the terrier, the results of which could not have been more immediate if the reprimand had been physical. The terrier stopped the chase, looked back over his shoulder, then trotted away, eyes rolling for fear of something worse. It was time to join the other dogs in the wood. He would be safer distinguishing the scents of night visitors, and grumbling at their smells amongst the frozen leaves beneath the trees.

The racket had awakened the gamekeeper's wife and children. The two boys looked out, then eased their way further into their warm beds. They knew by the degree of light in the bedroom that it was not yet time to get up for school. The gamekeeper's wife tried to stay awake. She had to get up. Her husband would expect his breakfast to be ready when he returned from feeding the pheasants.

Before he left the yard with his bucket of grain and can of water the gamekeeper put the dogs away. He never took them with him when he went to feed the pheasants. He always went alone. It made the job easier. He could have made the dogs sit at a safe distance. And they would have sat. They would have sat until the frost stiffened their fur if he had asked them to. But without them there was less chance of the unpredictable; a sudden rabbit, a chase, panic amongst the pheasants and possible desertion from the covert.

He called the dogs from the edge of the wood and held open the pen door for them to go in. The labrador and the springer came straight away and walked in. The terrier appeared reluctant to pass him, and he had to threaten it before it would come. Then it sidled up to the door, pretending not to look at him. He knew what it was going to do, and when it did rush past him, he was ready for it, and able to time a boot up the arse to help it on its way. He locked the door and looked at the split in the wood again.

'The buggers,' he said.

The gamekeeper picked up the bucket of grain and the watering can and walked across the yard towards the path which led to the feeding ride in the wood.

The smallholding was built in a clearing at the edge of the wood. The gamekeeper's cottage faced outwards across arable land. Three fields away was the main road, which marked the boundary of the Duke's estate, and across the road stood the houses and maisonettes of a new council estate. The back of the cottage faced the yard, and the outhouses, and directly behind them, the wood.

It was quiet amongst the trees. The loudest noise came from the gamekeeper's boots crushing frost, and fracturing twigs and rigid blades of grass. As he walked he looked about him and listened. He was looking for signs of trespass; a partly eaten rabbit, a bunch of feathers or undergrowth flattened by poachers and their dogs. He was concerned with these signs, not out of compassion for the victims, but out of professional necessity to discover the killer. A rat? a fox? a stoat? a feral cat? or just a dog on the prowl? What could kill a rabbit or a woodpigeon, could do the same to a pheasant or a partridge. Whatever it was, it was an enemy of game.

As he walked he listened for bird calls. He did not know many birds by their songs. He had never had the patience to stand with binoculars and watch a bird singing, then imprint the sight and the sound so that next time he heard those notes he could name the bird without looking for it. He knew them all by sight. He knew their flight, their habits and their habitat. On his rounds in the woods and fields he found their nests, their young and sometimes their bodies. He liked song birds. He did them no harm. They were not enemies of game.

The crow family was. Their harsh notes made him look upwards immediately. The rook and the crow, the magpie, jay and jackdaw were the gamekeeper's enemies. They sucked eggs and ate pheasant chicks. They had to be destroyed.

But walking through the wood on this dun-coloured morning, the gamekeeper heard no crows and saw no suspicious signs. He heard the high bare branches combing the wind, and he saw a blue-tit searching the wrinkled bark of an elm tree for food. Nothing more.

Before he reached the end of the path, which formed a T-junction with the feeding ride, the gamekeeper started to whistle; a staccato, one-note affair, repeated over and over. It was a functional sound, he could have been whistling a dog. But the pheasants hidden in the undergrowth, already alerted by the footfalls, now knew whom to expect. The reared birds had been fed to that whistle from birth, and the wild birds had also learned to recognize that it meant food.

When he reached the end of the path, the gamekeeper could hear the pheasants scuttling around under the rhododendron bushes which lined the ride. Along the centre of the ride he had spread thick litters of straw. A car tyre had been sliced in half to provide two drinking vessels, and close by these feeding points, slatted boxes had been positioned ready for catching up the game.

The pheasants watched him from the cover of the evergreens. The overlapping leaves formed dense green canopies. It was dark and safe under there.

First, the gamekeeper refilled the drinking vessels. There was still water in them from the previous day, but it had been fouled, so he turned both tyres over and emptied them. He reverted the tyres, then refilled them from the watering can, pouring until the water overflowed and slid down the sides, making the rubber as shiny as seals.

He did not have to water the birds. There were numerous drinking places close to the wood. There were the drains and ditches around the fields. There were the two ornamental lakes, and the old fish ponds which used to supply the Big House. But George Purse looked after his pheasants; by watering in covert he minimized the temptation to wander. By keeping them close to home, they were less available to poachers who might be stalking the hedges and fields. His job was to keep the birds alive for the official killers, not to provide a meal for a fox, or a trespasser with a gun.

The gamekeeper picked up the bucket and began to walk along the ride, whistling as he broadcast handfuls of grain. He did not throw the food on to the mat of trodden leaves where the pheasants could easily see it; he threw it into the litters of straw where it immediately disappeared from sight. This was to make the pheasants work for their food, to make them scratch about and search the straw, to prolong their meal and keep them occupied. If the grain were just thrown on to the ground, the pheasants would quickly eat their fill, and then be off, foraging along the hedgerows, and across the nearby meadows.

The straw also made it difficult for other woodland birds to get at the buried grain. Gamekeepers use various feeding methods to try to keep the food exclusively for their pheasants. Some use hoppers made from cleaned-out oil drums. They cut three or four vertical strips near the bottom of the drums and stand them up on two bricks. The slits are just wide enough to allow the grain to trickle out when it is pecked by the pheasants. They make sure that the bricks do not protrude from underneath the oil drums, or other birds might perch there and scrounge a meal.

There are variations on this hopper. An inverted screw-topped drum can be used, with a small grille like a letterbox built into the lid. The drum is then secured to a post or tree at a height which allows the pheasants to walk underneath it and feed by pecking upwards, so that the grain trickles through the wire mesh. This precludes all small birds from feeding.

Birds of the crow family can be discouraged by hanging the body of a dead rook over the hopper, but even this draconian measure does not deter finches and sparrows, which when hungry, still try their best to eat.

The gamekeeper threw several handfuls of grain into the rhododendrons, and it rattled on their leaves like hailstones. He scattered food in and around the catchers, so that the pheasants, to whom these slatted boxes were as familiar as the bushes and the trees, would step through the doorways and feed contentedly inside.

The following morning, after he had baited the catchers, he inserted wire-netting funnels into the doorways. Then he picked up his bucket and watering can and returned home through the wood, leaving the pheasants feeding busily on the ride.

Some of the birds worked their way around the catchers, pecking and scratching for the grain amongst the leaves. They poked their heads between the slats to get at any grain they could reach inside, and then they approached the doorway to go in. But they balked at the funnel, they were unfamiliar with it. They strutted around the entrance, eyeing it. Some poked their heads into the funnel, and some even had a peck at the wire. But they would not go in to feed.

But, during the morning, when there was no grain left in the shrubbery, and it was hard work finding it in the straw, one hen pheasant ventured down one of the funnels for easy pickings inside. And during the afternoon, a second hen entered another one.

Once they were inside, and they had eaten all the grain, they did not know how to get out. They strode around the boxes poking their heads out between the slats. They jumped on and off the funnel, and occasionally tried to explode their way out by flying. One thing they did not do was walk out through the funnel, the way they had come in.

And they were both still there the next morning, when the gamekeeper arrived with his sack to carry any captured birds back to the laying pen.

The pheasants panicked as he approached the catchers. They ran two strides back. They pushed their heads between the bars as far as they would go, eyes staring, necks so taut that spaces appeared between the feathers, and the skin on their necks was visible. Then, as they withdrew their necks the bars backcombed the feathers, and they overlapped into place like a row of dominoes going down.

But the gamekeeper did not allow them to dash around for long, he did not want the birds to injure themselves. Injured pheasants were no good for breeding. He quickly bent down at one of the catchers, lifted it high enough to slot his other hand underneath and grabbed the bird across the back, clamping its wings to its sides. He stood up, holding the brown mottled hen in both hands to examine it for signs of disease or injury before placing it in the sack.

Its eyes were big and bright. It was well-feathered, and when the gamekeeper stroked one hand firmly down its back, the bloom came up on the plumage. He scuffed up the breast feathers to look for lice on the skin, spread both wings to examine the flights, then checked the legs and toes. He nodded. It had passed its medical; it was fit to breed. He opened the mouth of the sack and placed it inside. It would be quiet in there, it would not panic in the dark.

The laying pen had been built in line with the gamekeeper's cottage and allotment, along the boundary fence which separated the wood from the fields. It had been sited in the clearing so that the pheasants could get the sunshine, yet it was still close enough to the wood for the trees to take the sting out of the cold winds which blew from the north and the east.

The pen was made of rolls of wire netting six foot high, which had been nailed to posts spaced out to cover an area the size of a tennis court. Sheets of corrugated iron had been laid end to end around the bottom of the pen to give further protection from the wind and the rain. The more protection the pheasants received, the more reliable the egg production would be. Clumps of evergreen and conifer branches had been placed around the pen, some in the grassy central space, others

27

against the corrugated iron walls. These branches formed little tunnels and retreats, which provided necessary privacy and cover for the birds.

The laying pen had no roof. A roof was unnecessary because the pheasants would be unable to fly out. They would have one wing brailed before they were put into the pen.

The gamekeeper put the sack down in the yard, and walked across to the outhouse where he kept his tackle. As he opened the door he turned round and called across to the house,

'John!'

He stood poised to enter the building, waiting for an answer.

'John!'

'What?'

'Come here! I want you to give me a hand with these pheasants!'

'I'm having my breakfast!'

'Now! You can finish your breakfast when we've done!'

He went inside and walked across to the bench. He seized the knob of the middle drawer and yanked it. It did not budge, and this immobility jerked him forward against the bench. He tried again, this time bracing his left hand against the bench, and flexing his knees, his force directly in line with the pull. The wood squealed. He pulled again. He could now get hold of the sides of the drawer with his thumbs inside, and, jerking it from side to side, he fought it open.

The drawer contained the leather brails and tapes, which the gamekeeper fastened to the pheasants' wings to prevent them flying out of the laying pen. He had checked the numbers and the condition of the brails the previous week, but apart from that occasion the drawer had not been opened for months, and the wood had swollen with the winter damp. The gamekeeper

28

picked out two brails and half a dozen paper fasteners, left the drawer open, and went out into the yard.

Two boys were crouching over the sack. Ian, the youngest one, was just untying the string to peep inside.

'That's it, Ian. Let the buggers out.'

Ian left the string alone, and both boys quickly stood up and stepped away from the sack.

'We were only having a look, Dad.'

'You'd have been having a look at summat else, if they'd have got out and taken off.'

Both boys were quiet, and thought about this. And although the threat remained unspecified, they were glad that the two pheasants had not escaped.

'Anyway, Ian, you go back inside. I only want our John.'

The seven-year-old ran back a few paces, to where he could enjoy a tantrum in relative safety.

'It's not fair. I don't want to go in. I want to watch. I want to watch, Dad!'

His wellingtons, his brother's cast-offs, were too big for him, and when he jumped up and down they scarcely left the flag-stones. His father advanced on him, and it was surprising how well-fitting his footwear suddenly became. Safe again, near the house, he began to stamp one foot, and his leg, sliding in and out of the wellington, was reminiscent of a bicycle pump at work.

The gamekeeper turned away from him and went back to the sack, where John was still waiting.

'The young bugger. I'll tan his arse for him when I get hold of him.' He bent down at the sack and looked up at John.

'I'll get 'em out for you, John. You know how to hold 'em don't you? Firm, but don't squeeze 'em to death.'

29

John nodded. He knew what to do. They had moved here ten years ago when he was two. He had been brought up handling animals. He knew how to handle them when they were alive, and when they were dead.

His father untied the sack, reached inside and had one of the pheasants out before the other bird realized that there had been any chance of escape. He gave it to John, who took it cleanly, with both hands spread across its back to keep its wings closed. The hen pheasant looked big in the boy's hands, and he had to hold it close to his chest to take some of the weight off his arms.

The gamekeeper took one of the brails out of his jacket pocket and prepared to attach it to the bird's left wing. A brail is a leather fastener with two short straps and one long strap. All three straps have holes punched in them like a belt.

'Right, John, let's have hold of its wing.'

John shifted his grip to release the pheasant's left wing. His father took hold of it, wrapped the two short straps around the bird's wing just above its elbow, checked this loop for tightness, then pushed a paper fastener through the appropriate holes to secure it. This left the long strap hanging loose. He passed it underneath the bird's wing, slotted it up between the end two flight feathers, then bent it back to meet the other two straps, and fastened them all together with the paper clip. It was like putting the pheasant's wing into a sling. It stopped it from straightening its elbow, which meant that it could not fly.

The gamekeeper tried to bend the sharp ends of the paper fastener under the metal head to complete the job, but his big cold fingers did not have the necessary fine touch. During the operation on the bird he had not noticed that Ian had crept up close again to watch, and when he suddenly turned round and shouted his name, the little lad thought he was going to cop it again, and he started to cry.

The gamekeeper laughed at the way he had startled the boy.

'O, you're there are you? Well, stop roaring, and go and fetch me them little pliers from the outhouse.'

Ian was away across the yard, as fast as his slobbing welling-tons would carry him. He was still small enough to go through the bottom half of the stable door and leave the top half closed.

There was the grind of a drawer being opened; then the sound of objects being moved around.

'And I don't want the pincers, or owt daft like that, Ian! I want them little pliers with the pointed ends!'

He underestimated the boy. Ian knew what he wanted. He knew the difference between pliers and pincers, and he quickly found the right tool.

'Wonders'll never cease,' was all his father said when Ian handed them over. He bent the sharp ends of the paper fastener neatly under the metal head, checked the brail to make sure that the pheasant's wing was not completely immobilized, then told John to take it up to the laying pen.

When John opened the wire-netting door and put the pheas-ant down, it ran away from him and tried to take off. Its right wing lifted it into the air, but without assistance from the other one, it overbalanced and came down on its left side. John stood in the doorway and watched a whole series of these lopsided take offs and landings. He did not laugh at the bird's failure to fly; he watched its efforts seriously, concerned at its plight. He wanted to wait there until the bird had settled down, but his father called him away to help him brail the second pheasant.

When it was done, Ian wanted to carry the bird up to the

laying pen. His father said he would drop it. The little boy immediately began his dance, but this time, having overestimated his bargaining power on the strength of the successful pliers errand, he did not retreat first, and immediately received a skelp across the back of his head.

He ran across the yard, and into the house, crying. John carried the second pheasant up to the laying pen. But he had not time to stand and watch it, for he was immediately called away by his father for school.

When they got into the house, Ian was sulking. He would not look at anybody, and he was not talking either. He was sitting at his place at the kitchen table with his head down, taking it out of the fried egg on his plate. He attacked the yolk so viciously with his bread, that he even destroyed the yellow clot at the bottom, leaving the egg a mere raggedy-ruff beside the untouched rasher of bacon. He pushed the mess away from him and started to climb down.

At the sound of the plate sliding, and the chair legs scraping against the tiles, his mother turned away from the stove to see how much he had eaten. When she saw, she stayed his action with one hand, and pulled his plate back in front of him with the other.

'Finish your breakfast now, Ian, and stop being silly.'

'I don't want it. I don't like white.'

'You liked it until this morning. And what about your bacon?'

'I don't want it.'

The gamekeeper sat down at the opposite side of the table to the boy.

'Just pop that bacon back in the pan. I'll have it if he doesn't want it.'

'You would an'all.'

'Well, it's no good wasting it is it?'

'You're not going to waste it, are you, love?'

And she tried to tempt him by cutting his bacon up into small stickable pieces.

'It's no good trying to force him, Mary. He'd eat it if he was hungry.'

'I know, but he'll be starving by dinner time if he doesn't eat a bit more.'

'It'll serve him right. He'll eat his breakfast tomorrow then.'

Mary Purse turned away to prepare her husband's breakfast at the stove.

'It's all your fault, anyway.'

'That's it, blame me.'

'You hit him, didn't you?'

'He should do as he's told.'

'He only wanted to carry a pheasant.'

'He's not big enough.'

'You could have helped him, couldn't you? Anyway, what could have happened? It was taped wasn't it?'

'What if it had broke loose, and we'd have been chasing it all over the yard? Pheasants have been known to go sterile when they've been scared bad.'

'Don't exaggerate, George. It'd have had plenty of time to settle down. They'll not be laying for another couple of months.'

'I'm not taking any risks, Mary . . . Anyway . . . look, am I getting any breakfast, or what?'

And that was the end of that.

Mary Purse made as if to continue the argument; then she shrugged and turned back to the stove. She sliced a tomato into the frying pan, and the reaction of the juices on the hot fat created a furious energy, which jiggled the slices around, and produced a hissing sound like an angry cat.

John had brought a cat home once. He was five, just started school, and did not know any better. He did not know that his father was a gamekeeper.

A girl in their class had brought three kittens to school in a cardboard box, lined with an old red cardigan to keep them warm. Her dad said that if she could not get rid of them, he was going to drown them. Some of the children said they would like one, but they had already got pets, and their parents would not let them have any more. Some of the children said they would like one, but pets were not allowed in the new flats. John said he could have one. The teacher asked him if he was sure. They had got lots of animals at their house he said, a kitten would not make any difference. He did not mind which one he had. They were all nice. They were tabbies, with different-sized white bibs, and different-sized white socks on their paws. They all had blue eyes, and they seemed to smile every time they said mew. One of the girls said that the kittens could have her bottle of milk at playtime. Some more children said that the kittens could have theirs as well. Then the teacher said that there was no need to argue about it because there would be a spare bottle anyway; and she took the kittens along to the staff-room for the morning, so that they could get on with some work.

John took his kitten home at dinner time. He carried it down his jerkin to keep it warm. He kept running a bit and walking a bit, and every time he stopped running he looked down his jerkin at the kitten clinging on to his jumper.

When he arrived home his mother was hanging nappies out in the yard. The new baby was asleep in the pram. When she saw the kitten she dried her hands on her pinafore and took it from him. It pulled itself up her jumper and clung to her shoulder, mewing. She held it there, and stroked its back, and told him that he could not keep it. He started to cry and said that he would look after it. His dad did not like cats, she said. They killed the pheasant chicks if they got chance. Then his dad came out of the wood with his gun. 'Where's that thing come from?' he said. His wife told him the story. 'Well, he can take it straight back,' he said. 'There's enough cats get here off that estate as it is, without bringing them here. They all ought to be drowned,' he said. John took it back to school after dinner, and another boy took it home at four o'clock. He never saw the kitten again.

Mary Purse served out her husband's breakfast, then took Ian's duffel coat down from the peg behind the kitchen door, and helped him to put it on. John made no move to get ready. He just stood in front of the fire in his stocking feet, watching. A decision had been made, and he was now waiting for the outcome.

His father looked across at him from the table.

'Isn't it time you got your things on, John?'

John looked from his father to his mother. Still fastening the toggles on Ian's duffel coat, she reciprocated the look; it was a kind of telepathic baton passing. She turned to her husband.

'He says he doesn't want to go this morning.'

'Why, what's up with him?'

'He says he doesn't feel very well.'

'What's up with you this time, John?'

35

John looked at his stomach, then marked its position with his hand.

'I've got stomach-ache.'

The gamekeeper levelled a forkful of egg at him. The portion of white, hanging over the prongs, looked as languid as a Dalí watch.

'Stomach-ache my arse. You're telling lies again, John. Now then, what's the matter with you? Why don't you want to go to school?'

The boy looked to his mother for support. But she shook her head at him. The game was up. But although she would no longer comply with the deception, she was prepared to defend the fear which had caused it.

'I'll tell you what's the matter with him. He's getting picked on again at school. I've a good mind to go up and see Mr Newton about it.'

'You're not, Mam. You're not going up there.'

The gamekeeper shook his head in agreement. Although he knew nothing of the merits of the case, he agreed with the boy in principle. Parents, especially mothers, no matter what the circumstances, should keep away from school.

'Who's picking on him this time?'

'That eldest lad of Docherty's.'

'What, Sammy Docherty's lad? Well, you know why that is, don't you?'

'Of course I know.'

'I'll tell you what. I'd have had his mate an'all that morning, if his dog hadn't started growling and warned him.'

'Who was it?'

'Joe Price.'

'Well, I'm glad you didn't catch him. Our John'd be all right with Price's team ganging up on him. How many have they got, six? Seven?'

'I don't know, but they all ought to be gassed in their beds like they do rabbits. And they're all taking after their father. I'm fed up of chasing them out of the woods. And the lip they give you when you say owt to them. When I was a kid, if we were caught on private land we knew we'd done wrong and we'd just get off, thankful that we didn't get some stick, or get reported. But these days . . . Pu! . . .'

And he took two substantial drinks of hot sweet tea to fortify himself against modern times.

'The way they talk back to you; you'd think they'd the right to trespass. You'd think that the woods belonged to them.'

And he was so indignant at the insolence of the Price family, who by now embodied the evils of a whole generation, that he forgot about the immediate problem confronting his own family, and continued with the demolition of his breakfast.

Ian was now ready and waiting for someone to take him to school. If John was not going, either his father or his mother would have to take him up the cart track through the wood, and see him across the main road which separated the Duke's estate from the council estate.

The mother and the two boys stood there, watching the game-keeper eat, waiting for a decision; until he became aware of them watching him.

'Hey up, it's not a sideshow you know.'

'We're waiting. Is our John going, or isn't he?'

The gamekeeper was surprised at the question. He thought he had settled it minutes ago.

'Of course he's going. If they see he's frightened of them, they'll pick on him even more. I know it's not very nice for him; it'll be the same for our Ian when he gets older. But I've a job to do. Every time I catch somebody poaching I can't stop and think to myself, has he got any kids who might bash our John up at school? He'll just have to put up with it, that's all. I mean, what do you want me to do, give me notice in and go and work back at Brightside Steel?'

As the two boys left the house in their wellingtons and coats the gamekeeper said to the elder boy,

'Remember, John, you stick up for yourself. If they see you're not frightened, they'll stop bothering you.'

All John wanted was to be friends. He did have friends at school, but these relationships were never cemented because he saw so little of the other boys after school.

Sometimes he stayed to play at someone's house on the estate, and sometimes, on Saturdays, he went to play football on the recreation ground. This was all right. But the trouble was, John could rarely ask anyone home in return. His father was always uneasy when there were strangers around the place. He occasionally allowed an individual friend. But a gang, never. And this frustrated the boys. They could not understand it. All they wanted was to play. So, when things went wrong between them, and John became involved in an argument, and they reached that point where reason fails and irrelevant accusations begin, John's opponents always used his father as their first point of attack. In similar circumstances some boys have the handicap of obesity or foreign birth, crossed eyes or an impediment of speech. John's handicap was having a gamekeeper for a father.

Because the boys loved to visit John's house if the game keeper happened to be away for a few hours. They thought it must be the best place in the world to live. They would have gone on their holidays there. It was a real cottage in a wood. They burned logs on the fire, and there was even a wooden trestle to saw them on, like in Hansel and Gretel. There were old dark stables with creaky doors filled with ancient and mysterious tools. There were dogs and hens and hutches with ferrets in. And sometimes, when you looked warily into their rancid dens, there was the shocking sight of a dead rabbit or a bird in the sawdust, and the ferret staring up at you from the hole in the flesh.

There was usually something dead about the place; a load of rooks or woodpigeons, or sometimes a hedgehog or a hare. Something for the boys to turn over with their foot, and make them jump, when the flies exploded off it.

And in the summer, swallows zipped in and out of the outhouses, and when you peered upwards into the cool gloom you could see the mud bowls of their nests moulded to the rafters, and the high places up on the walls.

It was magic land. You could play hide and seek, and in less than a minute be crouched down in a bracken cave, so secure that nobody could find you, and eventually you were forced to crawl out to make a game of it.

But the gamekeeper could not allow this. He could not allow gangs of boys to race around the house when the pheasants were in the laying pen. The noise and the excitement would terrify the birds, and might affect their fertility. Then, when the poults had been released in covert, he could not allow the boys to rampage through the woods, Tarzaning up the trees, and adventuring in the undergrowth. They might scatter the birds and force them to leave covert, and then there would be less pheasants for the guns to shoot when they came in the autumn. He could not allow that. He was paid to keep game, not to administer a public playground.

And so the Purse boys were lonely boys. Their main companions were each other.

George Purse wiped his plate clean with a piece of bread, washed the bread and grease down with the remains of his tea, then stood up. He picked up the unopened newspaper from the table and walked across the kitchen to have a look at it by the fire. Mary Purse cleared his dirty dishes and put them into the sink with the other pots. She scalded them with water from the gas heater on the wall, and the rising steam misted up the kitchen window. She immediately wiped a clear patch on a pane. She liked to look out while she was working at the sink.

Her husband stood on the hearthrug letting the fire scorch the backs of his legs. When they became too hot he stepped forward a pace, then back a pace as soon as the heat decreased. He was secretly messing about, daring himself, experimenting with mild degrees of pain. He had nothing special to do that morning; yet while he stood there, reading the paper, taking a step forward, then taking a step back, he never considered helping his wife with the pots, even though she had a lot of work to do and would still be doing it at bedtime. There was rigid demarcation in the Purse household. He did his job. She did hers.

Mary Purse had the radio on to keep her company while she worked. It was a record request programme, and the compère

40

talked as though the whole country was having one big coffee morning while they listened to the show. She hummed the tunes, and joined in the words when she knew them. All those songs, all about love, love, love. Some banal, some risible, some true. Relayed over tannoy systems to women in factories; over radios to mothers at home; some dreaming, some consoling themselves, all trying to make sense of the promise of it all.

George Purse was not trying to make sense of it. He had finished courting as soon as he had got married. Courting had been a necessary embarrassment. It had been an uncomfortable time, when he had been forced to endure jibes from the rest of the lads. It had been the same with them all. The general idea seemed to be to get a girl, get her courted and get her wed; then start getting out with the lads again. Crazy.

George Purse was trying to make sense of something he was reading in the paper, about a stray dog that had been caught with tattoos on its ears. Experts were puzzled by it, it said. So was George Purse. He shook his head at the story.

'It's a pity some folks have nowt better to do with their time. I hope they catch them. And when they do they want to tattoo their bloody ears. They want to write silly bugger, on each one.'

He dropped the newspaper on to a chair and set off across the room for his jacket.

'I don't know, there's some rubbish in the papers these days. If it's not dogs with tattooed ears, it's a picture of some silly sod looking out of a bedroom window next to a sunflower. What about that bloke up on the estate who had his hand off last week, because his machine guard was faulty? I never saw that in the paper, did you?'

Mary Purse was listening to Frank Sinatra on the radio.

When love congeals
It soon reveals
The stale aroma of performing seals.
I wish I were in love again.

George Purse took his jacket down from the hook on the back of the kitchen door and put it on. He took his deerstalker hat out of one of the side pockets and put that on. He was now dressed in his full gamekeeper's uniform; hat, tweed knicker-bocker suit and woollen knee stockings. That hat and socks he had had to buy for himself. The suit was provided.

The Duke's gamekeepers were issued with one suit per year. They were made by a tailor in Harrogate. An old family firm which specialized in country wear. Once a year the tailor drove down from Harrogate to measure up George Purse and the other gamekeepers for their new suits. The Duke selected the pattern. It was a family tradition. Once a year he looked through the swatches of green tweeds and decided on the check. The game-keepers always knew how old each other's suits were when they met each other.

George Purse was wearing his last year's suit. He always wore his last year's suit for work, and saved his best suit for attending country shows in the summer, and for the shooting season later on in the year.

He straightened his tie in the mirror. Except for the times when he was doing jobs at home, he always wore a tie. He had instructions to do so; whether he was on his rounds in the fields and woods, or up in the village, or out anywhere else on business. He had been told to look neat and tidy at all times. Gamekeeping is a very respectable profession.

It was a green tie, pure wool, handwoven in Scotland. He had bought it one year at the Country Landowners' Association Game Fair. He had been drinking all lunchtime in a marquee, and had emerged into the sunlight, staring and reckless. He had bought the tie for himself and a pair of sheepskin slippers for his wife.

When he took the tie out of the bag at home, he wasn't sure. He thought it was a bit gaudy; more blue than green perhaps. But it had cost him two pounds so he had to wear it. He was glad there hadn't been any red ties on display, or any with polka-dots or zig-zags on them. His wife said that sheepskin made her feet sweat. She had told him before. But the slippers had also been expensive, and eventually she wore them out.

He tucked his tie down his sweater. It was a green sweater. Not the same green as the tie, or suit, or socks, or hat. None of them were the same green as each other. But they all toned in well enough, as the different greens in a wood tone in. Game-keepers always wear green. According to pictorial evidence, moving and otherwise, so did Robin Hood and his merry men.

Mary Purse turned round from the sink for the tea towel, and saw her husband adjusting his tie at the mirror.

'Are you going out?'

'I thought I'd have a walk up to the yard. See if I can get a bit of timber to mend that pen door.'

'While you're up there, see about that window frame again. And tell them if they'd have come and put a bit of paint on the house, it wouldn't have rotted in the first place.'

'Do you think I haven't told them?'

'Well, tell them again. The only way you get anything done round here is by pestering their eyes out.'

She was right. This is what George Purse had done to try and get his bedroom window frame repaired. First, he had reported it to the Head keeper, and then he had mentioned it casually in conversation to the other keepers. He felt obliged to tell the Head keeper because, although he had nothing to do with the repair of window frames, he was George's immediate boss, and to circumvent him during the process might lead to offence, and perhaps repercussions, or the withholding of favours at some later date.

He did not have to say anything to the other keepers, but they usually told each other their external domestic grievances. They derived comfort from each other's troubles. When George told them that the frame was rotten, and the wood was as soft as shit, they told him he should get up to the yard and get it reported. Their approval was important, it gave him confidence and strength; he felt he was acting as a delegate when he issued his complaint. Another reason they told each other, was that none of them wanted the others to think that they were obtaining favours surreptitiously. If they acted in this way they would appear to be humble and cowardly, to be bosses' men. The gamekeepers liked to be thought of as men of independence, brave and open in their dealings.

Besides, it was bad enough having to be openly subservient during the shooting season, without demeaning themselves in such matters as new window frames, or kitchen sinks.

The Head keeper then came to George's cottage and stuck his penknife into the rotten wood. 'Yes,' he said, when the blade disappeared right up to the mother-of-pearl handle, 'it wants reporting.'

So George reported it at the builders' yard in the village. The builders' yard had formerly been a farm. Now, the yard contained timber and bricks and other building materials, and the house and the stables had been converted into offices and workshops, to deal with the improvement and repair of the Duke's tenanted houses and farms.

George went into the joiners' shop. There was a joiner in there making a new board for a no-trespassing sign. They were always making them. They needed a lot of boards because there was a lot of land to trespass on; a lot of gates that people could not open, leading into woods and fields that people could not walk through, up to hills that people could not climb, down to streams and ponds that people could not sit beside. And the notice boards were always disappearing off the gates, and children used the ones which were nailed high up on the trees for target practice.

George told the joiner that he wanted a new window frame. The joiner told him that he had better see the Foreman Joiner about it. He was somewhere around. He might be in the blacksmith's shop. George went out, but he did not go to the blacksmith's straight away, he went to visit the other workers in their shops, the painters, the plumbers, the electrician, the bricklayers. He knew all the workers personally. He went out of his way to know them, and to know the stock which they stored in and around their shops. A length of timber, or a roll of chicken-wire were quite often negotiable for a couple of rabbits, or a pheasant dropped outside their kitchen doors.

But not a new window frame. George found the Foreman Joiner talking to the blacksmith. Wanting and getting's two different things, George said. He told the Foreman Joiner about the window frame. The Foreman Joiner told George that he had better go and see the Building Manager about it.

So George went to see the Building Manager. His office was across the yard in the old farmhouse. George took his cap off before he went in. The Building Manager was cordial, but he did not ask George to sit down. He wrote down the nature of the repair, and said that it would be attended to. George was going to say that the house needed painting as well. But standing there, with his cap in his hand, before a man with his head down, writing, it suddenly seemed unreasonable and inopportune to ask for two things at once. He would see about the decorating some other time.

So, at the end of the month, the file containing the cards requesting improvements and repairs was sent across the village and through the Park, for the attention of the Estate Agent, who had an office in the west wing of the Big House, and who was directly accountable to the Duke. The Estate Agent inspected the cards and marked them; Deferred, Passed or Investigate. He wrote Investigate on George Purse's card, with the added instruction to ascertain whether a completely new window frame was required, or whether a replacement for the rotten length would suffice.

The file was returned to the Building Manager, who told the Foreman Joiner to go and have a look at it. The Foreman Joiner sent a joiner to George's house. The joiner stuck his penknife into the wood, and, with half a dozen fresh bantam eggs in his tool bag, reported back to his foreman that he thought the whole window frame was rotten. But he had better go and look for himself. So the Foreman Joiner went to look, and when George talked about pheasants and Christmas, he agreed. He reported back to the Building Manager that the whole frame was rotten and was in urgent need of repair.

46

At the end of the month, the Building Manager sent the Foreman Joiner's report along with a new batch of cards, across the village and through the Park to the Estate Agent's office; and two weeks later the card came back; the repair had been approved.

The Building Manager passed the card back to the Foreman Joiner, who passed it on to one of the joiners, who told the apprentice to put it into the box with the rest of the cards. By this time the Foreman Joiner had had a definite offer from one of the other gamekeepers for a brace of pheasants for Christmas. George Purse's card would have to take its turn with the rest.

And now it was February, the shooting season had ended. The Duke was taking a holiday in Switzerland, before flying south for a month's safari in Kenya. And George Purse was back at the builders' yard, still waiting for a new window frame.

He went to the joiners' shop. The apprentice was working there, creosoting fence posts, but the foreman and the other joiners were out on a job he said.

Perhaps it was time to see about the house being painted? The Foreman Painter was in. He was stencilling, TRESPASSERS WILL BE PROSECUTED in white, on a freshly painted green board. Yes, he agreed, it must be ten years since George's house had been painted. He'd better go and see the Building Manager about it. But he was out on a job somewhere. So George went back to the joiners' shop and bartered with the apprentice for a length of 2″ x 2″ to repair the jamb of his dog pen. The lad said he didn't like game. So George said that he'd give him a young ferret for the timber. The lad said

47

he'd see. He didn't know whether his mother would let him have a ferret . . .

Every morning the gamekeeper walked through the wood to feed the pheasants, and to bring back the captured birds to the laying pen. He bred around a thousand poults, so he needed about one hundred hens, plus fourteen or fifteen cocks to serve them.

He told his wife and boys not to go near the pen. He told them this every year. And he shouted at the dogs if they went close. He wanted no unnecessary disturbance while the pheasants were settling in. When he fed and watered the birds, he always whistled the same familiar notes as he approached the pen, so that they would know who was coming. He always wore the same green garb so that there would be no danger of mistaken identity; and once inside the pen, his movements were slow and deliberate, so as not to startle them. He never stared at the pheasants. Staring made them nervous. He risked nothing that might impair their fertility.

These early months were the quietest time of the year for George Purse. The shooting season had ended, and the breeding season had not yet begun. It was the closest he got to having a holiday. He had not been away in the summer since he had become a gamekeeper. The holiday season clashed with the breeding season and merged into the shooting season, and that was a busy, vital time of the year for the gamekeeper.

His wife sometimes took the children away. Her sister had a caravan at Mablethorpe. When they did go away, they always went there. The boys liked it. There was the sea. And it was cheap. It had to be. On the gamekeeper's wage, it was all they could afford.

They all could have gone away now, for a few days, in February or March, but even at this slack time of the year it all seemed too much trouble. First the gamekeeper would have to get permission from the Head keeper, then arrangements would have had to be made for one of the other keepers to visit the house every day to feed the pheasants and the dogs, the ferrets and the hens. And as soon as the boys at school had got to know that John was on holiday, they would have been rampaging through the woods scattering the pheasants, or worse still their fathers, armed with guns and dogs.

Anyway, where could they go? The seaside? The caravan site was closed for the winter. The countryside? They already lived in it. And they certainly could not afford to go abroad. So the gamekeeper used the time to go rabbiting instead. He had an arrangement with the butcher in the village, and the two butchers on the council estate, who promised to take all he could kill. He spent whole days at it, starting out as soon as he had fed the pheasants in the morning.

And the money he earned from rabbiting, he gave to his wife to buy new curtains or sheets, or new pullovers for the lads.

The gamekeeper went into the outhouse to fetch the ferreting tackle. The ferret hutches stood against the end wall of the outhouses, out of the cold north winds. As soon as the dogs saw the gamekeeper at the hutches they crowded to the door of the pen, whining and wagging their tails. The labrador and the springer went rabbiting in turn. The terrier never went, but he never seemed to learn, and he stood there every time, whining and wagging his stump with the other two.

There were two ferret hutches; one on legs, and the other one on top of it. They were as big as rabbit hutches, and strongly built with half-inch tongue and groove boards. Their roofs had been tarpaulined, and the rest of the wood was dark with creosote. The outer doors of the sleeping compartments closed as snugly as sideboard doors, and the little brass bolts which secured the doors were precisely aligned with their little brass barrels. The gamekeeper had built the hutches. The material had come from the builders' yard.

He kept two ferrets; a hob in the top hutch, a jill in the bottom one. He called the hob ferret, Sam. He did not call the jill anything. His wife and the boys called her Marilyn, because Mary said that she was as blonde as Marilyn Monroe. Marilyn was an albino ferret with eyes the colour of pomegranate seeds. She had been confiscated in the previous autumn from a boy caught poaching near Duck Lake. If the gamekeeper still had her in the spring, he would put Sam in with her when she was on heat again, and let her have a litter. In the meantime, if someone came and offered anything over a pound for her, they could take her. The gamekeeper had worked her, and she was adequate, no better, no worse than many of the ferrets he had kept. But that was all, she was just another ferret. She was negotiable.

Sam was not. Sam was a long, strong pole-cat ferret; he had a blonde undercoat, overlaid with wisps and patches of brown. He looked like a peroxide blonde letting his hair grow out. He was two years old and the gamekeeper had bred him himself. When he had first peeped into the hutch while the mother was feeding in the other compartment, he had quickly noted that amongst that seething heap of new-born ferrets in the corner, there was one big one and one runt. The big one was Sam. He killed the runt two days later. He held it in one hand; it was as bald as a worm and no bigger than a whiff. It kept trying to curl up into the foetal position, and its eyes were so tightly shut that it appeared to be making a conscious effort not to open them. The gamekeeper squeezed its neck between his forefinger and thumb, and nipped out its life in the same way as he would have nipped out a lighted cigarette.

Anyhow, it was a waste of the mother's good milk. There would be more to suckle the strong now. And what if he had let it live; what could he have done with it? Who would have bought it? Who wants a wreckling?

He never told his wife about the runt. She would have wanted to keep it. Then they might have had it for years as a useless pet.

Sam ran from one end of the hutch to the other as he waited to go to work. He kept close to the wire mesh, and his body was so supple that when he reached the ends, he was able to turn so sharply that his back legs were still going forward while his front legs were coming back. He had trailed wood shavings into his empty food dish and water bowl. The shavings had soaked up the water, and taken on a richer colour, as though they had been varnished.

Sam stopped running and reared up with his front paws against the wire mesh. His claws were so long that they curved through the honeycomb pattern and were on the outside of the cage. They were not like a cat's claws, or the claws of a bird of prey. Their claws snag and hold like crochet needles. Sam's claws were longer, more slender with a shallow curve, like the shape of a foil when it touches its mark.

As Sam stood there on his back legs, looking up at the gamekeeper through the wire netting, he opened his mouth and revealed his ivory-coloured teeth. The two canines were like little daggers. They were the longest, strongest teeth the gamekeeper had ever seen in a ferret. He always told the boys to be careful with Sam, and even though Sam was his ferret, and he had known him from birth, he never forgot that this flue brush of an animal was a professional killer. He handled him with care. One bite of those teeth could pierce clean through to the bone. These, and not his claws, were the ferret's chief weapon.

The gamekeeper opened the front of the hutch, and Sam stretched out his neck over the precipice and crinkled his nose to sniff at the outside air. The gamekeeper picked him up like a telephone and popped him into the ferret bag. When he drew the string across the top it looked like a bag of ready cash.

He closed the hutch door, and walked across to the dog pen. All three dogs were waiting at the door, ready for off. He waved his arm, and shouted at them to back off. Reluctantly they obeyed, and when they were three yards from the door, he ordered them to sit. It took three brusque shouts and a violent threat before they were all down, and even then the labrador lowered his haunches so slowly that he appeared to be anticipating a tin tack, or some other painful disclosure on the concrete.

So there they sat, in rapt, higgledy-piggledy formation, mouths open, tails brushing the concrete, like some absurd audience enthralled by an amazing performance in the doorway of the pen. The gamekeeper called the labrador and held the door ajar for him to run through. As soon as he shut the door the other two dogs were back at it; and they were still there barking, long after the gamekeeper and the labrador had walked out of sight into the wood.

The winter wood was striped grey and black, with a lick of moss green down the sides of the trunks exposed to the prevailing wind and rain. The labrador ran ahead, exploring random scents in and out of the stripes, and the gamekeeper could still see him when he was a hundred yards away, because the grass had died back, and the leaves were down on the undergrowth. The wood was a cheerless place; the black earth, the chill air, the bare trees all seemed locked in winter. But there were subtle signs of change; already the sycamore buds were green, and somewhere high up, a cock chaffinch was singing amongst the filigree of twigs and branches.

As George Purse came out of the wood, he looked up to watch a flock of fieldfares and redwings flying over the field next to the wood. Just then the wind blew the clouds apart, and the low sun flashed silver on the underparts of the fieldfares. It was so well synchronized with the gamekeeper's emergence from the wood, that it appeared to be an elemental warning, a transmitting of a secret semaphore to the creatures down below.

The gamekeeper climbed the fence and crossed a sloping field of winter wheat; then he climbed a steeper field, making for a high stone wall at the top of the fields. A gang of bullocks galloped across to meet him, twin plumes of steam issuing from their nostrils. They looked as though they meant business, but the gamekeeper just glanced at them and carried on walking at the same pace. Ten yards from him they stopped and stood in a line. They looked bemused, as though they had suddenly forgotten the original intention of their charge.

When he reached the high stone wall, the gamekeeper rested. He crouched down on the bank with his back against the stones and looked back over the land he had walked; dark plough, pallid meadows, and smudges of woodland, with the main road just visible in the distance. He could see the roof of his own house in the side of the wood, and the blue smoke from the chimney drifting across the dark bulk of the trees. Looking down on the wood, the space that had been cleared for the smallholding looked like a bite out of a slice of bread.

The bullocks in the field below him had drifted back to the fence by the cart track, and were rummaging amongst the remains of a bale of hay that the farmer had thrown in the previous day. Their heads were in clouds as they snuffled for the scattered wisps.

It was a quiet, solitary place by the wall at the top of the hill. There were no machines working in the fields, and the tiny vehicles moving slowly along the distant road were too far away to hear. The clouds had shut out the sun, and the deterioration in light and diminished perspective all added to the silence and seclusion. It was a tranquil scene; the bullocks in the field, the keeper by the wall, the ferret sleeping in the bag.

It was also a private scene. All the land that he could see belonged to the Duke. This was his beat, five thousand acres, and there were four more gamekeepers with equivalent acreage to police. And this was only the Duke's small estate. His main estate was in Wiltshire.

At Christmas, one of the gamekeepers had transferred to the Wiltshire estate. To give him a send-off, the other gamekeepers decided to have a do in the pub in the village.

But they didn't. They would not risk the word being spread that all five gamekeepers had assembled under one roof with the sole intention of getting drunk. None of their pheasants was going to emerge illegally from hot ovens on Christmas day if they could help it. The thought of those unsporting steel-workers and miners stealing through the woods at night even outweighed the prospects of a rumbustious evening with a departing friend.

They discussed a rota system in desultory fashion. First of all they were each going to patrol the estate an hour at a time. An hour at a time? That's five hours. Who's going to be boozing for five hours? Anyway, what about Doug? He can't go out, he's supposed to be the guest of honour. So it was decided that they would go out in pairs and patrol for an hour. But what about the last hour? Whoever's turn it is'll be pissed up by that time. Some use they'll be if they drop on any poachers . . .

It was never organized, the evening was never held. Instead, three of them, who happened to be at the builders' yard one lunchtime, went to the Arms, and bought a round each and three pork pies.

The Duke also owned a few acres in Ireland, two grouse moors in Derbyshire, and rented an adjoining third. Unfortunately for the Duke, the lease on this moor was due to expire.

It belonged to George Brown's, the steel makers. As he grew older, old George Brown's sporting activities had been curtailed by severe arthritis, brought on by too much standing around on damp moors, his family always said. As his eldest son was still too young to take on the shoot, he had leased the land to the Duke.

When he died, young George became Managing Director of the firm. Young George was now a shooting fanatic. His main function in life had not transpired until after his father's death, so he had had ample time and opportunity in which to sample all manner of sporting activities. At school, he had played cricket and tennis, rugby, golf and squash. He had hunted the school pack of beagles, and he had ridden to hounds. He had ski'd in Switzerland and Austria, and he had raced as a crewman on a yacht. He had discovered that shooting seemed as exciting and as sociable a way as possible of getting half the year over at least.

Being Managing Director of the firm did not interfere too much with his sport, so now he wanted his moor back. The lease expired at the end of the year. The Duke would only have two moors of his own to shoot then.

The gamekeeper stood up and brushed the stone dust off his back where he had been leaning against the wall. The wall was twelve feet high, and looked like some kind of fortification. It was called the terrace wall. On top of it were the ornamental gardens of the Big House. Guests at the House would stroll along the gravel paths of the terrace and stand at the top of the wall to admire the view; the same view that the gamekeeper had just been looking at.

George Purse had once stood under the terrace wall with Jim Buck, the old Head keeper, who was now dead, and Jim Buck had told him that when he was a young keeper in the service of the 11th Duke, and they had kept a pack of hounds at the House to hunt the deer in the park, he had stood on this very spot, and watched the hunted deer leap from the top of the wall into the field, with the hounds pouring over after them. Sometimes the deer got up and ran on, he said, but sometimes the jump broke their front legs, and the dogs killed them. Some of the dogs broke their legs as well, he said, and if the deer did get up and run on, the injured dogs would be yelping with pain, but they would still be trying to struggle up and run after them with the rest.

The bank on which the terrace wall was built was undermined with rabbit burrows. The labrador knew what to do without being told. As soon as the gamekeeper started to move along the bank the dog was at it, tail wagging, nose down, sniffing each hole in turn.

'Seek 'em, Jack. Seek 'em, boy.'

And the nose went in, explored and moved on. The gamekeeper grinned, he enjoyed his dog's enthusiasm for its work. He enjoyed its expertise, which he had developed in its early years by systematic training. And even now, after twenty years of working with dogs, he never ceased to be amazed at the refinement of a gun dog's nostrils.

Sometimes, when he was certain that no one was looking, the gamekeeper would kneel down and sniff at a few burrows himself. He would sniff at a hole which the dog had analysed and left, then one which the dog had marked. And what did he smell? Nothing. To him there was no difference. It was the same air at the entrance to both burrows, as it was six feet higher when he stood up.

And what did the labrador smell? Rabbits; there were always rabbits. Their smell, in varying degrees of strength, permeated the tunnels. It lined the walls, and their droppings littered the packed earth floors. What else? The tang of the soil. A worm. A mole. It broke through the wall of the burrow, lifted its nose in the greater, vaulted space, then carried on, to engineer its own, familiar, fitted habitation. Leaves, blown and scuffed in underfoot. A sleeping hedgehog, lodging for the winter. A mouse. A rat, running the tunnels because they were there. A stoat, running the tunnels with purpose.

The dog marked a hole. He thrashed his tail and whined with excitement. He tried to push his head into the hole, and when it would only go down to his eyes, he backed out and started to enlarge the opening by digging with his front paws. The gamekeeper called him off and made him sit down. He sat down three yards away, still looking at the hole; then he got down on his belly with his chin on the ground, so that he could see further in.

George Purse stuck his spade into the soil, took the purse nets out of his jacket pocket and placed them on the bank at the side of the ferret bag. Then he looked for other, nearby holes, from which the rabbit might bolt.

The holes were easy to see in the winter, when the grass and the flowers had died back. But in the summer, when the vegetation was rank, the holes were completely obscured, and it was easy to miss a bolt hole and lose a rabbit, or even a ferret emerging and walking unobserved into the rough. Summer was the gamekeeper's close season for ferreting.

Now the bank was a pallid green, as though diluted by the winter rains. But the coltsfoot were pushing up their furry stalks, the bank would soon be starred with yellow, and the green would deepen when the spring arrived.

The gamekeeper found five holes which he reckoned were close enough to be connected to the marked hole. They were all above the marked hole; two side by side like big nostrils, then above them, the other three, forming a rough dotted line parallel to the wall. Looking up from the bottom of the bank, the marked hole was the apex of an inverted triangle, and the six holes formed a pattern like a frame of snooker balls.

George Purse blocked the bottom hole with the spade, then quietly started to net the other five holes. He spread a purse net loosely across each hole, and pegged it securely into the earth. The nets covered the holes as a hairnet covers a woman's head.

The ferret bag was rippling on the bank. The gamekeeper picked it up, pulled it open, and lifted Sam out. He held him round the body just behind the front legs. The ferret did not struggle, he just hung there, placid, body slightly curved like a comma. The gamekeeper removed the spade and placed the ferret at the entrance to the hole. He did not rush around to relieve his confinement, or dash straight down the burrow. He just stood there for a moment, extended his head, snake like, to confirm the judgement of the dog, then calmly walked into the dark. There was nothing extravagant about his movement. Yet he was all the more dangerous for his calm.

In a cartoon featuring Sam, the temptation would be to cast him in a pinstriped suit, with a trilby pulled low over his pointed features. And he certainly would not get the jill at the end. But that would be wrong. Morality does not enter into it with predators. There are no goodies and baddies in the animal world. Their behaviour is functional, that is all.

As soon as the ferret was inside the hole, the gamekeeper netted the entrance. He went to the top of the bank and called the dog to him. Any rabbits which came to the surface would not see them there. If they waited directly in front of a hole and a rabbit appeared, it would see them and turn back. They waited. Quiet down below.

A blackbird flew across the ornamental gardens of the Big House, touched down on top of the terrace wall, saw the gamekeeper and his dog directly below and took off again before it had folded its wings. Chattering and scolding, it skimmed back across the terrace and dropped a mute into a star of purple crocuses.

George Purse looked up at the noise. It had startled him. He never saw the bird. The dog just kept looking towards the holes.

'The noisy bugger.'

He walked down the bank and knelt down over the warren with one ear to the ground. He could not hear anything; but the ferret had not yet appeared. He was just standing up when there was a bumping, a galloping in the earth. It stopped. Then a rabbit appeared, full tilt into a net. It was as though it had run into a string bag. The peg held, the draw string tightened, and the more the rabbit squealed and struggled, the more entangled it became. It was all too much for the dog. It rushed at the writhing heap, snarling and biting. The gamekeeper shouted him off, but he had to smack him across the back, and push him away with his foot before he would obey. He bent down and picked up the rabbit, net and all. He held it up by its hind legs and started to unravel the net. The rabbit just hung there, limp. It could have been dead, except for its eyes. The gamekeeper pulled the net off its front legs and let the net drop. Then he held the rabbit firmly in both hands, and now that it was right way up, and it was close to his face and his smell was stronger, it began to struggle and squeal again. But not for long. The gamekeeper put his hand over its face and shoved its head back until there was the soft crunch of bone as its neck broke.

He dropped the rabbit on to the bank and picked up the net to straighten it out. The ferret had still not appeared, so he decided to re-net the hole. The rabbit was still kicking on the ground. Every time it kicked its hind legs it rolled a little further down the bank. Then it stopped kicking and its body began to stiffen. A wave of movement, emanating from its middle, passed

60

through its body, down its legs and up into its ears. The rabbit lay still. It was really dead now. A trickle of blood from its nose emphasized the vertical furrow below its nostrils, and the slit between its lips. Its eyes had lost their clarity, and already a film like a thin sheet of ice was forming over the retina.

The gamekeeper was right to re-net the hole. He had only just shoved the peg in, when a second rabbit ran out of one of the holes above him. The net pursed, and the rabbit was caught. When he picked it up, this one did not hang there, it struggled intermittently, like a fish on deck. The gamekeeper broke its neck and threw it down beside the other. Reflex action made it kick and twitch and it rolled away down the bank. Then it died like the first, stiffening and stretching simultaneously.

Then the ferret appeared, walking calmly into the light. It slipped through the net, then stood there on the bank. And as it lifted its nose to test the air, there was that aura about it, that ability to create tension in the watcher that is discernible in all predators when they are at work.

The gamekeeper climbed the bank and put the ferret into a tunnel at the bottom of the terrace wall, which had been formed by dislodged stones and erosion. The dog had marked strongly. There was a rabbit in that tunnel. There were three little door-ways out. The gamekeeper blocked the first two with stones and netted the end one. The ferret was in, it was just a matter of waiting now until the rabbit ran into the net. But it did not. Its head suddenly appeared through a hole two feet above the ground half-way along the tunnel. The gamekeeper clapped his hands and ran towards it to try to make it go back in, but he was too late; it jumped down and fled along the bank, like an adulterer escaping from a bedroom window. The dog chased

61

it. But he could not catch an adult rabbit, and the gamekeeper called him back before he ran it out of sight.

After they had worked the length of the bank, the gamekeeper hid the rabbits in a tangle of brambles, to be picked up on the way home.

The gamekeeper worked Duke's wood next. It had been given this name by the villagers and the estate workers because it was the favourite wood of the 9th Duke. He had enjoyed walking here with his dogs. Not that there was anything special about the contours of the land here, or the composition of the trees which grew on it; they were of the same hardwood variety as the rest of his woods on the estate. No, the 9th Duke had favoured this wood simply because it was close to the Big House. It was only two fields away from the high wall which surrounded the vegetable gardens, therefore it was unnecessary to arrange transport when he fancied a walk.

He never went in his other woods on the estate. The nearest he got to them was the adjacent fields during the shooting season, where he waited to kill the pheasants as they were driven from the cover of the trees and over the waiting guns.

The 9th Duke had had his favourite hunter buried in this wood. A bay mare, which, after long and faithful service in the field, had died peacefully in the stables one night.

The gamekeeper passed her grave, which had been made beside the main ride in the wood, so that the Duke would be reminded of her as he passed by. The dedication on the arched gravestone read:

MERLE

1854–75

There had never been a formal grave with a defined boundary, but the Duke had ordered the keepers of the time to keep the ground clear of any growth which might obscure the headstone. Now, a tangle of ivy and grasses concealed the lower part of the headstone, right up to the date, and a holly bush, rooted amongst the bones of the horse, formed a natural tribute to the animal.

The labrador cocked his leg and marked the stone. The gamekeeper let him. He did not like foxhunting. He thought it was cruel. Once, watching an argument on television about foxhunting, he had heard a woman quote somebody called Oscar Wilde on the subject. 'The unspeakable in pursuit of the uneatable,' he had said. The gamekeeper had liked that. It made him laugh and he remembered it. It was the only line of any writer he had learned since childhood. He hoped he would be able to use it one day in an argument.

The 12th Duke did not keep hounds on this estate. He kept his pack in Wiltshire and hunted there. The nearest hunt to George Purse's beat was centred on a village called Eccleshall, six miles away. The hounds (15½ couple) were kennelled there, and the Master of Hounds was a knight and a farmer. Once, he had invited the keepers from the Duke's estate over to Eccleshall to do some earth stopping, the day before a hunt. Earth stopping is sealing off the entrances to foxes' dens, so that they have fewer places to escape to when they are hunted.

When the keepers arrived, the Master of Hounds made them members of the Eccleshall Hunt Earth Stoppers Society. The Master of Hounds treated the Earth Stoppers Society to an annual supper, in an upstairs room of a pub during the week preceding the Hunt Ball in November.

George Purse and Charlie Taylor went out into the fields to stop some earths. They bolted two foxes that afternoon and George Purse shot them both. Six miles was no distance for a fox to travel if it was hungry. The shots were heard in Eccleshall, but the gamekeepers buried the carcases, and they were never discovered.

No foxes were sighted the next day, and no halloos were called. George Purse never went earth stopping again. And he was never invited to the annual supper of the Eccleshall Hunt Earth Stoppers Society.

The holly bush on the horse's grave was one of a cluster of hollies growing beside the ride. Even after a winter's foraging by birds, several of them were still rich with fruit. There had been no other demands on their resources. Nobody had cut the holly for Christmas.

Holly was cut for Christmas in some of the Duke's woods. The estate had a contract with a wholesale greengrocer in the City. The woodsmen employed by the estate cut the branches and gathered them together, and the wholesaler sent vans to collect them. The wholesaler's drivers and the Duke's woodsmen were all given orders to handle the branches carefully, so that the berries did not drop off. They took no notice, and threw them into the backs of the vans just the same. The drivers could always blame the rough state of the cart tracks when the doors were opened, and the berries were all over the floor.

During hard winters, when the frost and the snow came early, the birds could no longer forage in the fields, so they moved into the hedgerows and the woods, and fed on the haws, the rosehips and the hollyberries. During these winters, there was a shortage of holly with berries for Christmas, and the estate was able to charge the wholesaler more for its stock. The wholesaler still bought all he could get. He knew that even when he had raised his own price to the retailer he could still sell the stuff. And the retailers in the City regretfully passed on the price increase to their customers. The customers balked at the price of those horny sprigs; but those clusters of ruby beads worked their magic, and the holly was sold. After all, Christmas comes but once a year.

The gamekeeper left the ride and walked between the holly trees. A thrush flipped out from a low branch and flew towards a spread of rhododendrons straight ahead. The gamekeeper stood underneath the holly tree and looked up into the foliage. It was dark up there. The dense leathery leaves filtered the cold. It was a good roosting place.

The gamekeeper followed the thrush to the rhododendron bushes. Rabbits lived beneath them. It was a good place for rabbits; there was cover above the ground, and the soil was light and easy to dig. The labrador disappeared into the shrubs to smell them out. The gamekeeper ducked down and followed him in. He hated working in here, crouching and scrambling, being scratched and slapped in the face by bunches of leaves, tripping over roots and branches and having his hat knocked off. He was so preoccupied with his own progress, that he did not notice the dog underneath him, scenting a hole. He stumbled into the dog, it yelped, and the gamekeeper finished up on his knees, cursing and throwing soil after it as it retreated through the bushes. He was glad that he was alone and that Charlie Taylor had not seen the incident. He would have laughed at George's fall, and would have referred to it during the rest of the day. Sometimes, when they worked the rhododendrons together, Charlie would sit back and watch George at work.

'What you puffing at, George? I don't know how you'd have gone on in them two-foot-six seams that we used to work in.'

'Don't start on about that again. You miners are all alike. You'd make folks think you're the only ones who ever did any work.'

'Some of them seams were that thin, that if you crawled on to the face with your shovel upside down, you'd to crawl back out to turn it over.'

'And there's some light jobs, even down a pit. Anyway, it was no picnic where I used to work.'

'The only thing that's light about the pit is the money.'

And they crouched there under the green canopy, dogs and rabbits forgotten.

The dog barked, and sent the leaf mould spattering against the hard gloss of the rhododendron leaves as it dug in with its front paws. There was always a rabbit under these bushes. The gamekeeper had never failed to take one yet. He called the dog off and looked about him for bolt holes. He was too impatient to fiddle with the nets; he wanted to be out of these bushes as quickly as possible. So with his spade, he chopped away the soil above the surrounding holes and blocked up their entrances. Then, kneeling down at the open hole, he took Sam out of the bag and buckled his little leather collar round his neck. There was a line clipped to the collar, and as the gamekeeper unwound the line, it looked as though he was going to take the ferret for a walk. Instead, he placed it at the entrance to the hole and allowed the cord to slip through his fingers as the ferret walked in.

The rabbit was crouched in the dark, nose twitching, ears angling to catch the sounds outside. Then it smelled the ferret, turned round and padded away. No hurry. It branched left up a short slope; but there was no way out that way. It touched the fresh fall with its nostrils and the tang of the soil momentarily overpowered the smell of the ferret. It started to scratch at the loose pile. The ferret's stink. No time, it turned back, ran on and branched right, hind legs pushing hard up the steep crumbling slope. No exit. Down again, running hard, the stench pervading the narrowing tunnel. Stop. The rabbit pushed the hard soil with its face, scratched the wall, then crouched down as it was overwhelmed by the stink and the scuffle of the ferret behind it. The rabbit blocked the tunnel. The ferret could not squeeze past to attack the rabbit's neck, so he started to scrabble at its rump with his claws, quickly wearing a bald patch, a bloody patch in the pile. The rabbit squealed and turned its head in at the pain, and this turning and squirming movement made a gap between the rabbit and the burrow wall. The ferret filled this gap and shoved his face through the fur at the back of the rabbit's neck. The rabbit tried to buck him off, but there was insufficient room for the action, so it just squealed and shook its head. Driving in, the ferret pierced the flesh with its canines, one bite, two bites and he snapped the spinal column. The rabbit was dead.

At the other end of the line, the gamekeeper watched the line vibrating. He had heard the rabbit squealing, waited for a few seconds, and now he twitched the line to fetch Sam off. He did not want the rabbit spoiling. There would be no sale for a bloody mess. He jerked the line again, and this time it went slack. Sam was on his way out.

When he appeared, the gamekeeper did not pick him up straight away. The ferret became excited when he tasted blood, so the gamekeeper left him alone for a minute and kept his fingers clear. Sometimes, the ferret would not leave a kill, and the gamekeeper had to dig both the ferret and the rabbit out. When this happened the rabbit was always spoiled by the time he reached it, and he had to use it for the family's dinner, or throw it in for the ferrets. Sometimes, if the rabbit was only small, the gamekeeper dragged ferret and rabbit out together. But this time the ferret had been persuaded to detach himself. The gamekeeper let him stand for a few seconds looking back down the hole, then picked him up, unbuckled his collar, and placed him back in the bag.

The soil was as loose, and as easy to dig as sand. Working on his knees, the gamekeeper quickly unearthed the rabbit, shook it free of soil, then carried it out of the bushes, where he could stand up straight and stretch his back. Even if there were any more rabbits in there, he had had enough. His back ached and his thighs ached. It was a large estate. There were easier places to catch rabbits than this.

The pheasants started to lay in April. It was time to clean out the incubators and prepare the nesting boxes for the broody hens.

The incubators were situated in one of the outhouses directly across the yard from the cottage. The only other furniture in the room was an old kitchen table containing papier mâché egg trays. The table stood against the back wall. The incubators were spaced out in a line in the middle of the room so that the air could circulate all round them when the eggs were inside.

They were heated by electricity, and the wires ran down the wall together, then branched out across the stone flags.

It was a good place for incubators. The ventilation could be regulated by opening and closing the two halves of the stable door, and because the building was made of stone and roofed with stone tiles, there were no violent fluctuations in temperature. It was cool and clammy inside, like a church.

The nesting boxes for the broodies were sited in a line in front of the laying pen. They stood with their backs against the corrugated iron wall of the pen, so that they could receive the warmth of the sun in the morning, then, as the sun passed overhead, the shadow of the wall would lie across them in the afternoon. The hinged lids of the nesting boxes sloped downwards from back to front to let off the rain, and holes had been drilled in one side of each box for ventilation.

The gamekeeper made the nests by cutting out a round sod, shaping the hollow and lining it with hay. He was careful how he shaped the nests. If he made them too deep, or the sides were too steep, it made it difficult for the hen to turn the eggs in the centre. If they were too shallow, eggs which were accidentally pushed away from the clutch might not roll back underneath the hen, or newly hatched chicks might escape to the corners of the next box and die of cold in the night.

He preferred broodies to the incubators. They were more reliable. They looked after the eggs and the chicks. He only had to look after the hens. But he could never get enough to supplement his own stock. He approached all the farmers on the estate, and all the men in the village who kept hens on their allotments. Some of them did not have hens which were broody at that time. Or if they did, they wanted them for breeding purposes of their own, or they wanted too much money for them.

The gamekeeper managed to buy nine. He could have had three more but rejected them because of their condition. He had to be particular when buying broody hens. Sitting a clutch of eggs for twenty-four days is hard work for a hen, and if she is in poor fettle at the start of the sit she will not have the necessary stamina for the long job ahead. When he picked the hens up he looked for clear eyes, and smelled to see if their breath was sweet. He looked for well-feathered thighs and stomach, small feet and above all, clean legs. A scaly-legged bird can pass on infection to her chicks. One hen, borrowed from a farmer on the promise of a brace of grouse, had scaly legs, but was otherwise in good health. So the gamekeeper took it home in a sack, and got rid of the scales by dipping her legs in a mixture of Lorexane and paraffin, and holding them there for a minute.

He bought a Rhode Island Red off the landlord of the Sutcliffe Arms in the village. The gamekeeper offered him 50p for it. The landlord wanted 75. They finally settled at 75 with a pint of bitter thrown in to settle the difference.

The landlord led the way through the back room behind the bar, where all the crates were stacked, and out into the stable yard where his hens were strutting around the cobbles. The Sutcliffe Arms had formerly been a coaching inn, and the landlord housed his poultry in one of the old stables. When the gamekeeper saw the hen sitting on the nest, he said he didn't think it looked broody. The landlord immediately bet him a pint before he picked it up. The gamekeeper bent down and the hen began to cluck loudly. She mantled her wings, puffed out her feathers and raised her hackles in defence. The gamekeeper lifted her gently off the nest and placed one hand beneath her with his fingertips upwards. She squeezed his fingers between her wings, and he could feel her breast, bare and warm. She was broody all right. He did not go back into the pub. He paid the landlord 75p and took the hen straight home.

The gamekeeper also inquired after broody bantams for sitting partridge eggs. He always reared two or three clutches of partridges in addition to the pheasants. He collected the eggs from any wild nests he found on the extremities of his beat, where he felt they might be robbed by bird-nesters. So he brought them in and set them under broody bantams in the nesting boxes. Hens are too large and clumsy for partridge eggs. When the chicks hatch they are likely to be crushed beneath the heavy tread of the hen's big feet.

The pheasants in the laying pens did not lay their eggs in nests. They dropped them in the grass or under the tents of conifer branches which the gamekeeper had spread around for their protection. He collected the eggs every morning, moving around the pen carefully and systematically, so as not to frighten the birds or tread on any of the eggs.

One morning he found a broken egg with the contents partly eaten. Instinctively he looked up at the sky. He wanted to see a crow and blame it on that. But he knew that it was probably a young hen pheasant which had pecked at the shell out of curiosity, broken it, then found that there was food inside. This practice had to be stopped before it became a habit. He left the pen and crossed the yard towards the outhouses. The dogs watched him from their pen; the springer and the terrier close behind the wire mesh, the labrador sunning himself on his side on the wooden platform behind them. He lifted and turned

71

his head until the gamekeeper entered the outhouse where he stored his equipment, then his head flopped back to its original position on the warm boards.

The gamekeeper took down an Oxo tin from the shelf and eased off the lid. There were four last year's pheasant eggs inside. He took one out, replaced the tin, then carried the egg back to the laying pen. He collected the rest of the fresh eggs, settling them carefully into the basket, then placed the old egg on the bare earth near the feeding hopper.

Next morning the egg had been broken. The stinking slime had congealed about the fractured shell. There were no broken eggs the following day; and that was the end of egg eating for that season.

The gamekeeper left the pen and placed the basket of eggs on the ground so that he could close the door. A cock pheasant, perched on a fir branch close to the wire netting, watched him. Its head was iridescent in the morning sun, and its long barred tail feathers trailed to the ground like a rope ladder. He was the master cock of the pen. He had fought and asserted his mastery over all the other cocks. The gamekeeper whistled to him as he clicked the lock shut. The pheasant looked back with an eye as bright as pitch. He lifted his ear flaps and tilted his head towards the sound, and this slight change in position was sufficient to slide the blues and greens to turquoise, and shade the bronze to purple on his chest.

The gamekeeper picked up the basket and carried it down the yard towards the incubator house. John and Ian were playing football in front of the cottage. Ian was in goal and they were using a fishing basket and an empty sack for goalposts. The gamekeeper shouted to them to be careful until he had gone into the outhouse and closed the door. The boys immediately stopped playing. John stood with his foot on the ball, and Ian sat down on the basket. They would never have seen their ball again if it had gone near the basket of eggs, never mind hit it. The gamekeeper had to be careful how he carried and handled the eggs. Jolting the basket or handling them roughly could produce cracks or damage the eggs internally. He closed the outhouse doors behind him and switched on the light. John, noticing that the goalkeeper was still sitting on his post looking at the outhouse door, pushed the ball slowly with the inside of his foot into the goal. Ian jumped up and said it wasn't fair. John said he should have been ready, and the goal counted. Ian ran at the ball and kicked it out of the yard and into the edge of the wood. Then, before John could catch him, he escaped into the house, crying, to tell his mother all about it.

The gamekeeper placed the basket on the table and began to take out the eggs. He turned them round between his fingers to inspect them, then placed them blunt end upwards in a papier mâché tray. Any eggs which were fouled, he kept on one side, and when he had emptied the basket he took a pad of wire wool out of the table drawer and began to rub them down.

When he had finished, he was still not satisfied with the state of two of the eggs; he would have had to scrub them with the wire wool to get them clean, and that might have damaged the contents; so he went to the door and told John to fetch a bowl of warm water from the house.

In the yard, a house sparrow picked up a wisp of white down in its beak and carried it up towards the cottage roof. It dropped it, and as the tiny feather zig-zagged to the ground, the sparrow tried to catch it again. But the flurry of wings only sent the feather zooming and bobbing away from it, and in the end the sparrow tired of hovering and had to land and wait for the feather to float down to it. It was nesting time. The swallows would soon be back. Two years ago a pair had nested in one of the outhouses, and raised five young. They had returned last year and started to build again. Then the outhouse window had blown shut one night, and the swallows had been unable to get in. The gamekeeper did not notice the closed window for several days, and when he did see it and open it again, it was too late, the birds had lost interest. They stayed around the house for the summer, but they did not breed. Their part-built, forsaken nest was still there, a pat of dried mud up in the apex of the rafters. The gamekeeper hoped they would return. He opened the outhouse window while he remembered; then John came across the yard concentrating on the bowl of water. The gamekeeper wedged the window with a piece of stick, then walked back into the incubator house to wait for him.

He washed the two scruffy eggs in the warm water, then dried them on his handkerchief and stored them with the rest of the clean eggs on the egg tray.

John carried the bowl outside and slewed the water on to the flagstones. While the water was still finding its level, Ian came out of the house eating a biscuit. John immediately ran at him, looking into the bowl and screaming. He trapped Ian against the kitchen door before he could turn the knob and pretended to hurl the contents of the bowl all over him. Ian cried out, cowered down with his arms up, in anticipation of the deluge. When nothing more than a string of drops came out of the bowl and he remained dry, he started to cry. Not a wet sorrowful cry, but a furious bawling cry compounded of shock and humiliation.

Dodging swipes and kicks, John laughed and taunted Ian, then, to crown the success of his hoax, he fitted the bowl over his brother's head. Ian knocked it clattering on to the flags. Hens scuttled across the yard squawking, necks out, wings flapping like dusters. The dogs started to bark. A cock pheasant called Kok Kok in the laying pen. And the gamekeeper and his wife appeared in the doorways of the outhouse and the kitchen, threatening both boys as they came.

Every morning the same routine; feeding and watering the pheasants in the laying pen, collecting the eggs, cleaning and stacking them in the egg trays. The eggs were never stored in the trays for more than a week. They were only kept there until there were enough to fill an incubator. The incubators were like wooden chests on legs. The hinged front opened like a drawbridge, and inside was a metal tray for holding the eggs. Underneath the egg compartment was a narrow space which held the water tray. The gamekeeper had to keep this tray full all through the incubation period in order to maintain the humidity inside the incubator. Humidity is important for successful hatching. During incubation, the egg loses water by evaporation through its porous shell. This gives the chick space to manoeuvre when it breaks out of its shell. If it loses too much water the growth of the embryo will be stunted and it will die.

The gamekeeper sorted and graded the eggs before he set them in the incubator. He tried to make up a trayful of roughly the same size, shape and texture. Large eggs do not hatch as well in incubators as medium-sized eggs, so he used these along with any others he considered not sufficiently uniform, to help make up the clutches for the broodies.

He lined the egg tray with a square of clean sacking to give the chicks something to grip with their feet when they hatched out; then he set the eggs neatly in rows until the tray was full. He filled up the water tray and closed the door. That was one incubator at work. He would fill each incubator in turn when he had collected enough eggs. It would take twenty-four days for the chicks to hatch out. The gamekeeper chalked the date on the incubator door, picked up his basket and went out.

Before he set the broodies on their clutches he had to disinfect them with insect powder. He used a cocoa tin with holes punched in the lid like a pepper pot, and while John held the clucking hens, he shook powder under their tails and wings and round their thighs and vent. Then he allowed John to place them in their nesting boxes, each of which contained two white dummy eggs. The old dummies were made out of pot, the new ones out of plastic. They sat the dummies for three days to enable them to settle down. Then the dummies were replaced by the real pheasant eggs, sixteen or seventeen per nest.

The gamekeeper let the lads put the eggs into the nests. At first he said that Ian could not do it. He said that he would smash all the eggs. So Ian ran in to his mother, crying. She came out into the yard with the boy and said at least he ought to give the lad a chance. So he did; and Ian handled the eggs just as carefully and as confidently as his elder brother. Counting aloud, they placed sixteen eggs into the saucer of hay, eight each, each one handled as seriously as a bomb. Sixteen olive-coloured eggs, each one containing a tiny window of light in the curve of its glossy surface.

The boys moved back to allow their father to place the broody hen on the nest. Clucking softly, she fluffed out her feathers and settled herself gently over the eggs. John quietly closed the lid of the nesting box, then started to walk down the yard with his father. Ian watched them go, and when they went into the house, he knelt down and inched up the lid of the nesting box to have a last peep at the hen, sitting there with her eyes open in the dark.

The wind was pushing dabs of cloud across the sky. Every time a cloud passed in front of the sun the colour drained from the land. Then, when the sun reappeared it was like a silent celebration. The clear morning light stretched the horizon, and the sky, tracing the curve of the world, was as blue as a dunnock's egg.

It was a day to run across a field and launch a kite. Above the fields, higher than any kite, skylarks were singing. And below them in a ploughed field, a blackbird sat sunning himself on the crest of a furrow, his wings spread about him like a cloak. The opening buds of the hawthorns which separated the fields covered the hedgerows with a green haze, and in the woods the beech leaves were unfolding from their brown sheaths like little fans.

The gamekeeper went into the house for his shotgun. It was time to shoot a few nests out before the foliage grew any thicker and concealed them.

The gamekeeper kept his guns on a wall rack in the living-room. He owned three guns: two twelve-bore shotguns and a single-barrel .22 rifle. He stored the cartridges on the top shelf of the cupboard out of reach of the boys. They had been threatened with violence if they climbed anywhere near that shelf. The gamekeeper lifted down his oldest shotgun from the rack then looked round to see where his wife was. He could hear her talking to the dogs out in the yard, so he stood on the arm of the settee to reach up into the cupboard for a box of cartridges. He put two handfuls of the red number 6 cartridges into his jacket pocket, replaced the box and stepped down. His wife opened the kitchen door. The gamekeeper brushed the arm of the settee with his hand, picked up his gun and quickly left the room, closing the door behind him.

He was after crows and magpies, jays and jackdaws. The rooks could wait until their eggs had hatched out, and the fledglings were swaying in the branches beside their nests. Enemies of game, all of them. Especially the crow.

On his rounds, the gamekeeper looked for any new nests, or signs of the rebuilding of old ones. Jackdaws' nests were the most difficult to find because they built in holes. With them, he just had to be lucky enough to see the parents fly in or out of the hole; or hope that people would tell him of any nests that they had found.

He sometimes missed jays' nests because they built in the forks of trees. But while the foliage was still thin, crows' and magpies' nests were easy to see, especially the magpies', which sat up in the branches as bulky as hampers.

He did not find every nest. There were a lot of trees and miles of hedgerow on the land which constituted his beat. But vigilance, and years of systematic persecution with the gun and poisoned baits, allowed few families to thrive for long on his territory.

The gamekeeper knew a crow's nest in an oak tree in a hedgerow close to the Duke's wood. He had stood in the edge of the wood and watched the crows carry sticks and grasses to the tree.

He had allowed them to build on purpose; there would be eggs in the nest now. On his way through the wood the gamekeeper visited a robin's nest which he had found in the roots of an upturned stump. When he was ten yards away, he could see the mother sitting there, rust-coloured face and chin, watching him over the mossy rim of the nest. He backed off so as not to frighten her off, and as he retreated he ruffled the crushed grass with his gun barrels to obliterate the path which he had made to the nest.

At the edge of the wood the gamekeeper stood under the canopy of a horse chestnut tree, and looked across the field towards the oak where the crows had nested. No foliage was visible at this distance, its silhouette still belonged to winter. The gamekeeper reached up and felt one of the swollen brown horse chestnut buds. It was as sticky as a toffee apple. Some of the buds were unwrapping and revealing pale clusters of down-covered leaves. They looked more like the legs of hairy spiders than leaf shoots sprouting from their buds.

The gamekeeper walked along the edge of the wood until he came to the place where the hedgerow met the wood at right-angles. He climbed the fence into the field, then, under cover of the hedge he loaded his gun. Right barrel, left barrel, the two cartridges fitting snugly into place, brass caps flush with the end of each barrel. He closed the gun by lifting the stock and not the barrels. This kept the barrels pointing at the ground, and with the gun at this safe angle, left hand supporting the barrels, right hand on the stock, he began to move quietly along the hedgerow. Although the hedge had not been cut back for years and the hawthorns were feet taller than the gamekeeper, he still assumed a crouching position as he approached the oak tree. The crow's nest overhung the far side of the hedge. The gamekeeper was moving up on the blindside, and as he drew closer, he could no longer see it over the top of the hedge. Ten yards from the oak, he backed off into the field until he could see the nest. Then he released the safety catch on the gun, mounted it smoothly to his shoulder and fired both barrels into the nest, front trigger right barrel, back trigger left. There was a double explosion of sticks, feathers, grass and mud. The sitting crow was knocked up into the branches, where she hung for a few seconds before her dead weight dragged her loose and she dropped to the ground.

The gamekeeper squeezed through the hedge and stood under the oak tree looking up at the nest. He could see the sky through it. It was like looking up through the rafters of a derelict house. The debris had settled round the tree, sticks, grass, crusts of earth and sticky fragments of egg shell. The gamekeeper walked across to look at the dead crow. It had landed on its stomach with its beak pointing forward and legs tucked underneath it. There was blood on its beak, and with its wings spread, it lay in the grass like a black arrowhead. The gamekeeper turned it over with his boot, then picked it up by its stiffening legs and hurled it further into the field so that its mate could easily spot it as he flew in. Then he walked back to the hedge and crouched down under the overhang of the branches, making sure that his gun was in the shade, so that the barrels would not reflect light from the sun. He quietly reloaded his gun, then settled down to wait.

The death was soon forgotten. Life quickly returned to the fields and hedgerow. A bird landed in the top of the bush directly above him and started to sing. He looked up slowly, but he could not see it for the green fuzz of buds between them.

So he sat and listened to it. A run of staccato notes then a long wheeze. What was it? The gamekeeper stepped out from under the bush and looked up. The bird flew off immediately, but he saw enough of it to have a guess at its identity. Yellow. A canary? Two white feathers on its tail. It must be a yellow-hammer. He would check it in John's bird book when he got home. He ducked back under the bush. The yellow-hammer had flown, but he could still hear its song in his head, Te Te Te Te Te Te Teeee . . . He would know what it was the next time he heard one singing.

A hare loped across the field close to the dead crow. It could have been a dog at first glance. It stopped, ears and nostrils working, its slender legs lifting its stomach well clear of the ground. It was an animal built for running, and it was ready to run any moment now. In the mythical world of elves and fairies, messengers ride hares under full moons, carrying royal notes to distant Kings under distant woods. A fabulous creature, the hare.

Then the gamekeeper heard the crow. It had flown in behind him, and was up in the oak tree making its din. The gamekeeper eased off the safety catch, crooked his finger round the front trigger and stepped out from under the hawthorn, pivoting and mounting his gun as he looked for the crow. It was perched swaying and cawing on two twigs at the top of the tree, looking down into the field. Its legs kept splaying, and it had to flap its wings to keep balance. The gamekeeper fired his first shot before it had time to fly, but it was too hurried and he missed. The crow threw itself sideways out of the tree, but it had barely cleared the branches before the second shot sent its feathers flying and tumbled it into the top of the hawthorn hedge. The gamekeeper walked up to the hedge and looked up at the crow. It was hanging upside down, eyes staring, opening and closing its beak and trying to flap its wings amongst the tangle of thorny branches. The gamekeeper broke open his gun, and there was a reek of powder as the cartridge cases ejected themselves. He pushed a fresh cartridge into the right-hand barrel, aimed carefully, and blasted the life out of the crow in a fresh puther of feathers. The force of the shot lodged the crow even more firmly amongst the branches. The gamekeeper left it hanging there and walked on.

Grey down was still drifting down when he reached the end of the hedgerow and climbed back over the fence into the wood.

The two bird-nesters were so busy that they did not hear the gamekeeper coming up behind them. The bigger boy had made a stirrup by linking his hands, and his mate, who had taken his jacket off to climb the tree, was standing in the stirrup and reaching up for the first branch. He grabbed it and pulled himself up while the boy on the ground helped him by shoving his feet from below. The boy on the ground let go and examined his hands, which were stinging from the pressure of the climber's boots. The climber stood on the first branch looking up the tree, working out his route.

'Now then, what you doing?'

The shock nearly fetched the climber out of the tree. But even as the boys jumped and spun they were still looking for a way of escape. The boy up the tree had no chance. Unlike Tarzan, he had no convenient creeper at hand. The sight of the gamekeeper's gun was enough to deter the other boy.

'Don't you know you're trespassing?'

The boys just looked at each other.

'Right then, where do you come from?'

Again no reply.

82

'Come on! Or I'm taking you straight to the police station, both of you.'

'Woodside.'

'I thought so. It ought to be wiped off the face of the earth that estate.'

He took a last year's *Shooter's Year Book* from the breast pocket of his jacket and opened it at random. Both pages were blank. The gamekeeper had had no engagements that week. At the bottom of the right-hand page in small type it read,

The Game Conservancy provides an expert advisory service for shoot improvements. Write to Fordingbridge for details.

The gamekeeper read it. He agreed. Between five and six million pheasants are shot in a season, about two million grouse and large numbers of woodpigeon, partridge and mallard. Many of these would not exist to be shot without the help of the Game Conservancy, which advises landowners how to build up their gamestocks. The Game Conservancy is a new name for the Eley Advisory Station. Eley Ammunition is a subsidiary of Imperial Metal Industries, which is in turn a subsidiary of I.C.I. Eley produces around eighty per cent of all the cartridges shot off in Britain each season, and makes the cases for all the cartridges produced in Britain. Imperial Metal Industries subsidizes the Game Conservancy with a yearly grant, and Eley published the *Shooter's Year Book* which provided the information about the Game Conservancy.

The gamekeeper found an inch of pencil in the same pocket and licked the lead.

'Now then. What's your names?'

Neither of them spoke, so he nudged the gun barrels in the direction of the boy standing under the tree.

'You, what's your name?'

'David Smith.'

'David Smith! And I suppose your mate's called John Brown?'

'Honest, mister. That's what they call me, don't they, Mart?'

The boy up the tree nodded.

'They'd better, lad, or I'll be straight up to that school to find you out. Where do you go to, Dame Edith Sitwell?'

'Ar, worse luck.'

'Well the headmaster up there's a mate of mine, so you'd better not be lying. And where do you live?'

'Five Duke's Close.'

The gamekeeper repeated this information to himself as he pretended to write it down in his diary.

'Da-vid Smith. Five Duke's Close.'

He looked up into the tree.

'And what's your name?'

The boy up the tree had not moved. He was still standing on the bottom branch with one arm round the trunk.

'Martin Clarke.'

'Mar-tin Clarke. And where do you live?'

'Twenty-five Manor Drive.'

'Twen-ty, five, Man-or, Drive. Right.'

The gamekeeper underlined the blank addresses with two sharp strokes, as if to emphasize to the boys how seriously he was treating the matter. Then he replaced his pencil and diary and took a firmer grip on the gun.

'It's a court job this, I can tell you. I'm fed up with you lot off that estate.'

'We didn't know we were trespassing, mister.'

'Didn't know! What do you think all them boards are round the side of the wood, invitations to come in?'

'We didn't see any boards, did we, Mart?'

'No, you probably ripped the buggers down and chopped them up for firewood.'

The boy up the tree shifted his position and his foot slipped. He grabbed the trunk and the branch shook, frightening the boy underneath it, who thought the lot was coming down on top of him. He ran out with his arms up, looking backwards and up.

'Fucking hell, I thought I'd had it then.'

The gamekeeper had to say something or he would have started laughing.

'And what are you doing up that tree?'

'Nowt.'

'Nowt! You ask a question and nobody's ever doing owt. There's a nest up there isn't there?'

'I don't know.'

'Don't you know that it's illegal to take birds' eggs?'

'A jackdaw flew out. I was just getting up to have a look.'

'How do you know it was a jackdaw?'

'We saw it. It was black with a grey head.'

'Well, get up and have a look then.'

The boy looked from the gamekeeper to his mate, but he just elevated his shoulders and depressed his lips, so the climber started to climb. The going was easy. It was a beech tree with branches as accessible as a step ladder. Near the top the boy stopped and looked into a hole which had formed where a branch had broken off the trunk.

'It's here. There's young 'uns in. Four.'

'Right. Come down now then.'

The boy started to climb down. When he reached the bottom branch, he lay across it on his stomach, eased himself off until he was hanging full stretch by the hands, then dropped the few feet to the ground. When he stood up, his shirt was out of his trousers and there were twigs snagged in the front of his sweater.

'Can we go now, mister?'

'What else have you found?'

'Nowt.'

'Have you got any eggs?'

The boy shook his head. His mate shook his as well, even though he was standing behind the gamekeeper, and the question had not been directed at him. The gamekeeper turned round.

'We'll soon see.'

He walked across and held his hands in a clapping position close to the boy's jacket pockets.

'Have I?'

'You can please yourself.'

The gamekeeper slapped both pockets, then his jeans pockets, front and back, and finally his chest, just in case he had inside pockets. The last two slaps were hard enough to make the boy step back.

'Satisfied?'

'No.'

He walked across to the jacket under the tree and picked it up. Underneath it, in a shallow depression in the leaf mould, lay a hybrid three-egger; woodpigeon, songthrush and chaffinch.

The boys looked at each other, then glanced around as though contemplating escape. But the gamekeeper was still holding the jacket.

'Right. That's three things I can do you for now. One, trespass. Two, illegal acquisition of birds' eggs. And three, intent to deceive. You'll get six months apiece for this.'

He threw the jacket and the boy who had climbed the tree caught it and started to put it on.

'We haven't done owt wrong. We've only taken one out of each nest. There were plenty left, they'll not desert.'

'It must have been a funny woodpigeon's you found if there were plenty left in that. They only lay two.'

'Well, we left one in. Anyroad, what about when folks go round shooting woodpigeons?'

His mate agreed, and moved forward to his side.

'That's right, I've seen them. They shoot them in hundreds.'

The boys seemed to be gaining confidence, so the gamekeeper took a quick step forward and made a show of taking a fresh grip on his gun.

'They're not trespassing though, are they?'

And both boys stepped back.

'Have you blown these?'

He bent down and picked up the three eggs. He could tell immediately by the weight of the woodpigeon's and thrush's eggs that they were still whole. But he checked the ends of the smaller chaffinch's egg just to make sure.

'Good. Right now you can just take them back where they came from.'

He gave them an egg each and kept the woodpigeon's for himself.

'You ought to be ashamed of yourselves. Lads of your age taking eggs.'

'We can't take them back. We've forgotten where we got them from. Haven't we, Mart?'

'Well you'd better remember then, 'else I'll have the bobby waiting for you before you've got home. Now go on.'

The boys turned round and started to walk away, with the gamekeeper close behind. Making sure that they were not looking, he flicked the woodpigeon's egg backhand against a tree root and smashed it.

'Have you lads found any pheasants' or partridges' nests on your travels?'

Half turning, the boys shook their heads.

'If you have and you show me where they are, I might let you off this time.'

'We haven't found any.'

They found the thrush's and the chaffinch's nests, and when they had replaced the eggs, and the gamekeeper had looked into them to verify that they had been telling the truth, he let them go.

He stood and watched them walk away through the trees, waiting to see if they would start abusing him when they thought they were far enough away to outrun him. If they did, he would cut them off and frighten them by firing both barrels close enough for them to hear the lead shot overtaking them.

But they did not. They just conversed quietly with each other, and kept glancing back. When they had gone, the gamekeeper walked back through the wood and climbed the tree to the jackdaws' nest. The young birds were still skinny and bald. Their large heads and scaly legs looked out of proportion to their bodies, and when the gamekeeper put his hand into the hole, four black beaks blossomed into orange gapes in anticipation of food. The gamekeeper took them out one at a time and killed them by banging their heads sharply against the tree trunk. He dropped them to the ground, then reached into the hole and pulled out all the sticks, wool and paper, and dropped that after them. He climbed down, spaced out the dead jackdaws around the tree, then loaded his gun and settled down behind a holly bush to wait.

Busy days; the eggs were set in the incubators and all the broodies were sitting. After breakfast, the gamekeeper's first job was to turn the eggs in the incubators. He did this by licking his forefinger, then, working along the rows of eggs until he had completed a whole tray, he turned each egg half a roll to the right. He looked as though he was dialling a long number. He pushed each tray back into the incubator, topped up the level of water in the water tray from a tin jug, and closed up the front. This turning had to be done every day, morning and evening at twelve-hour intervals. In the evening he turned the eggs back half a turn to the left. If he had rotated the eggs in one direction only, the strands which held the yolk would have become strained, and fewer chicks would have developed.

The gamekeeper wedged open the outhouse door to make a draught, then went outside. The yard was in the shadow of the cottage, and the air was still cool. But by mid-morning the sun would have cleared the house top and warmed the flagstones, and the stone tiles on the outhouse roof.

His next job was to feed the broodies. He went next door, where he kept his feed. The window was still wedged open, but the swallows had not come back to nest yet. The gamekeeper ladled half a bucket of poultry pellets from a sack under the bench, walked across the yard and filled a watering can with a hosepipe through the kitchen window. He carried the bucket and the watering can up the yard to the laying pen, where the row of nesting boxes was sited. At the front of each box there were two earthenware pots and a forked stick like a catapult straddle. A short cord was tied to each stick with a slipknot at the loose end. The dishes were for water and grit, the sticks to secure the broodies while they fed.

The gamekeeper threw the old water out of each pot, swilled it round with fresh, then half filled it and replaced it beside the pot of grit. He dropped two handfuls of pellets outside each box then lifted the lid of the first box. The brown hen blinked at the light, and started to cluck and depress herself as the gamekeeper reached down to lift her off her nest. He placed his open hand beneath her, but before he lifted her out of the box he felt under her wings to make sure that she was holding no eggs there. He tethered her by the leg to the Y stick, then left her to feed and drink while he lifted the lid of the next box and picked out the second hen.

He had to work quickly. The hens had to be out long enough to eat and drink and excrete, but if they were off their nests too long there was the danger that the eggs would go cold and the hatch would be impaired. This morning, the sun was up, and the wind was mild from the south-east, so the gamekeeper did not have to scuffle. He reckoned fifteen minutes each, as the morning was fine.

By the time he had tethered the last hen, it was time to replace the first one. He tested the eggs with the back of his hand. Yes, they were still warm. The hen had finished feeding, so he untied her, replaced her gently on the nest and quietly closed the nest box lid. Before he replaced each hen he made sure that there was a dropping at the front of the nest box. If there was not, he made the hen shit by gently pushing her around for a few moments. A few clucks and it was there. This mild persuasion never failed.

When all the hens were back in their boxes the gamekeeper removed all the droppings with a shovel; then he picked up the empty bucket and the watering can, and started back towards the outhouses, watering the ground as he went, until the can was empty.

After he had put the feeding utensils away, the gamekeeper went into the house. His wife did not hear him come in. She was in the living-room using the vacuum cleaner. He felt at the teapot, looked at the dark brew inside, and decided against it. The motor died next door, and the ensuing silence was so profound that it seemed to be generating a hum of its own.

'Are you coming to help me let the pheasants go, Mary?'
'What?'

She had forgotten that she had switched off the machine.

'What you shouting at? I'm not deaf you know.'

She came through into the kitchen, pushing the vacuum cleaner with one hand, and reeling in the flex with the other.

'What did you say?'
'I said I'm not deaf.'

She left the vacuum cleaner at the side of the dresser and walked across to the sink.

'Nobody said you were. Do you want a cup of tea?'

She picked up the kettle and shook it to see how much water there was in it.

'I'm going to let the pheasants go out of the laying pen. Are you coming to help me?'

'The kids'll help you when they get home. They like doing things like that.'

'Why don't you come and help me?'

'I've no time. I've work to do.'

She emptied the teapot into the sink, then turned the tap on to flush away the mess.

'I've told you before. You'll be blocking the sink up doing that.'

She ignored him, and kept the tap running until every tea leaf had disappeared.

'Anyway, I'd look well now, running about that pen chasing pheasants.'

'Why would you? You used to. You used to enjoy it as well. You used to kill yourself with laughing.'

'Well, that was different. I'd no choice then had I? Somebody had to help you.'

She looked about her, then nodded in the direction of the dresser.

'Pass me the tea, George.'

The gamekeeper picked up a biscuit barrel with a chrome handle off a pile of women's magazines on the dresser. The magazines partly concealed a square of lining paper with a picture painted on it. The gamekeeper could see enough of the picture to make him pull it out and look at it.

The top half of the picture was blue, the bottom half green. A large brown tree dominated the left side of the picture, and on the right hand side a man appeared to be looking up into the branches through a long black telescope. There were black blobs in the branches which were obviously nests, and smaller black blobs which were recognizable as birds because they had beaks. Two birds shaped like aeroplanes were falling from the branches, and heading for the ground with the finality of Kamakasi pilots. The ground was littered with birds, and there was a lot of activity in the sky around the tree by birds shaped like lance corporals' stripes. In the bottom right-hand corner of the picture it said, Ian Purse. And below that, in sloping rapidly diminishing letters which just made it before they ran out of paper, my dad rook shooting.

The picture made the gamekeeper laugh.

'When did he do this?'

'It must have been last week sometime. He brought it home on Friday.'

'Look at them all. It looks more like Custer's last stand.'

'He said Miss Morris said it was good.'

'It's a good job that rifle isn't longer though, or I wouldn't need any bullets. I'd be able to knock them out of the branches with the barrel.'

'He said she thought it was cruel though.'

'Cruel. What's she know about it?'

He slapped the picture back on to the dresser.

'Let her stick to her job and I'll stick to mine!'

'It's no good shouting at me. I'm only telling you what our Ian said.'

'You agree with her though, don't you?'

She filled the teapot, and the steam and the hiss of the boiling water scalding the metal seemed to emphasize the tension between them.

'What's she know, anyroad? She's only a kid. Straight from school to college, then back into school. Nine 'til four and three months' holiday a year. She doesn't know she's born.'

'Pass your cup and stop shouting.'

'She's never had to get up at half-past five in a morning and work shifts. She's never come home black bright, or come home in an ambulance with metal splashes on her. If she'd worked in some of the places I've worked in she wouldn't be so bloody fussy about killing a few rooks.'

'She's a right to her own opinion hasn't she?'

'She doesn't know enough about it to have an opinion. I mean, what was there to look forward to? Eight hours of purgatory, week in week out, until I was sixty-five?'

His wife pushed his cup of tea across the table, making the level tilt like a seesaw. They watched the tea until the motion had subsided.

'Yes, it's better for you, I'll give you that.'

'Well, it's better for you isn't it?'

Mary Purse said nothing, so the gamekeeper interpreted her silence and answered his own question.

'You what? We've got a nice little house in a nice place, all rent free. What more do you want? Some folks would give a fortune for a place like this.'

'Yes, but it would be theirs then, wouldn't it? What would happen to us if you got the sack, or got lamed or something and had to find a fresh job? Where would we go? We've no savings for a mortgage, and there's a waiting list for council houses as long as your arm.'

'Well, you can't have everything.'

'Everything! We haven't got anything. We've no security at

all. At least when you worked at Brightside, you brought home a decent wage.'

'Money's not everything.'

'And suppose we're still here when you retire. They're not going to let you stop here, are they?'

'Well, they'll not just chuck us out on to the streets after all them years, will they? They'll find us a cottage somewhere else on the estate.'

'Perhaps they will. But all the time we're having to rely on them. They seem to have us over a barrel, that's what gets me.'

'It's a bit late to start grumbling now, Mary. We knew what we were doing. Let's face it, they didn't force me to take the job at gunpoint.'

'I know, I know. I didn't know as much then, though.'

And they drank their tea, and ate biscuits from a packet standing on the table between them. Every time they took a biscuit, they held the packet so that it would not fall down.

Mary Purse looked past her husband at the outhouse across the yard. The sun had just lit the top row of roof tiles and made the rest of the roof look dirty. A magpie landed on the apex of the roof and ducked forward to look into the yard. Its tail disappeared down the other side of the slates and suddenly it looked a much smaller bird. There was something there, and it swooped down, describing a curve across the window pane like a rapid drop on a sales graph.

'You know, I did think it was romantic when we first moved here, a cottage in the wood and all that. It is beautiful, but even that wears off. I mean, you can get fed up of looking at trees and fields all day.'

'What do you mean all day? Anybody would think that you never went out.'

'And where do I go? I go cleaning up at the House three mornings a week, and shopping in the village.'

'And what do other women do that's any different?'

'Nothing, but that's no consolation to me is it? Do you know we've been here ten years and I hardly know anybody. I feel uncomfortable on the council estate because of you. And they're that close up in the village, honestly, some of the older end still look on me as a day tripper.'

There was a squawk from the yard followed by a cackle. It sounded as though the magpie had played a trick on one of the hens. The gamekeeper looked round at the window.

'Is that a magpie?'

And his tone could have been no more incredulous if he had heard the voice of God. He jumped up and hurried to the door. In the yard there were hens and a pair of house sparrows. When they saw him the house sparrows flew up on to the slates. The hens continued to strut about, jerking their heads and pointing their toes.

'The crafty bugger. Where's it gone?'

He stepped outside and looked around. But there was nothing there. He walked to the house end and looked across the fields. There was nothing there either. So he went back inside and finished his tea standing by the table.

'Do you want another cup?'

'No, I'll get off now. I'll release the pheasants later.'

'Where are you going?'

'I'm going for a walk round.'

'Will you be back for your dinner?'

'I'm not sure. I might call in at the Arms and have a sandwich or something.'

'Well, I want to know, don't I?'

'No, don't bother then. I'll have my dinner at tea time with the kids.'

He fetched his rifle and some bullets from the living-room, then went out. Through the window his wife watched him walk away across the yard. When he had gone she switched on the radio.

> It's only a paper moon
> Sailing over a cardboard sea ...

It was bluebell time. They grew so thickly that they coloured the floor of the wood, pale in the clearings where the sun came through, darkening to indigo in the shadow of the trees. A blue haze hung over the bluebells and tinted the light between the trees. This light set off the fresh foliage which concealed the birds singing in the branches. The air was sweet with the scent of bluebells, and George Purse breathed in this scent as he walked through the wood. He might have sung too if he had not been a gamekeeper. But he could not sing when he was working. How would he catch anybody? They would hear him coming a mile off.

Nobody else was allowed to walk through the wood to appreciate the bluebells. Poachers, abroad on their nefarious activities, sometimes saw them. They even trod on them. But they never lingered on the floral carpet, discussing subtleties of light and shade. They just called their dogs to heel and sneaked knee deep through its pile.

And sometimes little girls crept into the edge of the wood to pick the flowers. At first they kept quiet, whispering while they worked. But as they became absorbed in their task they forgot where they were. All they saw was a field of flowers, bluebells, green stalks turning to white as they pulled them from the soil. They kept sniffing them, thinking that the strength of the whole crop was contained in the single flower. Bees made them scream, made them laugh. They could see their mothers' faces when they took them home. They could see them in vases, on the sideboard and on the window sill. And they never knew when to stop. They competed for the biggest bunch. They picked and picked until they had to nurse the flowers in their arms like sheaves of corn. They never saw the man until he was standing over them.

The gamekeeper was very stern. He told them that they were trespassing, then asked them if they knew what that meant. He told them that he had a wild dog which guarded the wood, and he put one finger up to make them listen. But they could not hear it, so he said that it must be asleep somewhere, and that they were lucky it had not found them. Then he sent them out of the wood, and told them that he would take them to the police station if he caught them again. But he always let them keep their flowers.

Once, John had painted a bluebell. Then he had painted a fairy dressed in one of the bells. His father had seen the painting and called him a right little puff. You'll be turning into a bloody fairy if you're not careful, the gamekeeper had said.

He came out from the trees and stood looking across the fields. He was not looking for anything in particular. He was just enjoying the sun on his face, and savouring being there. It was mornings like this which made him become a gamekeeper.

When he worked in the steel industry, he used to turn the alarm off, turn over for five minutes, then get up and walk across to the window to have a look at the weather. He would look at the clouds to see which way the wind was blowing, and when he saw that it was going to be fine, it made him even more miserable. Then he would go down for his breakfast and watch the sky brightening as the sun came up. And if it was Friday it was all too much, he would take the day off. He would go fishing, or work in his allotment, or go out with the ferret and the dog. Whenever he did miss a shift, he never made his wife suffer a drop in wages. On the next pay day he always gave her the same housekeeping money, and stood the loss himself.

George Purse had always enjoyed being outside. When he left school there had been two choices. It was either the steel industry or the pit. Some lads chose the pit. George Purse chose steel. At least there was only a roof and walls between him and the sun there.

The first time he was offered a job as a keeper, he turned it down. He would not be able to live, he said. The keepers on the Duke's estate were only paid the same rate as the farm labourers, and he earned twice as much as that as a moulder. Two years later the job came up again. This time he took it. He had had two more years of working shifts, of lifting boxes, of strained backs, of fierce heat, of dust, of metal burns. He took the gamekeeper's job at half his previous pay. But there was a rent-free cottage with the job; that was a bonus.

The gamekeeper was on his way to look at his traps. He had traps set all over his beat; in hedgerows, in wall bottoms, in copses and in woods. He had to walk round every morning to see what they had caught, and to re-set the ones which had killed.

His first trap was set in a hedgerow which separated two fields of wheat. He had diverted the end furrows in both fields by digging channels which led straight into a tunnel through the hedge. He had blocked the furrows with soil, so that any animal travelling down the furrows would be encouraged to take the short cut through the tunnel into the next field. Two sticks, and a stick lintel marked the entrance of the tunnel, and the stick rafters had been roofed with turfs. A Fenn trap was set inside the tunnel. When an animal ran across the metal plate the jaws sprang to and crushed it. The trap was empty. The gamekeeper found a stick and touched the trigger pan. The jaws clanged shut and snapped it. He re-set the trap, replaced it carefully in the tunnel, covered the chain and peg with soil and moved on.

The Fenn trap is now used instead of the gin trap, which was made illegal in 1958. The gin trap had two iron jaws with blunt teeth. When an animal stepped into the trap the jaws snapped to, smashing and gripping it by the leg. The jaws broke the bone and held the animal by the tendon, and as it struggled and pulled to free itself, the tendon twisted round and round like an elastic band. Sometimes the tendon snapped and the mutilated animal would limp away, leaving a leg or a paw still fast in the trap. Sometimes the pain was so fierce that the trapped animal gnawed its leg until it severed the tendon and released itself. If it could not pull its leg off, or if it was caught by more than one leg it had to wait there until the gamekeeper or the poacher came back to kill it next day. Young rabbits died in the night from shock and exposure. Adult animals, weakened by pain and hunger and fright, would start to struggle all over again when they heard the footsteps and smelled the man approaching.

George Purse had never used a gin trap. When he was a boy he had once seen a white bull terrier stagger down their street with a gin trap clamped to its face. It had dragged the peg out of the earth and the chain was trailing along the ground like a broken lead. The right ear was nearly off, and that side of its face was raw flesh where the iron teeth had combed its face, as it tugged itself free. It kept whining and shaking its head, and spots of blood splattered the paving stones and fronts of houses as it passed them. The noise brought people out into the street, and some of them followed the dog home, gathering on the pavement when the dog walked down the entry. A minute later Sam Johnson ran up the entry and everybody moved back. He was white even underneath his pit muck. 'I'll kill them. I'll fucking kill them.' And at that moment he would have done. He set off running for the vet, two miles through the pit yard and over the fields in his pit muck and slippers. Somebody phoned the vet while he was still running, and the vet had already left when Sam Johnson arrived. When he got back home he gave his wife a good hiding for letting the dog out on its own. The dog died five days later. Sam Johnson never found out where the trap had been set or who had set it. When George Purse went back to school after the summer holidays he wrote a story about it. He got seven out of ten and underneath the mark, watch your spelling.

The gamekeeper's second trap was set at the bottom of a wall which bordered a copse of birch trees. He had leaned a flat stone against the wall and set the trap inside. He bent down and raised the stone from the wall. There was a dead rat in the trap. It was still in a running position, eyes open, mouth ajar. It had been travelling along the wall bottom, seen the tunnel and decided to investigate. Then smack. It looked surprised to be dead just for that. The gamekeeper threw the rat into the field, re-set the trap, and climbed the wall into the copse.

New fronds of bracken were unwinding under the trees. Last year's rusty growth was festooned around the tree trunks and branches like flotsam marooned at low tide. The gamekeeper followed a narrow path which separated the bracken like a parting through curly hair. It was the only path through the copse. The gamekeeper had set a snare on it. Anybody else walking along the path would not have seen it, because the wire noose was disguised with old bracken stems. The gamekeeper hoped a fox would not see it either. The pear-shaped noose was set a hand's width from the ground and fastened to a peg hidden in the bracken at the side of the path.

Head down, hunting, the fox would push its head through the noose, feel something brush its throat and jerk away. Caught. And the more it panicked and pulled, the tighter the wire bit into its neck until it had to relax because of the lack of air, and resume the struggle at intervals.

When the gamekeeper did his rounds on the following day he would not waste a cartridge on it, he would just nobble it on the head and kill it that way.

But snares are unselective. They catch other animals which walk into them. The gamekeeper once found a dead cat, eyes bulging, head like a football from the pressure of the blood which had pumped through its brain as it had struggled to pull free. He once found a sheepdog, fretting and vicious after a night with the wire noose chafing its neck. He tried to release it, but every time he went close, the dog wrinkled its face and showed him its teeth. It snarled and growled in its throat and the gamekeeper's soft words were useless. It just watched his hands approaching its head then snapped at them, making him whip them away. Finally, the gamekeeper lost his temper and clubbed the dog with the stock of his shotgun. But he hit it too hard, and when he slackened the noose, he realized that it was dead. It lay in the bracken with a sore collar worn into its ruff. The gamekeeper buried it in the wood and said nothing.

The snare in the copse was empty. The gamekeeper touched up the bracken camouflage, checked the shape of the noose, then stepped over it and walked on.

At the edge of the copse there was an oak tree with a tunnel running through the roots directly at the base of the trunk. The entrance was as perfectly arched as a mousehole in a cartoon. If children had been allowed in the copse they would have knelt down and peeped through it. Small animals liked the tunnel too and the gamekeeper had set a trap in there. He knelt down and peeped in. It had caught a hedgehog. The spring jaws had crushed and snapped its quills when they had sprung to on its sides. Fenn traps did not always kill big hedgehogs. Their armour and stout bodies did not allow the springing jaw full bite, and all they did was maim the animal and hold it alive until the gamekeeper arrived to kill it.

The hedgehog was no real enemy of the gamekeeper. They sometimes destroyed a wild nest of partridge eggs, but he much preferred to trap a stoat, or a rat, or a weasel, they were the real enemies of game. The gamekeeper released the dead hedgehog and threw it down on top of some others which were piled like logs at the bottom of the tree.

The gamekeeper came out of the copse at the back of a barn in the corner of a field. Along the edge of the field adjacent to the trees, rabbits had nibbled away a twenty-yard strip of wheat shoots. The gamekeeper moved quietly up the far side of the barn and peeped round the front. Six rabbits were feeding in the field. Mounting his rifle, the gamekeeper stepped out from the corner of the building and started to shoot. The first bullet forced up a spray of earth. The nearest rabbit sat up and cocked its ears. It appeared to be unaware that a bullet had just missed it. It did not look over its shoulder to see how close the bullet had landed, it just looked towards the gamekeeper, then started to bob away, white scut winking, making for the cover of the trees and the bracken in the copse. All the rabbits were running now. The gamekeeper fired again, knocked a rabbit over, and fired at another one before they all vanished into the copse. The shot rabbit was travelling with them, squealing and pulling itself along with its front legs, and it made cover before the gamekeeper could reach it.

He stood looking into the bracken near the place where the rabbit had disappeared into the copse. All the rabbits were in there now, listening, safe amongst the fronds. The gamekeeper stepped into the bracken, poked around with his rifle barrel, separated a few stalks with his boot, then looked at the expanse of curly green stretching away under the birch trees. He was not going to search that lot just to find one injured rabbit.

The wounded rabbit heard the bracken rustling, then the sound receded as the gamekeeper moved out and walked across the field to have a look at his next trap. Still the rabbit did not move. It just lay there with its head up, panting, shattered leg stretched out behind it, listening now for danger from more immediate animal sounds.

A good morning's work done, time for some lunch. Thursday, pork pie day! Home made pie and a pint of bitter. The gamekeeper nearly started running.

He walked across the fields to the Big House and took a short cut through the vegetable garden. A trodden earth path bisected the garden. Three long greenhouses containing tomato plants and flowers stood on one side of the path, and the land on the other side was planted with vegetables. One of the under-gardeners let him through a locked door in the high wall which surrounded the garden, and he came out at the war memorial at the end of the village street.

The war memorial had been erected by the Duke in memory of his tenants who had been killed in the two World Wars. It consisted of two open stone books leaning back to back on a plinth. The pages of one book were engraved with the fatalities of the First World War, the other book with the fatalities of the Second. The books were set at an angle like a tent, and there was a triangular tunnel between them. The plinth was surrounded by stone flags and there were two benches, one facing each book. Anybody sitting there with nothing to do could read the stone pages of one book, then move round and read the stone pages of the other.

The gamekeeper had always thought that the tunnel between the books would be a good place to set a Fenn trap. But he had never mentioned the idea, in case friends or relatives of the deceased found it offensive.

The village had one main street. Most of the houses on the street were built in short terraces opening straight on to the

105

pavement. Some formed closes with a communal lawn, and there was the occasional detached house, with its gable end to the street, its garden enclosed by a high stone wall.

There was a farm half-way down the street, and a trail of cow dung led from the gateway down to the far end of the road. There were other farms in the fields behind the houses, and in the spaces between the houses there were allotments and lawns. Fruit trees, laburnums and flowering cherries were in blossom, and above these, softening the skyline of the village, grew the wild, self-planting trees, the sycamore and ash, horse chestnut and elm. The ash trees were still knobbly with buds, their swelling black tips just splitting and shading to green, while the horse chestnut leaves were as long as a hand, and the white lights of their candelabra were already dimmed.

Most of the houses were built of stone, a few of rough narrow bricks which had been baked in the estate kiln. They had foot-scrapers set into the walls by the doors and the oldest ones were roofed with stone tiles. None of the houses had been built this century. Every house was painted the same colour, every window frame and door, every gatepost and fence, cream and brown; the estate colours.

An old man in shirt-sleeves and waistcoat came shuffling up the middle of the road, in carpet slippers. As they passed each other, the gamekeeper said, 'You'd better watch out, Tom. There's a hansom cab due any minute.'

The old man nodded in senile agreement and shuffled on. The gamekeeper passed the post office, and the postmaster immediately turned from his customer and looked through the window. Only small animals and midgets could get by that shop without being seen. The gamekeeper glanced at the window display as he walked by; bottled sweets and postcards showing black-and-white views of the Big House, half a dozen flowered pinafores and a small pyramid of tinned peas.

He passed the telephone booth. The bottom pane in the door had been kicked in. The village stocks used to stand where the telephone booth stood. In the nineteenth century, one of the incumbents of the Church, who was also a Justice of the Peace, used to lock offenders in the stocks on Sundays, so that church-goers could view them as they walked past.

The telephone booth and the letterbox were the only fixtures in the village which were not painted in the estate colours. Even the Duke could not swing that one.

The gamekeeper crossed the road by the Co-op. It was a low stone building with a bow window at each side of the door. But it was self-service now. The interior had not been redesigned in any way, there were no alleys and trolleys, all it meant was that the customers fetched their own goods from the shelves behind the counter and paid at the till as they went out.

The butcher's shop was in the same terrace as the Co-op. Through the window, the gamekeeper could see the row of one-pound pork pies on the block behind the counter. There were no customers in the shop. The door was open. The butcher turned round for a pie as soon as he saw the gamekeeper outside. He brought one forward to the counter and placed it on a wad of greaseproof wrapping paper. On top of the pie four pastry petals had been arranged to form a flower. The gamekeeper looked at the pie on the paper. 'Who says I want that? I could have come for a pound of sausages, or a couple of pigs' trotters for all you know.'

The butcher pretended to take the pie away.

'Please yourself then. Anyroad, they're still a bit warm just yet. Might give you indigestion, George.'

'I'll risk it.'

The butcher picked up a carving knife from the counter.

'How much do you want?'

'Half.'

The butcher cut the pie in two, was about to remove one of the portions, then halved it instead and wrapped up three quarters of the pie. He charged the gamekeeper for half. Nothing was said. The favour would be returned.

There were two cars parked by the kerb in front of the Sutcliffe Arms. The gamekeeper looked into them as he walked past. In one of them, there was a corgi sitting on the back seat. It had its tongue out, panting, and when the gamekeeper stopped to look at it, it stood up and yapped at him. He felt at the roof of the car and looked at the windows, then turned away to go into the pub. As he walked under the hanging sign over the door, the thin oscillating shadow on the pavement slid up his body and momentarily shaded his hat.

It was immediately darker and cooler inside. The bar had a flagged floor and bare stone walls decorated with shields, bearing the Sutcliffe coat-of-arms. A brass urn engraved with the same insignia concealed the cold ashes in the grate, and above the mantelpiece a framed family tree traced the Sutcliffe family back to the eleventh century. There were three customers in the room; two of them were sitting separately on the cushioned wall bench, talking to the landlord who was standing behind the bar. The third man was standing at the bar. There was a pause in the conversation when the door went, and suddenly there was the sound of dominoes being shuffled in another room.

The landlord turned a pint glass over and started to pull the beer while the gamekeeper was still walking to the counter. When he reached it he turned to the man standing there.

'Is that your dog outside, mister?'

'In the car? Yes. Why?'

'It could do with a bit of air. It must be like an oven in there with the sun braying down on it. You could do with a window open.'

'Well, I shall be going as soon as I've finished this drink.'

'I wouldn't leave it too long if I was you, or you might find a dead dog on your hands.'

The conversation between the landlord and the two customers on the bench was never resumed. They were all watching the man at the bar now, and he knew it. He did not gulp his drink down and rush out. But he drank it quicker than he would have done if the gamekeeper had not come in interfering. And he did not say anything to anybody when he left.

They listened to the engine start, then fade away. The gamekeeper picked up his drink and went to sit down.

'Thoughtless sod. The poor little bugger was panting its heart out in there.'

He placed his glass and pie on a table, and sat down on the long bench between the other two men. He took a long drink of beer which half emptied his glass and left the foam streaming down the sides. Then he smacked his lips and sighed loudly in a parody of satisfaction. The others watched him start to unwrap the parcel, and when the contents were revealed the landlord slowly shook his head in mock censure.

'He's a right 'un isn't he? First he drives my customers away, then he brings foreign pies on to the premises. Just imagine if this room had been full of strangers and they'd have seen him come in and unwrap that lot. I mean, who's going to buy one of my pies then?'

He turned his head to indicate the small wrapped pies and miscellaneous sandwiches under glass at the end of the counter.

'They're going to think Sweeney Todd's made them aren't they?'

'No offence, Stanley, I just prefer these, that's all.'

He took his penknife out of his pocket and raised the large blade with his thumbnail.

'And don't be having crumbs all over either.'

'Stop nattering man, you don't have to clean them up do you?'

He patted his pockets to locate his handkerchief, felt it in his trousers, then leaned sideways and stretched one leg to take it out. He produced a crumpled khaki rag which disguised the dirt, but still showed smears and dark blotches which the others surmised to be blood. They watched him clean the blade with his handkerchief. He kept holding it up to the light, then rubbing again. There was still a bit of something stuck to one side. The gamekeeper scraped it with his nail; then he licked his finger and rubbed, and whatever it was sticking there rolled up like a tiny cigar and dropped off. Satisfied, he dried the blade, then stuffed the handkerchief back into his pocket.

'Now then, who wants a bit of pie?'

The landlord stayed the knife by pointing at it.

'Nobody if you cut it with that, you dirty bugger.'

'That's what I was hoping.'

'Well just hold on a minute.'

He went through to the back room and came back with a bread knife.

'This is more like it.'

He lifted the drawbridge at the end of the counter and walked across to the gamekeeper's table. George Purse held out his hands to take the knife, but the landlord ignored it and brought it down to the rim of the pie.

'Now then, who wants a bit?'

'Hey up, whose pie is it anyroad?'

'Don't be so bloody greedy. Anyroad, look at the state of your hands. I bet they've been delving inside rabbits and allsorts this morning.'

'I know you. All I shall finish up with is a lump of jelly if I don't watch myself.'

The landlord turned to the man sitting next to the fireplace.

'Jack?'

He could not make his mind up, so the landlord turned to the other man.

'Frank?'

He looked across at Jack, then nodded.

'Go on then, I'll force myself.'

Now that Frank had accepted, Jack felt that he could force himself too. The landlord cut the small portion of pie in half, then cut a slice off the large piece for himself. He bit the narrow end of the wedge as he walked back across the room, using his other hand as a plate to catch the crumbs on.

'We might as well get summat out of you keepers while we've chance. What do you say, Jack?'

Jack could not say anything without spraying the table before him with masticated meat and crust, so he just nodded slowly and watched the gamekeeper. The landlord shut himself in behind the counter, stood his pie up on a clean beer mat and pulled himself a glass of bitter.

'He keeps going to bring me a rabbit in, but it's a long time coming.'

'Don't worry, Stanley, I'll see you right.'

'You keep saying so.'

Frank stood up and walked across to the counter to have his glass refilled.

'Old Jim Buck was the worst though wasn't he? He wouldn't have given you the snot off his nose. I've seen rabbits lying about in the back of that van of his for days, 'til in the end he's had to throw them away.' He shook his head slowly as he remembered. 'He brought me one once, though. You've never seen owt like it. I'm not kidding, it must have been older than me. Anyroad, I popped it in the pot to see what I could make of it. It must have been on for two days. I kept pouring water in and sticking it with a fork, but it was hopeless. In the end I finished up having a drop of gravy with a bit of bread dipped in, and I gave the meat to the dog. I mean, I'd no chance with false teeth, had I? I'd have finished up with lockjaw.

'I'll tell you how tough it was. Even our Bess couldn't manage it. Can you remember our Bess? She had a couple of goes at it then went back to her bone.'

'Old Jim,' the landlord said.

Jack finished his pie, finished his beer, and set the empty glass deliberately on the beer mat before him.

'He was a right cunt, old Jim.'

The others looked at him.

'He'd have walked on water if the Duke had told him to.'

The gamekeeper finished his drink, and waited to see if Jack would offer to buy him another.

'He was one of the old school, old Jim. Them days are over now.'

'So everybody keeps telling me. Every Christmas my father used to say, "Another year older, and not a penny richer." He worked all his life on the land and he hadn't a penny to scratch his arse with at the end of it. And as far as I can see it looks as if it's going to be just the same for me.'

He picked up his glass and walked across to the bar. The landlord was turning the pages of a newspaper which he had spread out on the counter. Jack allowed him to reach the middle then he tapped the paper with his glass.

'Hey up, Stanley. Have you gone self-service in here then or what?'

The landlord reached for the glass without looking up.

'Do you think self-service pubs will ever come, Stanley? No reason why they shouldn't I suppose.'

'It's to be hoped they don't come in my time that's all.'

'It is old lad, else you'll have to go out and work for a living then.'

'I wouldn't mind that if I could find a job like I've just been reading about in here.'

He turned the pages back until he found it, then rubbed his hand across the page to smooth it out.

'"Judge does his own love test in sports car." What about that then? Apparently the girl reckoned she'd been raped in this sports car, so the judge went outside and sat in it with another girl to see if it was physically possible. Now if I was made redundant, that's the sort of job that I'd like to put in for. What do you say, Frank?'

'You've no chance, Stanley. You need qualifications to do a job like that.'

The landlord refilled Jack's glass. Jack had a sip to make it safe to carry then went back to his place.

'Ar, you never hear of them buggers being thrown off do you?'

Frank winked at the landlord.

'What about that judge who gave that miner a year for poaching the other week? Did you read about that, Jack?'

'Read about it. I should think so. Them days are over though now, everybody keeps telling me.'

The gamekeeper was just about to stand up, but he forgot about his drink and stayed where he was.

'It served him right. It wasn't the first time he'd been done. Some folks never learn.'

'I know, but bloody hell, a year for a few brace of pheasant. It's a bit stiff isn't it?'

'He shouldn't have been trespassing. He knew what to expect.'

'Trespassing. And where did they get their land from in the first place, anyroad? They just grabbed it didn't they? Or the king dished it out to courtiers and pimps and royal bastards born on the wrong side of the blanket. That's where they got it from, so don't talk to me about trespassing, George.'

Frank started to laugh.

'It's like that joke Soft Mick once told us, about when the old Duke met that miner up on the moor.'

'Soft Mick,' the landlord said.

'Soft? He never did a day's work in his life. I can't see owt soft about that,' Jack said.

'He said the old Duke was out walking on one of his moors, when he came on this miner with his gun under his arm. Anyroad, they had a right argy-bargy about private property and trespassing and such like, and in the end the Duke finished up saying, "Do you know my ancestors had to fight for this land, my man?" And the miner said, "Right then, get your coat off and I'll fight you for it now."'

Even the gamekeeper had to laugh; it was an appropriate time to fetch another drink. Jack was not amused.

'He was a right cunt, the old Duke. He was as hard as nails with poachers, especially the miners who worked at his pits. Straight to court, no messing, then it was a heavy fine or prison. He tried his best to discourage them. He had to, because if they'd had a good night's poaching they wouldn't go to work for the rest of the week.'

The gamekeeper turned round from the bar.

'The law's the law, Jack. And that's all there is to it.'

'Ar, but whose law is it, George? That's what I want to know. The Duke and the judges and such like, they're all in the same team aren't they? Everybody knows that.'

'I don't know about that. All I know is that I've a job to do. And it's as simple as that.'

'You wouldn't do us though, would you, George?'

'I'd do anybody, Frank, no fear or favour with me, they all come alike. It's the only way to do it.'

He stayed at the bar to finish his drink.

When he had gone, Jack said, 'He's a right cunt, old George.'

The gamekeeper stood on the pavement, staring. Everything was brighter than when he had gone in. The air was clearer, the greens were greener and the trees and buildings stood out in sharp relief. When he looked along the road, the heat was shimmering above the tarmac.

He walked back through the village the way he had come. A car passed, riding its own shadow like a raft. Then a man on a bicycle, riding so slowly that the gamekeeper was able to watch the valves on the rims going round as he rode past. The postmaster watched him walk by, and when he reached the war memorial at the end of the street, two old men interrupted their silence as he walked past them.

'Mornin', George.'

'Mornin'. It's quiet.'

'Ar, it usually is when everybody's at work.'

The gamekeeper crossed the road and walked along the pavement in the shadow of the high wall which surrounded the vegetable garden of the Big House. The old men watched him until he reached the end of the wall; then he climbed out of sight over a fence into a field. They went back to their silence. Behind them in the elm trees rooks kept flying in with food for their young. There was incessant cawing communication which intensified as the parents landed. The fledgelings flapped and tottered in the branches as they stretched and gulped, and the food itself altered the pitch of their notes as it was thrust down their throats.

As he walked across the field, the gamekeeper took off his jacket and unfastened the top button of his shirt. There was a dark rosette under each arm and the way his shirt stuck to him revealed the contours of his back. He now had his jacket over one arm and his rifle under the other. They were suddenly heavy and awkward. The sun and the beer and the pie had tired him. But he had the rest of his traps to see to. He might just have a rest first though. Find some shade and sit down. Just for five minutes. Better get away from the road though. Always somebody ready to make something out of it if they saw him settling down. The next thing he'd know, the Agent or the Head keeper would be winking and cracking jokes about it in the Arms.

The field ended at a steep bank with a stream at the bottom. Across the stream another bank rose to another field. The gamekeeper strode down the bank, out of sight of the road, and sat down in the valley. The running water made the air cooler down here. He would sit here for five minutes, then move on to inspect his other traps. There was cress growing in the water. The gamekeeper dragged a handful out and the water was momentarily muddied as the roots came up. He chewed a few strands, threw the rest away then lay back on the bank. This was the only kind of sunbathing he would get this year. He took his tie off and unfastened another button. Just five minutes. Then he closed his eyes and pulled his hat over them, to shield them from the force of the sun.

A skylark woke him up. The cascading notes dribbled into his sleep until he realized that he was awake and listening. He did not open his eyes straight away, he just lay there sweating under his hat. He had a headache. He was hot. He was thirsty, and being asleep had made him even more tired.

The song stopped. The skylark must have landed, and he saw it land even though he had his eyes closed and his hat over them. It fluttered vertically down singing all the way, then, ten yards from the ground shut up, and swooped obliquely into the field where it was lost in the grass.

The gamekeeper sat up. The change in position made his head throb. He took his hat off and knelt at the stream and drank from leaking hands. Then he threw water over his face and head and sat back and wiped his eyes with the soft cloth of his hat. The sun had moved across the sky. He had no watch, but he could tell by its position that he had stayed longer than he had intended.

He was just about to stand up when he heard somebody coming. Trespassers! He looked around, but there was nowhere to hide, so he picked up his rifle and sat still.

A boy and a girl came walking along the top of the bank opposite. They had their arms around each other and the girl was resting her head on the boy's shoulder. When they drew level the gamekeeper could see that the boy's enfolding arm was supporting and gently kneading the girl's breast. He never moved, and they never saw him. They just walked slowly by, kissing and talking fondly to each other. The gamekeeper left them alone, and waited until they had gone before he stood up and put his jacket on. Then he climbed the far bank and stood still for a moment at the top. It was time to go home. He would look at the rest of the traps first thing in the morning.

The dogs could hear him coming through the trees before they could see him. As soon as they started to bark, Ian and John ran out of the house and looked at which side of the pen the dogs were standing so that they knew where to go to meet their father.

They ran across the yard and round the back of the outhouses. Ian was in the lead as the gamekeeper came out of the trees and into the clearing.

'Dad, my mam says that you're going to let the pheasants go.'

The gamekeeper walked past the boys and round the side of the outhouses, past the ferret hutches. He stopped and looked through the wire.

'I thought I told you to clean these ferrets out. I could smell them coming through the wood.'

The boys looked at the hutches, looked at their father, then looked at each other.

'It's our John's turn. I did them last time.'

'It's not. I did them.'

'You didn't.'

'I did.'

'You didn't.'

'I did!' Smacking Ian in the chest in time with the last syllable. Ian thumped him back, but John was ready for it. He had covered up and the blow caught him on the back of the shoulder as he was turning and fading. It hurt Ian more than it hurt John.

'I don't care who did them. But I want them cleaning out. Now.'

He walked across the yard leaving the dogs and the boys looking after him, and the ferrets looking at the boys through the wire.

'Will you then, Dad?'

'We'll see.'

'What did you tell them I was going to release the pheasants for?'

Mary Purse looked up from wiping the kitchen table. She had rounded up all the crumbs with a dishcloth and was about to drive them over the edge into her waiting hand.

'Because you said you were.'

'I wish you'd kept your mouth shut. I've got a wicked headache.'

'How was I to know that? You seemed dead set on it this morning.'

'That was this morning. Is my dinner ready?'

'It will be in ten minutes. I'm not a mind reader you know.'

'I'll have a couple of aspirins. It must be all that walking about in the sun.'

'Sun my eye.'

While the gamekeeper was at the sink taking the aspirins he looked through the window and watched the boys cleaning out the ferret hutches across the yard. Ian was taking handfuls of wood shavings from a sack and sprinkling them into the bottom hutch. Marilyn had been placed on top of Sam's hutch with her feeding bowls while her hutch was being cleaned out. She kept running to the edges and looking over. As Ian was reaching into the sack, John picked her up, held her close to the back of Ian's head, and tapped him on the shoulder, so that when he turned round the ferret was threatening his face. Ian stood up and threw a handful of shavings into John's face. He stepped back shaking his head, temporarily blinded, sawdust in his hair and mouth, the ferret struggling in his hand.

The gamekeeper turned away from the window shaking his head.

'The young buggers. Have they had their teas yet?'

'They had it as soon as they came in from school.'

The hutches cleaned out, the ferrets fed and watered, the boys came into the kitchen. They did not come in to do anything, they just mooched around, waiting for their father to finish his dinner, waiting to see what he was going to do next. But they did not ask him.

John still had shavings in his hair, curls of white wood tangled in his own mousy strands. The gamekeeper pointed with his knife.

'Been sweeping the hutches out with your head, John?'

John went to look in the mirror over the fireplace to see what he meant.

'It's our Ian, he threw a handful of sawdust at me.'

120

Ian turned round from the dresser where he was standing looking at a comic.

'It was your own fault. You deserved it.'

'Why did I? I didn't do owt?'

'Oo, you liar. He pushed Marilyn right into my face, Dad, and made me jump.'

The gamekeeper laughed.

'It's a good job he didn't push Sam into your face, lad, or you'd have been like the maid in the garden. He'd have snapped off your nose.'

He reached out and pinched Ian's nose between two fingers, then he showed the boy his thumb squeezed between them. Ian looked at it, and although he could see the cracked nail, and the ingrained dirt lining the prints, he felt at his nose to make sure.

'It's not, Dad.'

The gamekeeper picked up his knife and Ian's nose became his own thumb again. John, taking advantage of his father's levity, approached Ian, pointing at his face.

'You big baby. He thought my dad had pinched off his nose.'

Ian waited for the hand to come into range, then he swiped it down and ran round the table. John flicked his hand at the pain, surprised and annoyed that he had been too slow to avoid the blow.

'Right. You've had it now, lad.'

But before he could start the chase, the gamekeeper thrust his chair back and threatened to stand up.

'John! Stop it.'

'He's just hit me.'

'It serves you right. You started it.'

'I didn't do owt.'

'And stop telling lies. You started it out there an'all. I was watching you through the window.'

And that settled that. There was nothing John could say. He just stood there, threatening Ian with his eyes across the table.

'Now both of you, go out and play while I finish my dinner, and if there's no more falling out we'll see about releasing them pheasants.'

The boys rounded their eyes and made O's with their mouths, and ran out of the kitchen into the yard.

'Our John's nowt but a torment with our Ian.'

Mary Purse took his empty plate away from him.

'He's bored stiff that's why. He ought to be up on the estate, playing with kids his own age.'

The gamekeeper finished his meal with a cup of tea and two biscuits, then he went outside in his shirt-sleeves. The sun was still up, the trees filtered the breeze, and the air was still warm in the yard. Inside the house, Mary Purse sat at the kitchen table drinking tea, and looking through the open door of the living-room at the television. In the morning it was the radio; after lunch, the television. Any programme, as long as she had voices and faces to keep her company when she was alone.

John and Ian walked up the yard carrying sacks. The gamekeeper followed them carrying a landing net. He started to whistle as he approached the pen so that the pheasants would know who was coming, and he carried on whistling as they went inside and he closed the door behind them. But the pheasants were still alarmed at the presence of three people; they were used to seeing the gamekeeper on his own. They ran for the corners, and hid under the tents of evergreen propped up against the sides of the pen. The boys stood still waiting for their father to tell them what to do.

'I'll catch them, then you can take turns holding them while I take the brails off. All right?'

John nodded. Ian put his sacks down and sat on them.

'Can't we catch any, Dad?'

'No, you'll be running up and down frightening them to death.'

'Why will we?'

'I know you. We'll finish up with a stampede on our hands and a penful of nervous wrecks.'

'We'll not.'

'I'll send you out if you don't stop arguing, Ian.'

'It's not right, Dad.'

He sat with his head down, then scuffed a pheasant dropping into the earth with his plimsoll, as though it was something poisonous which had started to crawl towards him.

'All right then, I'll let you catch the last two if you behave yourselves and do as you're told.'

The gamekeeper selected a hen pheasant and walked towards it, holding the net at the ready. He could have been advancing on a butterfly. The pheasant ran to the end of the pen, then turned into a corner, and by quickly following up and feinting to right and left, whichever way the bird threatened to escape, the gamekeeper was able to get close enough to reach out with the handle and pop the net over the bird. It struggled, its feet became enmeshed and the gamekeeper held it down until John was kneeling by the bird; then he turned the handle to let the boy free the pheasant. He stood up with it, and held it still, speaking gently to it while his father felt amongst the feathers of the left wing and pulled out the paper fastener which secured the leather brail. The wing was free now. The bird could fly again. He gave the wing back to John to fold close to its body, so that it could not flap it, which might panic it and injure it in a struggle.

John carried it to the door of the pen, opened it, and put the pheasant down outside. It ran away across the clearing, then disappeared amongst the trees, leaving a faint slipstream behind it in the grass.

It was Ian's turn next to release the pheasant from the net and hold it while his father unfastened the brail. It ran under one of the evergreen hides.

'Go to the other end, Ian, and make it come back this way. But don't bend down and pop your face in there, I don't want it dying of fright.'

If John had been there on his own, the gamekeeper would have let him unfasten the brails. But not with them both helping. Ian would have caused aggravation if he could not have unfastened some, and it would have taken him too long to have undone them on his own.

When they had released half of the pheasants through the pen door, they captured the rest and placed them in the sacks, six or seven to a sack, ready to be loaded into the back of the gamekeeper's van, to be released in other coverts on his beat.

The gamekeeper could have kept his pheasants penned up longer. They would have laid some more eggs. But, by releasing them now, they still had time to build their own nests and lay clutches in the wild. The gamekeeper liked to produce a wild stock to supplement his own hand-reared birds. Wild birds tend to be stronger, more wily, more wary. They fly higher and faster than hand-reared birds, and a shooting man enjoys a difficult shot at a towering pheasant. It is good sport. And if he has enjoyed a good day's sport, he is more likely to reward the gamekeeper with a good tip at the end of the day.

So the gamekeeper would work assiduously to protect the wild nests. He would patrol his beat regularly to discourage poachers and trespassers. And he would poison, trap and shoot ruthlessly to eliminate the vermin.

The sun had gone by the time they had loaded the last sack of pheasants into the van, leaving the sky rosy over the fields, merging back through darkening shades of blue to violet over the woods, and it was already dusk amongst the trees. The boys went in for bed, and the gamekeeper drove quickly up the track towards the main road. He was in a hurry. He wanted to release the pheasants before it got dark, so that they would have time to find a safe roosting place for the night.

He emptied the sacks in Boundary Wood, and in a spinney called the Willowgarth. He placed the last sack on the ground near a hedge which separated the trees from the fields, and began to twitch the bottom, at the same time tipping the sack gently to encourage the pheasants out. A cock was first out. It ran through the hedge into the field and took off. It had to work hard to gain elevation. For twenty yards a fast dog could have run with and snapped it out of the air. It was slow and clumsy and heavy. It was the first time it had flown since February. The gamekeeper watched it through the hedge. The land sloped downhill so that the height gained by the bird as it crossed the field was out of all proportion to the power of its flight.

At the bottom of the field, two men with two dogs were kneeling by some reeds at the edge of a pond. They had heard the whirring and clapping of the pheasant's wings as it took off, and had ducked down, hoping that it would not see them, and that it might land near enough for them to sneak up on it and let the dogs have a run at it.

The gamekeeper only saw them because they lost the pheasant against a dark band of trees in the distance, and they stood up hoping that the new angle would bring it back into sight. The gamekeeper waited until they moved off, so that he knew which way they were going; then he picked up the empty sack and walked back through the trees to the van.

When he arrived home he walked straight through the kitchen, leaving the outside door open behind him, and went into the living-room for his shotgun. Mary Purse was in there, ironing and watching the television. She put down the iron in its place and watched him stand on the arm of the settee in his boots and open the cupboard doors.

'What's the matter with you?'

'Poachers.'

'Where?'

'Over near the Donkey Pond.'

'How many?'

'Two, I think.'

'Have they got guns?'

'I don't know. I couldn't see. They were too far away.'

'O, don't bother, George. It's too late now. They'll have gone by the time you get back round there.'

'They'll not. I know which way they're going.'

'Let them go, George. It's dangerous this time of night. Two of them in the dark, you never know what might happen.'

'I can't help that. That's a risk I've got to take isn't it?'

He lifted his shotgun down from the wall rack and went through into the kitchen.

'If it was up to you, Mary, I'd never catch anybody. They could knock on the door and ask for pheasants out of the laying pen and you'd never tell me.'

'I'm only thinking of you, George.'

'I know that, but I've a job to do and that's all there is to it.'

'Why don't you phone Henry or Charlie? They'll come and help you.'

'And what do you think them two are going to do while I'm waiting, just stand about 'til we all run up and grab them? Talk sense, Mary.'

She followed him to the kitchen door and watched him hurry away across the yard.

'Well just be careful. And if they've got guns leave them alone.'

But they did not have guns. They just had two greyhounds, and one of those was lame. It had not been when the gamekeeper had first seen the men. They were on their way home when they saw the pheasant. They watched it, lost it, then carried on round the pond.

A coot swam away from under the bank beneath them, black bird on dark water, white vizor leading. Further round, a grass snake swimming just below the surface, a living M a living W, the flowing change of letter too subtle for the eye.

They left the pond and crossed the meadow to take a short cut across a potato field. As they climbed the fence into the field, a hare materialized from its form in a furrow and raced away. It had crouched there listening to their approach, a smooth shape in its shallow mould. It smelled them, men and dogs; coming nearer, talking louder, smelling stronger. They might have passed it by without noticing it if it had sat still. It was the same colour as the dry earth. If it had been raining the hare's wet fur would have matched the soil just as well.

But as the poachers climbed the fence, the heightened voices, the sudden towering figures were too much for it, and it fled. The dogs were still in the other field. They saw the hare immediately, but they were trapped by the fence. They howled and whined as they squeezed sideways through the horizontals, then they were away, stretching out in pursuit across the grain of the furrows.

The hare disappeared through a hedge. Anybody coming across the scene at that moment would have thought that they were watching a greyhound race in a potato field. The leading dog yelped and stumbled, and when it stood up it was dangling one of its front paws. The poachers ran across the field to it, keeping to the tops of the furrows like men crossing a river on logs. Blood was dripping from the raised paw and dappling the soil. One of the poachers knelt down to examine the wound. The dog had gashed its pad. He dabbed the pad gently with his handkerchief to blot the blood, so that he could determine the damage before the blood welled back. Then he made a rough mitten for the paw, picked the dog up and carried it back across the rough ground to the grass.

His mate walked across to the hedge to see what had happened to his own dog. He dare not whistle it in case the gamekeeper heard. He looked over the hedge and the dog was loping back across a field of sprouting barley, empty-mouthed, looking about as it came.

It was a slow walk with the crippled dog. They took it in turns to carry the dog, but it was large and it weighed sixty-five pounds. They had to put it down every few minutes and let it limp along for a while. The owner of the dog tried carrying it across his shoulders like a sack. They could have carried it further that way. But the dog did not like it up there. It would not lie still, and when the other poacher saw it struggling to get down he wanted no part of the idea. He wanted no sore greyhound's jaws near his face. He knew the power of a greyhound's jaws.

He had once been walking his own dog along a pavement when a Yorkshire terrier had run out of a gate and started yapping up at it. The greyhound immediately snapped it up by the back of its neck and started to chomp and shake the life out of it. The terrier's yelping turned into a continual screech. The poacher shouted to his dog to drop it. He thumped it and tried to prise open its jaws with both hands, but the dog would not let go. A woman came running down the path. She saw what was happening, stuffed her knuckles into her mouth and screamed. She ran back into the house and a minute later a man came flapping out in carpet slippers and a striped pyjama jacket. He tried to pull the greyhound's jaws open while the poacher thumped it all over. Both men were shouting and cursing at the greyhound. The Yorkshire terrier was quiet now, its coat matted and stained with blood. A bus stopped across the road. The passengers looked out at two men, one in a pyjama jacket, fighting a greyhound which appeared to be holding an auburn hair piece in its mouth. As the bus drove off, they all strained backwards, trying to see until the last possible moment. Then the man in pyjamas started to pull one of the greyhound's ears. He seemed determined to rip it off if the greyhound did not let go. The poacher was just about to tell him to watch it, when the pain did force the greyhound to let go, and it dropped the bloody mess on to the pavement, dead.

There was nothing the owners of the Yorkshire terrier could do about it. The greyhound had been on a lead at the time.

When the lame dog was walking, its owner stayed with it, but that pace was too slow for the other man, and he kept drifting ahead with his own dog. He was twenty yards ahead, walking along a hedgerow towards the road when he reached a gap in the bushes. Through this gap he saw George Purse running at a crouch across a field towards them. He turned and ran back to his mate.

'Pursey, Arthur.'

'Here, take these then and run. There's no point in both of us being caught.'

He felt inside his jacket and produced two dead rabbits.

'Come on, man, run, the dog'll keep up.'

'It'll not do her foot any good though will it? Go on, run, I'll see you tomorrow.'

So he did, back the way they had come, stuffing the rabbits inside his own jacket as he went. His dog ambled along at his side looking up at him. He still did not understand these cross-country dashes by his master. They formed no part of his routine, and he was used to routine. He slept on his own blanket in his own box. Most days he was exercised at the same time in the same place, and he was fed at the same hour in the same dish. He had been reared from a pup by the same man. He knew the man's moods, but he did not know why sometimes, when they were walking through a wood or a field he would suddenly start sprinting. The activity was too infrequent to be part of any pattern. To the dog it was incomprehensible.

He was climbing a wall into a spinney when the gamekeeper ran through the gap in the hedge.

'Hey! You! Come back here!'

The other poacher watched his mate disappear up to his chest as he jumped down at the other side of the wall.

'He's bound to isn't he?'

The gamekeeper turned to him. He could not understand it; one running and one staying.

'Well, at least I've got one of you.'

'You wouldn't have though, if my dog hadn't been lamed.'

The gamekeeper looked at the dog. The bandage had come off, and it was standing there with its paw up like a pointer marking game.

'What's it done?'

'It stood on a bit of broken glass down the lane back there. I was cutting through the fields to get her home as quick as I can. It looks like a job for the vet to me.'

He fondled the dog's ears and adopted what he considered to be an expression of grave concern. A violinist, hidden behind the hawthorns, would not have been inappropriate at that moment to help him create a mood in which the gamekeeper might relent.

The gamekeeper was thinking the same thing, and decided to provide the accompaniment himself by making his shotgun into a violin, and scraping the trigger region with an imaginary bow, while at the same time humming *Hearts and Flowers*.

After a few bars, he restored his gun to a more functional position.

'Don't tell me any more or I might burst into tears.'

131

'It's right. I mean, anybody who thought anything about their dog would do the same, wouldn't they?'

'O, give up now, I saw you.'

'Who?'

'You and your mate. You were down near the Donkey Pond. I saw you.'

'Who was?'

'You two. You've been running rabbits and hares, so don't stand there lying about it.'

Having failed with pathos, the poacher was suddenly all wounded innocence.

'What mate? All I know is that my dog cut its paw and I was taking a short cut home to ring the vet. I don't know anything about rabbits. You can search me if you like.'

And to demonstrate his innocence, and make the task easier should the gamekeeper accept his invitation, he opened wide his jacket, to reveal a large square pocket stitched on to the lining at one side and a label advertising JACKSON THE TAILOR at the other.

'As though that proves owt. You don't have to catch a burglar with pearls hanging out of his pocket, you know. If you catch him on the premises, that's enough.'

'Well you're not nicking me for something I haven't done.'

It was time for the gamekeeper to start jiggling his gun around. Apart from the lame dog, he was familiar with the situation; he had seen and heard it all before. The rest of the dialogue would be predictable, it was just a question of how long it would last, that was all.

'Come on now, let's be having you. I'm taking you down to the village to report to Jack Anstey.'

'I'm reporting to no bobby just for walking across a field.'

'I know you're not. You're reporting to a bobby for trespass in illegal pursuit of conies, so come on.'

'And what if I don't?'

'What if you don't? First I'll shoot your dog, and then I'll shoot you if I have to.'

The poacher looked at him while he assessed the seriousness of the threat. The gamekeeper stared back, and in the end made him look away.

'You would as well, you cruel bastard.'

'Only if you made me.'

'You wouldn't half be in the shit then.'

'I'd get away with it, don't you worry about that. I'd only have to say that you were resisting arrest and tried to run away. They'd believe me before you.'

The poacher nodded his head sharply, and went, Huh!

'I know that, they always do.'

The greyhound had sat down while they were talking and was resting its injured paw lightly on the grass. The poacher touched its ears again, harder this time, rubbing them between finger and thumb as though feeling cloth.

'It'd have been a different story if you hadn't had that gun. Anybody can be brave behind a gun.'

The gamekeeper kept the gun at the same angle, pointing at a place on the ground equidistant between the two of them. At no time during their confrontation had he pointed the gun at the other man.

'Listen, I don't need this.'

And he took his finger off the trigger and tapped the safety catch with it.

'And if you want to make owt of it, I'll put it down and prove it.' But he did not have to prove it. When a man holding a gun is prepared to waive that advantage and still maintain his challenge, the gesture is usually proof enough.

It was time to go. The poacher nudged the sitting dog with his foot. 'Come on, Bett. Let's go.'

The rest had made the dog worse, and when the gamekeeper saw how badly it was limping, he stopped after a few yards.

'It's going to take us all night at this rate. It'll not do the dog any good either.'

The poacher turned round to him.

'Well, I can't carry her all that way.'

'The best thing to do is to tie her up here, and we'll nip back through the wood for my van. I can park up Flea Lane. It'll only take twenty minutes.'

'Good idea. You go and fetch it, and I'll wait here with the dog.'

'Like hell you will. You can come for a walk with me.'

'What for? You can see the state of her. Where do you think I'll have gone to?'

'I don't know where you'll have gone. All I know is that you'll not be here when I get back. So let's get her tied up and get cracking before it gets dark.'

They walked in procession across the field, the poacher at the front, followed by his limping dog, with the gamekeeper at the back.

At the edge of the field the poacher took a leather lead out of his pocket and tied the greyhound to one of the fence posts. He told the dog to lie down and stay, then he went off with the gamekeeper.

The dog watched him walk away across the field. Half-way

134

across it sat up. Then it stood up, and as soon as they disappeared into the wood it started to bark. The poacher half turned his head to listen.

'Come on, let's hurry up before she chokes herself, or breaks that lead or something.'

The air was calm, the trees were still, and they could hear the dog all the way through the wood. This background noise distracted from the immediate pleasures and shaded mysteries of the darkening wood. There were sudden rustlings, retreating shapes, but both men were too preoccupied with the nagging yap behind them to show interest. The gamekeeper grew tired of hearing it.

'Are you from round here?'

'The estate over the road.'

'I've never seen you before.'

'We've just come down from Northumberland. I used to work in the pits there.'

'I thought you sounded like a foreigner.'

They could see the lights of the gamekeeper's windows now through the trees.

'What's it like up there? I've never been.'

'Like here. You take your dog for a walk, and before you know it there's a gamekeeper or a farmer up your arse.'

After he had delivered the goods, and made his report to Jack Anstey, the gamekeeper went home. He replaced the shotgun on the rack, took all the cartridges out of his pocket and put them back into the box. The gun had been unloaded the whole time.

When the eggs had been in the incubators for a fortnight, the gamekeeper candled them. This means holding them in front of an electric light bulb so that you can see through them and assess the progress of the embryo. He had made a candling device with a cardboard tube. An electric torch was pushed up one end of the tube, and the hole at the other end was lined with a strip of draught excluder. This enabled the gamekeeper to press the eggs firmly against the hole and stop any bright light from escaping, which might dazzle him, and prevent him from seeing the contents of the eggs. The job had to be done quickly, so that they were not out of the incubators too long and did not have time to cool off.

He closed the outhouse door behind him to make it darker inside. There was a fluttering in the rafters, a small object whizzed twice round the room, then a house sparrow was scrabbling at the window to get out. It clung to the frame, and its beating wings billowed cobwebs in the angles of the dusty panes. The gamekeeper opened the door, then stood back to let it fly out. The swallows had not returned, but a pair of house sparrows had built in their place. He did not like them nesting there. Their droppings dirtied the floor, and litter from their nest dropped on to the incubators. He had been going to climb up and rag the nest all season, but it was too late now, their eggs had hatched.

He opened the door of the first incubator and slid the tray out. He switched on the torch inside the tube and blocked out the beam with an egg from the tray. He held it by the pointed end so that he could turn it while he held it sideways against the light-hole to examine it. The growing embryo inside could be seen as a dark shape occupying a third of the egg. He replaced the egg on the tray and picked up another.

Infertile eggs showed clear, like fresh laid eggs, and the eggs which had stopped developing after a few days also showed no shape, but these were more murky than the infertile ones. All the eggs with no obvious dark patch inside were placed on top of the incubators to be thrown away.

When he had finished candling the eggs, he went outside, and while the broodies were off their nests, tethered to their Y sticks feeding, he candled their eggs as well. There was no point in their wasting energy on dead eggs.

On the 19th day of incubation, the gamekeeper sprinkled the broodies' eggs with tepid water, and as the weather had been fine, he soaked the ground, front and back of the nest boxes with a watering can. Now that hatching time was approaching, humidity was important. The gamekeeper was trying to recreate the conditions of the wild, where, even if there was no rain for days, there was dew, morning and evening, collecting around the nests.

On the 21st day the gamekeeper turned the eggs in the incubators for the last time. He settled them in rows, with the blunt end slightly higher than the pointed end. This was the last time he would touch them before they hatched.

On the 22nd day he inserted a wad of cotton-wool soaked in hot water along the front of the trays, and filled the trays with warm water. He closed the fronts immediately, to avoid losing heat and moisture. Then he left them alone. The next time he opened the incubators, most of the chicks should have hatched.

Sunday. The church bells sounded across the fields and woods of the estate and the gamekeeper became aware of their melancholy music as he left the house and crossed the yard to the outhouses. He did not go to church. The Sabbath was no day of rest for poachers and predators, and in dealing with these problems the gamekeeper believed more in the efficacy of gun and trap than in the power of prayer. For him, Sunday was a working day like any other day.

Before he went on his rounds, he had to cut the grass on the rearing field, ready for the newly hatched chicks. The rearing field was a clearing in the wood just above the house. He started the rotary mower, and as he steered it along the path through the trees, the noise of the machine obliterated all sound of church bells.

It had rained during the night. Raindrops stood on each blade of grass and made the clearing silver and green. As it was the grass would have covered the chicks. It would have soaked them and some of them would have caught cold and died.

The chicks which were hatched under broodies would be placed on the rearing field in movable pens with their mothers. The incubator chicks would go in the brooder hut, which was a low shed with an infra-red lamp suspended from the roof, under which the chicks clustered to keep warm. Attached to the brooder hut was a shelter pen, and a wire-netting run like a hen run.

The gamekeeper decided that the grass was too wet to cut just yet, it would clog the cutting blades and keep stalling the engine. So he went across to the brooder hut to do a job there. As he walked across the clearing, he knocked the water off the grass, and left a green path behind him.

He opened the door of the brooder hut and took out a spade. Then he carefully worked round the run, checking that there were no gaps underneath the skirting board where chicks could squeeze out, or ground vermin squeeze in. If he found a gap, he cut a turf and blocked it with that. The run had a green nylon net draped over the top of it so that no predators could attack the chicks from the air. The net sagged with the weight of water. The gamekeeper pulled it, and caused a sudden square downpour inside the run.

He walked back across the clearing to the mower, and as he bent down to pull the starting cord, the sun came out and threw his shadow on to the grass before him. He stood up and looked around. Fresh grass and bracken stretched away under the trees in chequered areas of light and shade. The birds were noisy in the branches, and the leaves were still clean and growing. The year should stop here. Before the leaves lost their gloss. Before the chicks hatched. Before the early summer advanced into the grind of the shooting season.

After it had been cut, the rearing field was a pale green lawn with shaggy edges. The gamekeeper left the mower out in the yard to let the grass which had stuck to it dry before he cleaned it. He went into the house for his gun, and for the second time that morning reminded the boys that they had to rake up the grass on the rearing field. They had not forgotten. They were just waiting for him to get off somewhere, so that they could enjoy themselves while they worked.

They waited until he was ten minutes away from the house, then they fetched two grass rakes from the outhouse and ran up to the rearing field. They raked the hay into mounds, which they dived on to, burrowed into, covered themselves with and threw at each other. Then, when they were tired of playing, they gathered up the hay in armfuls and threw it away amongst the trees.

The field had to be cleared because chicks sometimes choke and die from eating dry grass stalks, and rotting heaps of hay might cause the development of fungicidal diseases like aspergillosis and moniliasis.

While the gamekeeper was on his rounds, and the boys were raking the rearing field, the pheasants inside the first incubator were starting to hatch. Cushioned in their sacs of water, protected by their shells, they had been growing for twenty-three days, and now they filled their shells. They stirred, they had to peck their way out, through the membrane, through the shell. They had to find room inside the packed darkness in which to move their heads to peck. Tap tap, pushing the membrane against the shell. Tap tap, hour after hour, resting and pecking, resting and pecking. And as they pecked they found their voices, cheep cheep, the anxious little sounds another manifestation of their urgency to be born.

After hours, after hundreds of taps at the same spot, a crack appeared. It could have been an eyelash fallen on the shell. Then others, radiating, and the membrane was visible, like a bladder in a split football. The beak pushed at the membrane, there was little leverage, its body was still curled tight, its legs tucked up to its stomach. But it pecked until it won, until the bump on its egg tooth was poking through the tissue, letting the humid air of the incubator seep through the puncture into the shell.

The beak pulsed, in and out of the fissure, enlarging it, perforating the shell around the blunt end. And all the time the chick was growing in strength, trying to flex its wings and straighten its legs, trying to supplement the power of its beak.

Then, with a shuffle and a push, the end of the shell fell off and the chick's head was hanging out. It rested a minute, with its head on the hessian bed of the tray. Then it recovered, and started to move slowly out of the rest of the shell. The shell stuck to its feathers, and followed it like a parachute. It wriggled free. It was out. It was born. It crouched there on big weak legs, wet through, feathers slicked to its body. Its legs wobbled, it was weary and weak. Its head lolled and it looked incredibly shrivelled and ancient. It was one minute old, and it would not look as old again until it was shot down and plucked in the autumn.

After it had rested, it tried to stand, tottered, fell, and tried again. But all the time it was growing stronger, standing longer. Its feathers were drying, and when the gamekeeper opened the incubator next morning, the wizened old bird had turned into a real chick, fluffy, two-toned brown, crowding together on the tray with the other chicks.

The gamekeeper picked one up. It was the same every year. As soon as he saw the first batch he had to pick one of them up and hold it. He made a nest with his hands. The chicken sat in it cheeping all the time. He wriggled his little finger. The chick pecked at it. He stroked the fluff on its head then carefully replaced it on the tray.

Some of the eggs had not hatched. The chicks lay curled and fully formed inside their shells, but had been too weak to peck their way through the membrane, or the membrane had been too tough for them, and in the end they had suffocated. Some had cracked their shells, and some had even managed to get their heads out, but they had not been strong enough to persevere, and the effort had killed them.

The gamekeeper slid the water tray out from underneath the chicks and placed it on top of the incubator. That would stay out now so that the chicks could dry off. Then he threw all the egg shells and unhatched eggs into a bucket and started to examine the chicks, touching them apart so that he could see them better. A few of them, although they were cheeping with the rest, had deformities which would not allow them to survive.

Three chicks were straddled on the hessian. They could not stand up, and were in a state of perpetual splits. They had to be killed. So did another with a wryneck, which appeared to have one eye cocked for falling objects all the time, and another, with its toes clenched into tiny fists.

The gamekeeper picked these out, threw them hard on to the stone flags to kill them, then put them in the bucket with the egg shells. He was now left with a tray of healthy pheasant chicks, ready to be moved out of the incubator as soon as they had all dried off.

Twenty-five days ago he had set 250 eggs on the tray. He had handled them carefully before they went on. He had turned them twice a day up to the twenty-first day. He had aired them for ten minutes each day from the eighth to the twenty-first day. He had lamped them on the fourteenth day, kept careful watch on the thermometer, and kept the water tray full to maintain humidity. He had done all he could do to help the eggs hatch. 185 chicks were alive and well on the tray. It was a good hatch.

Buttercups were in flower in the meadow. The hedgebank was white with beaked parsley, and their colour merged with the blossom on the hawthorn hedge. From a distance it looked as though the white rosettes which studded the bank had fallen from the hedge.

The gamekeeper walked close to the hedge so that he could smell the blossom. The same scent had also attracted bees and moths and multitudes of flies. A pair of swallows was feeding off these insects. They kept swooping along the hedgerow and nipping them out of the air. One of the swallows burst through a cloud of midges; if it had opened its beak it would have trawled some of them. As soon as the swallow had gone, the midges reformed, and started to jiggle up and down again.

A wooden fence met the hedgerow at right-angles and separated the meadow from a field of turnips. Working its way along the bottom bar of the fence was a magpie, which was being harassed by a pair of peewits. They had a nest somewhere in the turnip field and were trying to drive the magpie away from it. One of the peewits was stooping at the magpie, flying and corkscrewing down, calling pee-wit all the time. But the magpie looked in no way disconcerted by these threatening acrobatics above its head, it was safe on the bottom rung of the fence. Neither did it appear impressed by the histrionics of the other peewit, which was fluttering along in the meadow trailing one wing as though it was broken. The magpie knew all these tricks, and if it had found the peewits' nest, they could have fluttered and flown to distraction, but it would still have stolen their eggs.

The gamekeeper started to run towards the fence, hoping to get a shot at the magpie before it made the cover of the trees. The magpie just kept hopping along the fence in the same relaxed but purposeful way, and when it was twenty yards from the hedge, while the attacking peewit was still recovering from a stoop, and the gamekeeper was not yet in range, it flew into the hawthorns cackling, its rapid wing beats waving the three of them good-bye.

By the time the gamekeeper had arrived at the fence, the magpie had threaded its way through the branches and flown away across the field at the other side of the hedge. The gamekeeper looked up at the place where the magpie had flown in through the curtain of blossom and shook his head. 'The bugger.' The peewits flew back towards their nest, convinced that they had done it again.

For safety, the gamekeeper broke open his shotgun to climb the fence into the turnip field. Half-way down the field he had banked up the end furrow with soil and diverted the channel into a tunnel trap constructed in the hedge bottom. When he arrived at the diversion the tunnel was still there, but the trap had been removed.

The gamekeeper got up off his knees and looked round quickly, as though he still might see the culprit escaping across the fields. He walked out amongst the turnips and looked along the furrows to see if the trap had been thrown down there. He walked underneath the hawthorns to look up into the branches, then he squeezed through the hedge to see if the trap was in that field. He could not see it, and for the second time in a few minutes he was left standing, shaking his head at events and swearing. 'The bloody hooligans.'

The turnip field ended at a dry stone wall. Over the wall there was a cart track, then another wall, which enclosed more fields on the other side. As the gamekeeper climbed out of the field he dislodged one of the coping stones, which dropped in front of him into the long grass at the side of the track. As he reached down for it he nettled his hands, but he still reached through the nettles, picked up the stone, and wedged it back into place at the top of the wall.

The estate employed two masons whose job it was to maintain its miles of walls. They travelled the estate on bicycles to repair any damage reported by the tenant farmers, the villagers, and any other persons who lived on the Duke's land.

The gamekeeper tested the stone to make sure that it was firm, then turned away and set off along the track. A fledgeling blackbird preceded him, hopping away ten yards in front, trying to cock its stumpy tail. It kept chirping to keep contact with its mother, which was following it along the top of the wall at the other side of the track. The gamekeeper made no attempt to catch the bird, but when it darted into the long grass and he passed the place, he could not resist it. He could see where it was by the movement of the grass, and all he had to do to trap it was to push a handful of grass over it, then pick it up with his other hand. Its face poked out of the frame formed by the game-keeper's first finger and thumb, and when its beak was closed, the downward curve of its gape made it look more peeved than scared. He put it down and it sat back on its grown-up legs and squawked up at him. Its mother was in a state of extreme agitation, fluttering backwards and forwards along the wall, as though confined in a cage, and making tinny noises in her throat like a banjo. The gamekeeper walked away and left them alone.

In one of the fields, a tractor pulling a mowing machine was cutting silage. The cutter was laying the grass down in dark stripes, leaving pale stripes where the mowed stalks had just been exposed to the light.

When the driver turned the tractor round at the far end of the field, he saw the top half of the gamekeeper, which appeared to be travelling along the top of the wall. The driver waved to him, and the gamekeeper stopped and waited for the tractor to drive back down the field. At the end of the cut, the driver stopped the engine, climbed down, and walked across to the wall, knocking grass seeds and dust off his trouser legs as he came.

'Just the man I want to see.'

145

The gamekeeper took the cartridges out of his gun and laid it carefully along the top of the wall.

'Why, what have I been doing now?'

'I thought you might have been in the Arms last night, but I didn't see you.'

'The chance'd be a fine thing. I haven't time to breathe these days, never mind sitting in the Arms all night supping ale.'

'I was going to send our Terry up to your house with them if I didn't see you today.'

'With what?'

'Some partridge eggs. I cut a nest out yesterday. I killed the mother on the nest but the eggs are all right.'

Sitting tight. Listening. Long grass obliterating all but the noise. Louder. Fading. Coming back. Loud. Fading. Coming back. Too loud. Stirring. Too late.

'How many?'

'Sixteen.'

'Where are they now?'

'They're at home. I took them home in my cap and put them in the coalplace. It's nice and cool in there.'

'Good. I'll call for them on my way home. I've got a banty coming on broody so I'll be able to pop them under her. Have you seen many partridges about this year?'

'I've seen a few pair. Not many.'

'It's the same all over. Grubbing hedges up, and chemicals, that's what's done it.'

'There seems to be middling of pheasants about though, George.'

'It's not too bad round here, but in some places there's hardly a partridge left. You pull your hedgerows up and it destroys their cover and forces them out into the middle of the fields. Mind you, I'm surprised it nested in the middle of that lot.'

The driver looked round at the field he was working on.

'Why?'

'It's too thick, partridge like to run a bit. And there's nowhere for the chicks to dry off if they get soaked. A bit of draught or a dowsing and they've had it. Well, I mean, you know what partridge chicks are like? For the first few days they're no tougher than a dandelion clock.'

The driver nodded his head and looked at the standing band of grass.

'No there's not much room in there is there?'

The gamekeeper did a more general survey of the field before him.

'Don't you usually take the silage straight in when you've cut it?'

'We used to. But we've decided that it's better this way now. We let it dry out for a couple of days and then take it in. It doesn't lose anything in food value, and it's not as wet and sticky when it's stored.'

Half-way up the field a rabbit appeared from the standing grass and made its way unhurriedly and jerkily across the laid grass.

'An old milky doe there, look, Ernest.'

'There's plenty of them about this year, George. I don't think I've ever seen as many. I reckon they've got immune to myxi.'

'It's been a good year for them so far. A mild winter and spring and now plenty of lush grass. I reckon we'll have to have an onslaught soon or there'll be somebody complaining.'

'They're complaining already. Old Alec was in at the estate office last week. He says they're eating yards of corn off that field alongside the Boundary Wood.'

'We'd better get the long nets out then, and get some burrows gassed, before we all get the sack.'

The gamekeepers worked as a team when they were long netting. A long net is like a tennis net, only longer and lower, supported at intervals by sticks. Cloudy, windy nights were best, when there was no moon for the rabbits to see them by, and they could not hear them for the noise of the wind. A good place to set a net was a corn field adjacent to a wood, when the rabbits were out in the field feeding.

The keepers worked in silence, one of them walking backwards uncoiling the net, the others looping the top of the net to the sticks at intervals, and pushing the sticks into the ground. If it was a wide field, they set two nets side by side so that they stretched all the way across. They could set a net in the dark, in a few minutes, without as much as a whisper passing between them. When the net was in place, they walked quietly up the edges of the field to the other end, then spread out across the field and walked towards the net, making noises and tapping sticks on the ground.

The rabbits heard them now, and the wind brought their smell. All they had to do was to run back into the wood. But in the dark they ran into the net instead. The net had been set baggy enough to absorb them and most of them were soon entangled in the mesh. A few got out and squeezed underneath; while some escaped, then ran back into the net further along. All the gamekeepers had to do when they reached the net was to work along it, grab the struggling rabbits and swiftly break their necks.

Then they moved on to the next field, working through the night for as long as the darkness lasted.

'It's to be hoped they don't get too bad, or there'll be somebody in a laboratory somewhere inventing something else to kill them off. I hate myxi, I'd sooner be snided out with the buggers than do that to them.'

The rabbit in the field stood up on its back legs with its ears cocked, but the two men could not see what it was looking at.

'What's up with that one, George, is it out of range?'

'I should think so. What do you think I'm carrying, a bloody howitzer? Anyroad, the odd one or two's not going to make any difference. We're going to have to go the whole hog, if we're going to make any real difference.'

'Did Henry ever get them long nets back that he lost, George?'

'What, them that he hid in the wood?'

The gamekeeper laughed at what had happened to the nets, and the way that he laughed made the tractor driver want to know too.

'No, did he hell. When he went back for them they'd gone. Somebody had been. Anyway, the next thing he hears is that they've been seen up on the council estate. So he goes up and has a look round. And do you know what they'd done with them?'

'What?'

'They'd been cut up into lengths, and they were all over the estate in folks' gardens with sweet peas and runner beans trained up them. I'd have given a fiver to see Henry's face when he saw what they'd done.'

The tractor driver shook his head and put one boot up against the wall, as though needing this new stance to emphasize his disbelief.

'They're right 'uns aren't they? There's nowt too hot or too heavy for them buggers up there to handle, is there?'

'Mind, I'd have been furious if they'd have been my nets. But it serves him right, he's forever telling us to be careful with the tackle. Anybody'd think he paid for it out of his own pocket.' The rabbit stopped looking, turned round, and ran away down one of the pale green paths. The two men still could not see what it was running away from.

'Must have been a stoat, or a rat or something.'

The gamekeeper picked up his gun off the wall, straight up so that he did not scratch it.

'I'd better be going an'all. It's all right for some people, nowt to do but ride around on tractors all day.'

'Hey up though. Listen to him.'

And he looked to one side and jerked his head in the direction of the gamekeeper, as though he really was speaking to someone at his side.

'And what about this new settlement then? Another two hours off your week. You don't know you're born, you farm workers.'

'Two hours off, my arse. All it means is that them two hours count as overtime now. It pushes the basic wage up a bit, that's all. But we've still got to work all hours that God sends to make a decent wage.'

He walked back to the tractor and climbed up on to the seat. The gamekeeper tucked his gun under his arm and faced him over the wall.

'It's a good job they don't pay us overtime, or the Duke might have to start selling a few things to pay us.'

'It wouldn't take much to pay you, George. If he got rid of a bit of that silver I've heard about, they'd pay your wages for a lifetime.'

'And yours.'

'And mine.'

They looked up to watch a pigeon flying past. In the silence between them they could hear its wings beating the air. It was a red chequer flying straight and strong, obviously on its way somewhere.

'I wonder where that's going? I sometimes reckon that's what I ought to be doing, Ernest, back in my old job and racing a few pigeons. There's a lot to be said for it.'

They watched the pigeon disappear over the Duke's wood.

'There's still too much forelock-tugging round here for my liking. The Duke's only to walk down the street and say good morning to one or two people, and it sets them up for life.'

'Mind you, George, he's not a bad sort I don't suppose as that sort goes. He always seems pleasant enough when he pops into the Arms.'

'I should think so an'all. He's no excuse for not being has he?'

'Old Ned Mann's the best though. Have you seen that scrapbook of his? I'm not kidding, it's that thick it makes the Bible look like a pamphlet.' And he measured the thickness between his hands. 'It's filled with nowt else but cuttings and photos of the Sutcliffes. Pictures of the old Duke having tea in the gardens with King Edward and such like. They say old Ned's a bit simple, but he can answer any question you want to know about the family, from the present day right back to William the Conqueror when it all started. Dates an'all, uncles, aunties, the lot.'

The gamekeeper broke open his gun and pushed two cart-ridges into place.

'The silly bugger.'

'I know, but what can you do?'

'Well, I suppose if anybody really did want to do owt, they'd have to get rid of them, nationalize all their land and such like.'

'I don't know as I agree with that though, George. After all it does belong to them.'

'I'm not saying I agree with it. I'm just saying what would have to be done that's all. 'Cos let's face it, they're not going to give it away are they? A new generation'd grow up then and not know what it was all about.'

The tractor driver said something, but the gamekeeper did not hear what it was because he started up the engine at the same time. So the gamekeeper gave him a rough salute and walked away. The tractor turned round and started up the field on its final cut, laying the grass down gently behind it as it went.

The gamekeeper did not see the kestrel on the wall until he was fifteen yards from it. It had only let him come so close because it knew that it had not been seen. As soon as he saw it, it went sleek and got ready to fly. The gamekeeper kept on walk-ing, he had more chance of getting a better look at it behaving in the same way, than by suddenly stopping and staring. The falcon eyed him for two more strides, then raised its wings and let the wind lift it off the wall. The gamekeeper was close enough to see the separation of the primaries, the wind ruffling the down on the chest, and the feathery plus fours. It rode the wind a yard above the wall, looking at the gamekeeper as if to say, you can't do that. Then it banked, and flew low across a meadow, rowing the air with stiff wing beats.

The gamekeeper let it go. All the time he had been watching it, he had been close enough to shoot it. But he did not shoot birds of prey. He would have done if he had known that a hawk or an owl was systematically slaughtering his pheasant chicks, but he had no evidence of this, so he left them alone. He knew they must kill a few chicks during the rearing season, but he was willing to stand this loss for the pleasure of having them around. Generations of gamekeepers, then pesticides had done enough to decimate their population, and he did not want to continue the process.

Not all gamekeepers shared his sympathies, and even though all birds of prey in Britain are protected by law, gamekeepers, in the privacy of the moors and woods and fields of their employers are often in a position to make their own laws. Hawks and owls are still shot, poisoned, and worst of all trapped in pole traps.

A pole trap is a spring trap, set on top of a pole in a clearing in a wood, or in an open area of ground, where a hunting bird can easily see it. The trap is baited with meat and nailed by its chain to the top of the pole. When a predator sees the meat it flies down, reaches into the steel jaws with its legs, and as its claws clutch the meat, their weight releases the spring and the jaws smash to on its legs. It tries to fly away, but the chain jerks it to a halt and it just hangs there upside down, legs broken, bashing its wings against the pole until its efforts subside to a flutter and gradually, through a combination of exhaustion, shock and starvation, it dies.

153

In 1971 the Royal Society for the Protection of Birds started a campaign against the use of the pole trap, to inform the general public that, although it is illegal, it is still being used on some estates. After one year, the RSPB invited several interested country organizations to comment on the campaign.

They were supported by the British Trust for Ornithology, the Forestry Commission, the Game Conservancy, the Nature Conservancy, the Royal Society for the Prevention of Cruelty to Animals, and the Society for the Promotion of Nature Reserves.

The British Field Sports Society did not wish to comment until a working party on predatory birds had made their report. The Gamekeepers' Association opposed pole traps, yet attacked the Societies' campaign for being bogus, and the Country Land-owners' Association published this in its journal:

> The Director of the Royal Society for the Protection of Birds has recently informed us that for some time now they have been investigating the illegal destruction of birds of prey. There have been 13 prosecutions and 3 are pending. Altogether 90 pole traps have been found in England, Wales and Scotland. Under section 5 of the Protection of Birds Act, 1954, all such traps are illegal. The First Schedule to the Act now includes 59 species of protected birds, among which are nearly all birds of prey.
>
> To avoid painful involvements, members are recommended to ensure that their staff know the present legal position.

The tractor driver lived in a terraced cottage, opposite the war memorial at the end of the village street. The front doors of the cottages opened straight on to the pavement, and there was a communal yard at the back. A flagstone path formed a right of way past all the kitchen doors, and at the bottom of the yard there was a row of coalhouses and lavatories, all painted the same shade of brown.

The tractor driver lived in the middle of the terrace. On the flags beneath his kitchen window stood a bread pancheon with a hydrangea growing in it, and a stone trough set on two bricks, containing geraniums and pansies. Both containers had been sprinkled with bonemeal, and individual flecks of white could be seen mixed in with the soil. On the window sill above the plants stood a bottling jar half full of green water. The gamekeeper bent down and looked through the glass, but the water was too nebulous to see if there was anything in it.

The kitchen door was off the latch. The gamekeeper knocked on it and opened it a bit further so that he could get his head inside.

'Bring out your dead!'

The tractor driver's wife came through the middle doorway from the living-room. The gamekeeper could see the living-room behind her, and through the living-room window a segment of the street.

'O, it's you, George.'

'Don't sound so disappointed then. Who did you expect to see, George Best?'

'George Formby more like. Have you come for them partridge eggs?'

'Why, you haven't had them for your tea have you?'

'No, but our Terry's taken one. Ernest told him not to, but you might as well talk to that frying pan.'

She settled for that utensil in preference to all other accessories on view, because, as she was speaking, she was looking

155

in the direction of the cooker, and although the kettle was also on the rings, the frying pan was in the front position.

'I caught him blowing it over the sink at dinner time.'

'Was there any blood in it? Or was it just yolk?'

'I don't know, he'd washed it down the sink by the time I got there.'

'I just wondered if she'd started sitting or not. They're in the coalplace aren't they?'

'I'll get them for you.'

She moved to get past him, but he stepped outside before her, maintaining the same relationship of positions.

'No, I'll get them. Which one is it?'

'That one straight opposite. The one with all the dagger marks in it.'

The gamekeeper crossed the yard and opened the coalhouse door.

'They're up on the shelf in that shoe box.'

A milk bottle rack had been screwed to the back of the door. It was obvious what it was, but its function had still been branded on the back board, each letter bored out in dots with the tip of a glowing poker.

Inside the coalhouse there was about enough coal left to fill a wheelbarrow, plus a stack of logs against one wall, so that the gamekeeper was able to walk in, reach up off a firm floor and slide the box forward off the shelf.

'Are they all right?'

He checked the eggs and lifted a couple out as he crossed the yard.

'They seem to be.'

'Come inside a minute, and I'll see if I can find the lid.'

He followed her into the kitchen. She opened the bottom cupboard in the corner and a woollen jumper and an old vest fell off the shelf on to the floor. She put them back and started to rummage amongst a selection of dusters and old clothes. As she searched, she became more interested in what she was searching through than what she was searching for, and she started to pick out individual garments to see if she had made the right decision in relegating them to the duster cupboard. She held up a pair of boy's jeans by their belt loops, inspected the fronts, turned them round to look at the seat, then stood up with them.

'They're not too bad, these. I don't know how they've got thrown in there.'

'Hey up, Shirley, are we at a jumble sale then, or what?'

She bundled the rest of the stuff back inside and closed the doors fast, to stop it from falling out again.

'A patch or two on the knees and there's six months' wear left in them yet. Anyway, it's the fashion now isn't it, patches on things?'

'If it had been the fashion when I was a kid, I'd have been straight out of Savile Row.'

Shirley opened the tall top cupboard where she kept the crockery and glassware.

'I can't see it being in here, though.'

'Never mind it, Shirley, I can manage it like this.'

She stepped back to look on the higher shelves, but from where he was at the other side of the kitchen, the gamekeeper had been able to see immediately that it was not there.

'It's here somewhere. Well it was yesterday, unless somebody's burnt it. Ernest didn't put it on, he said they'd be better if they got some air.'

She went through into the living-room and opened the top drawer at the side of the fireplace and looked in there. The drawer was full to the brim, the top layer of its contents consisting of old Christmas cards, which rose even higher now that they had been released. She did not have the will to delve any deeper. If she disturbed those cards they would go spilling and sliding like slates, all over the armchair and on to the floor. So she pressed them down to close the drawer, holding them until she had to withdraw her fingers. To get into the bottom two drawers, she would have to move the armchair. The lid would have to stay lost, rather than face that.

'I mean, it can't be a million miles away in a house this size can it?'

The living-room contained all the downstairs furniture. The dining table was set in the middle of the room, and surrounding it, pushed back against the walls and into the corners, were a three-piece suite, a sideboard flanked by two dining chairs, and a television set on a table. This left a space on the hearthrug, and a track around the table just wide enough to accommodate two people standing side by side.

'Our Mandy was playing with it the last time I saw it.'

She lifted up the cushions on the settee, revealing only pressed newspapers and magazines. Then she dragged the settee away from the wall, just far enough to peer down the back.

'It's here, look.'

She reached down, head on one side like a thrush searching for worms, and came up with the shoe box lid.

'There's more stuff down there. Let me shove it back quick, before I find something I don't like.'

158

She pushed the settee back into place, then held up the shoe box lid to show it to the gamekeeper. Holes had been cut in it to make eyes, nose and mouth, and these features had been outlined with black crayon. The face had been further embellished with a beard, moustache and a sea of wrinkles about the forehead, and the mask completed with a length of elastic to hold it to the head.

The gamekeeper took the mask and covered up the beard.

'It looks a bit like Enoch Powell without the beard.'

'God help him then, that's all I can say.'

The gamekeeper held the mask in front of his face and looked at himself through the mirror over the fireplace.

'I reckon it's an improvement, George.'

He put it on properly, then his hat to complete the effect.

'I'll wear this when I'm out after poachers. They'll not come back in a hurry if they see this on a dark night.'

He took the mask off, and his grin underneath it was like the sun coming out.

'I'll cut you that elastic off, George, if I can find my scissors. It's funny in a little house how things are always getting lost. Things just seem to get shoved anywhere.'

'You want to get yourself organized. You're all alike you women, you're always grumbling and making excuses.'

'It's all right you talking, you're like Ernest, you're never in the house, only to eat your meals and go to bed.'

'We've no choice, have we?'

The gamekeeper looked about the room in mock concern.

'They don't build houses like this any more you know, Shirley. Just look at that wall.' He pointed to the window sill to illustrate its thickness. 'It's like the Great Wall of China.'

'I'm not on about the building. I'm on about the size.'

'What's up with you? You've just had a new bathroom put in. What more do you want?'

'I know, but that's not made the house any bigger has it? Cutting that back bedroom in two hasn't half made it a poky little place. We've had to change over to give them a bit more room. You can't get two beds in there now.' She reached across to the window sill for her sewing basket. Across the road, two boys were playing on the war memorial. One of the boys was balancing on the apex of the stone books, and the other boy was standing on the plinth trying to push him off. Shirley knocked on the window to attract their attention, but they were making too much noise to hear her, and if she had knocked any louder she would have been in danger of breaking the pane; so she left them alone.

'He gets worse, our Terry.'

'How do you think they went on in the old days when they brought six or seven kids up in houses like this? No electricity, no hot water, no vacuum cleaners; a cart load of them sleeping in one bed.'

'They had to manage I suppose, like us.'

'Those were the days.'

'Never mind the old days, what about these days? What are we going to do when our two get a bit older? We'll have to move house.'

'One of them'll have to sleep in the bath.'

'It's all right you laughing. You're lucky, you've got two lads.'

'I can't see what's lucky about that.'

Shirley opened the sewing basket. The scissors were on top.

'What they ought to have done, they ought to have extended

out at the back, and gave us more space, instead of cutting bedrooms in half.'

'You what? What do you think the Duke is, a millionaire?'

'I wish I was a million behind him, that's all.'

She snipped the scissors a couple of times, and held out her hand for the mask.

'No, I'll leave the elastic on. If I put it round the box it'll keep the lid on tight.'

He did and it did.

'Champion. I'll be off now then.'

'Are you going home, now?'

'Just for a bite of tea. I'll be off on my travels again then. You know what they say? A keeper's work is never done.'

In the street, he met the postmaster, who nodded in the direction of the shoe box under the gamekeeper's arm.

'Been buying some new shoes, George?'

There was a drawing at the end of the box showing a pair of dancing slippers with SILVER printed underneath. The keeper took the box from under his arm to have a look for himself, and revealed the mask with its elastic round the box. He saw the postmaster looking at it.

'Yes, I reckon they'll suit me, don't you? You get a mask an'all with this style. I'm going to wear them next time I get invited to a fancy dress ball at the Big House.'

He left the postmaster standing there, looking after him. That would be something to tell them in the Arms tonight.

On his way home, the gamekeeper turned in at the gates of the Big House. He wanted some bedding-out plants for his garden. One of the gardeners was raking gravel on the drive. It was no use asking him. He would have to ask Wilf Mott, the Head Gardener. Wilf was always willing to trade a few plants for a couple of rabbits, or the promise of a brace of grouse or pheasant in the season.

As the gamekeeper walked down the drive the gravel crunched under his boots, and he left rough footprints behind him. When the drive had first been laid in the eighteenth century, gravel had been scarce in the district and most paths were made of sand or shale. But the 6th Duke wanted gravel, and loads of it had been transported by sea, canal and road, all the way from Blackheath.

Lawns bordered the drive, and behind the lawns rhododendrons in full flower billowed up to meet the overhang of cedars and beeches planted behind them. The gamekeeper walked down the mauve and crimson corridor, which ended fifty yards away from the House, so that its full frontage could be appreciated on approach. The drive then widened out into a circular forecourt with a fountain in the centre. But there was no water sprouting from the dolphin's mouth, and the pond beneath the boy's feet was dry.

The gardener raking gravel had not seen Wilf Mott since dinner time, so the gamekeeper carried on across the forecourt. When he reached the fountain, he turned round to ask the gardener something else. But he was too far away, walking up the drive, and it was not important enough to start shouting or walking back for. At the top of the drive, between the gate posts, the tower of the village church formed a third column. The church was a mile away at the other end of the village. At the same time as the drive had been laid, the 6th Duke had had a private road driven straight from the park gates, through the woods and fields to the church, in order to save a detour of two hundred yards, which would have taken him along the village street. It was called the Duke's Drive. In the churchyard, the villagers were buried in the common graveyard at one side of the drive, and the Duke's family were buried behind railings in a private graveyard at the other.

The gamekeeper walked along the front of the House towards the West Wing. The stone façade had been built in the eighteenth century; the rest of the House was older. There had been a residence on this site since the thirteenth century, but these structures had been knocked down, rebuilt, remodelled and added to, right up to the present House, the earliest parts of which dated back to the sixteenth century. It was a simple façade with pilasters between the windows, and a portico in the centre like an entrance to a Greek temple.

The gamekeeper had been in the House, but never via the portico. During the season, he went in through a door on the east side to fetch the guns from the gun room, and after the day's shooting he sometimes carried in the grouse or the pheasants down to the kitchens.

He passed the windows of the George IV apartment, called that after a visit by the King, when a suite had been refurnished and redecorated for the occasion. The décor had not been changed since. The windows of the various rooms were too high for the gamekeeper to see the furnishings as he walked by, and all he could see were stucco ceilings, ornate friezes, and along the back walls, the heads and shoulders of enormous portraits. He passed the billiards room, with its collection of horse pictures by Stubbs, then the Van Dyck room, where he could just see the face of Henrietta Maria above the mantel. He could not see Jeffrey Hudson the dwarf, who was standing beside her with a monkey on his shoulder. Jeffrey Hudson, who was said to have been eighteen inches tall until he was thirty, when he shot up to three foot nine, was once served up in a pie at an entertainment given by the the Duke of Buckingham.

He reached the corner of the building and started to walk diagonally across the lawn which ran parallel to the West Wing. When he reached the shrubbery bordering the lawn, he turned round and looked across at the House. The ground floor of the West Wing consisted of the Old Library, the Music Room and the Adam Drawing Room, and on the first floor the Long Gallery stretched the full length of the wing. Between the velvet drapes he could make out gilt mirrors, landscapes and family portraits, and in the alcoves, shelves of books and marble busts on stands.

There was no chance of the gamekeeper being caught staring in. There was no one in the House. The Duke did not live there. He only visited for a few weeks during the shooting season, when he held house parties for his guests.

Wilf Mott was not in the Sunken Garden or the Japanese Garden. He was not in the pagoda either. The pagoda had been built as an aviary for canaries and other foreign birds, and incorporated a system of under-floor central heating to keep the birds alive during the winter.

He followed the paved walk between beds of roses, then crossed a lawn, passing beneath the branches of a yew tree, to reach the steps which led down the bank at the side of the old bear pit. The bear pit had been built into the bank, so that anyone strolling past could stand before the iron gate and look down into the pit, then if they wanted a closer look at the bears, they could descend the steps in the bank and look through the iron gate at the bottom. The gamekeeper walked down the steps which had been cut out of the rock and which descended the bank diagonally to reduce their steepness. The steps were flanked by sheer slabs of rock which oozed water, and had ferns and mosses sprouting from their fissures.

At the bottom of the steps the gamekeeper looked in through the bars of the bear pit. There were two sleeping dens inside and a stone trough which had been used for water. There was something scuffling around in the drift of dead leaves which had been blown through the bars by the wind. It was too dark inside to make out what it was, probably a rat, some bird, or a rabbit. It certainly was not Wilf Mott, and as he did not want to stand there until it showed itself, he passed on.

He passed a high wall with buddleia shrubs growing hard against it. It was a sunny, south-facing stretch, and the shrubs had been planted there because when they flowered, their violet cones attracted an assortment of butterflies, which provided a flickering colour show to anyone passing by. An outer wall of the maze bordered the other side of the path. The gamekeeper listened for the snipping of shears amongst the box privet corridors. Just birds. There was no one in there.

He looked through a window of what appeared to be a Greek temple built in glass. It had a shallow triangular roof, fluted pillars at each corner and Corinthian columns flanking the doors. The doors were locked. There were only azaleas in there, clouds of pink blossom and a layer of fallen petals on the stone floor.

There was no one in the kitchen garden, or in any of the greenhouses. There was no one in any part of the gardens. There were rabbits on the lawns and birds on the topiary. There were bees and butterflies about the flowers, and there were carp and goldfish in the ornamental ponds. There were sprinklers, sprinkling grass, and freshly painted white benches, set out in sunny places, and shaded places. But no people. All the gardeners had gone home, and the people they gardened for were in residence elsewhere.

The gamekeeper walked back through the gardens towards the South Front of the House, crossed the Terrace with its symmetrical walks and formal beds, and left the Park by a road called the Duke's Gallop. Spanning this road, half-way along it, was a construction like a church spire with an archway through it, called the Needle's Eye. It had been built in the nineteenth century, after the 9th Duke had boasted late one night to drinking friends, that he could drive a coach and four through the eye of a needle. In order to prove it, one had to be built, so the term was defined, and the design allowed a passageway with one foot clearance at either side. The masons were then set on, and when they had completed their work the Duke took up the reins, whipped up the horses, and charged at the archway. He passed through and galloped on, victorious, back to the Big House.

The bet was won. There was celebrating in the House, and in the Sutcliffe Arms that night.

After the chicks had dried off in the incubators, the gamekeeper placed them in cardboard boxes, twenty-five chicks to a box, and took them into the house to keep them warm until the brooder house was ready. He sprinkled a thin layer of gravel underneath and around the infra-red lamp which was suspended from the ceiling, then encircled this brooding area with a wall of corrugated cardboard to prevent the chicks from straying away into

166

the corners of the hut, away from the heat of the lamp, where they might catch a chill and die.

He turned on the lamp in the afternoon to warm up the air, then, in the evening, transferred the chicks from the cardboard boxes to the brooder house on the rearing field. They milled around in the dull red light of the cardboard corral, some quickly settling down under the direct heat of the lamp suspended a foot above their heads, some scratching and pecking at the gravel, and some just walking about, cheeping.

The gamekeeper watched them for a while, discreetly, through the crack in the open door to see what would happen when more of them settled down. If they all started to crowd together and pile up directly under the lamp, it would mean that they were not warm enough and he would have to lower the lamp a little. If they avoided the centre spot it would mean that it was too hot, and he would have to raise the lamp. But they started to settle down in fluffy bunches all over the brooding area, so he quietly closed the door, locked it, and left them to roost for the night.

Early next morning, he opened up the cardboard circle to give the chicks more room, and he fed them and watered them for the first time. He placed a papier mâché egg tray full of pheasant starter crumbs on the ground, and started to tap it with his fingernail, simulating the pecking of a parent bird they had never known. It appeared to work, and the chicks crowded around the tray, walking on it, pecking crumbs from the tops of the cones and from the hollows between them.

After breakfast, he came back and opened the pop hole in the brooder house, to allow the chicks to run through into the shelter pen, which was like a clothes-horse tent covered with

167

plastic fertilizer bags. As the chicks grew older, and they were allowed a free run of the grass pen, this shelter pen would provide protection from direct sunlight and from cold winds and rain, and when the brooder house was closed to them after five weeks, it would become their home.

As the chicks grew stronger through the first week, the gamekeeper removed the cardboard circle from around the lamp, and during the day, when it was dry, he allowed them out into the grass pen, so that now they were moving freely from the brooder, through the shelter pen and out into the open air to scratch and peck for insect food in the grass. But he still locked them in the brooder house at night. A cold wind, a downpour, or a hunting animal scratching under the skirting board of the grass pen, would have killed the lot.

The chicks which had been hatched under broody hens were also on the rearing field; they were housed in a row of movable pens, and they had their foster mothers instead of the lamp to keep them warm. The broody lived in a little coop, like a nesting box with bars inside the pen, and the chicks moved backwards and forwards through the bars from their mother to the grass run. At night, and when it was cold in the day, the broody, clucking softly, made a canopy with her wings, and the chicks burrowed beneath her into the warmth of her puffed-out feathers.

Because the pens only measured ten feet by six, the gamekeeper moved them along every week to give the chicks fresh herbage to range over. The boys helped him to move them. They lifted one end while he lifted the other, and as they slid the pens into their new positions, watching all the time where the chicks were running, the gamekeeper issued low threats, informing the boys what would happen to them if they crushed any.

Ascot week. The traditional week for the hatching of wild partridge chicks. It rained every day at the races. The thunder rolled, and the rain came down like rods. It rained every day in most places. Crops were flattened all over the country, and a river overflowed its bank in the south-west. But it was the weather at the race meeting which made the headlines. There were news items on television showing the horses splashing down the sodden course, and shots of punters in the paddock bearing up in most trying circumstances. The newspapers printed affectionate cartoons of the same people in crumpled morning dress, and there was one photograph of a smiling young lady with her flowered dress hoisted up to her knees to reveal a pair of wellington boots.

The gamekeeper wore his wellington boots that week as well. Every time it rained he pulled them on, grabbed his oilskins, and ran through the trees to the rearing field to make sure that the chicks were under cover. He closed up all the coops in the movable pens, then made sure that all the brooder chicks were inside, and slid down the panel over the pop hole in the shelter pen.

But he could not stay at home all the time, he had other jobs to do. On Gold Cup day the weather looked better. The sky was clear when he set out on his rounds after breakfast.

He heard the first thunder when he was in the Duke's wood. Because the trees were in full leaf he had not noticed the clouds come sliding across the sky. Then the wood went dark as clouds covered the sun, and by the time he reached the edge of the wood it was starting to rain. It rained so hard that the ground could not absorb it all, and when he got back to the rearing field, one of the chicks had drowned in a puddle which had formed in a hollow in one of the movable pens. That was the gamekeeper's fault. He should have checked that the ground was level before he had moved the pen there. And he knew it. The boys were lucky that they were not there to remark about his mistake. So instead, he delivered a tirade into the pen, vilifying the weather, his job, and the mental deficiencies of the corpse floating in the puddle. The mother crouched in the coop with the rest of the brood, pretending not to look at him. She was uneasy at the violence in his voice and croaked softly in her throat to reassure them.

Ten chicks were still out in the grass pen attached to the brooder house and shelter pen. They had panicked at the thunder, and run round and round the pen without finding the pop hole into the shelter pen. Now they stood huddled together in one corner, cold, saturated and exhausted. They looked thoroughly miserable. They were waiting to die, and although the gamekeeper caught them up and placed them in the brooder house under the lamp, the experience had been too much for some of them, and six of them were dead by next morning.

It was even worse for the wild broods out in the woods and fields. The sun was never out long enough to dry the grass, the chicks were continually wet, and the adult birds, being notoriously lax parents, did little to protect their chicks when the rain fell on them.

The few pairs of partridges which nested wild on the estate were more conscientious with their offspring. They did not wander away from their young, or fly over the walls and leave the chicks to follow as best they could. They tried to keep their broods together, and when the rain fell they mantled their wings and called their chicks beneath them. But partridge chicks are even more delicate than pheasants, the weather was harsh, and in spite of the efforts of the parent birds, predators ate well that week, without having to work hard for their food.

Not only did the weather kill some of the gamekeeper's chicks, but disease also reduced their numbers. He had to cope with an outbreak of gapes. The infected birds kept flicking their heads and sneezing. They were trying to dislodge the gape worms from their windpipes. The gamekeeper fed all the stock medicated pellets for a week, but he was too late to save some of the poults. The gape worms multiplied, until they completely blocked their throats, and choked them to death.

Simultaneously, some of the poults caught coccidiosis. The affected birds would not feed. They just stood around the pen with dozy eyes and drooping wings, as though they were too tired to hold them to their sides. To control the disease, the gamekeeper added a soluble drug to the drinking water, but when a poult had reached this stage it was too late. It was always dead when the gamekeeper came to feed the birds next morning.

What a week. Even the Duke, who had entered two horses at Ascot, saw them run unplaced.

Being cooped up for long periods when it rained, had led to an outbreak of feather-picking amongst the chicks. Overcrowded and bored, they had started to peck at each other as they milled about inside the brooder house and shelter pen. One of the chicks had been scalped where the others had plucked all the feathers from its crown, and some of them had sore patches where their feathers had been pulled from their necks and backs.

It was time to debeak them before the practice spread and the scraggy ones were pecked to death and eaten.

The gamekeeper carried out the operation first thing in the morning before he let the poults out into the grass run. He took Ian with him to help him. John would not go; he did not like debeaking even though it was painless for the birds. The gamekeeper unlocked the door of the brooder house, went inside and pulled the door to until there was a crack left just wide enough for Ian to peep through, but not wide enough for any of the poults to get out. He caught the first bird, held it in one hand, forced open its beak, then clipped off the tip of the upper mandible with a pair of nail clippers. He passed the bird out to Ian, who placed it in the grass run, then picked up the second bird and did the same thing.

He debeaked all the birds in the brooder house, then moved on to the movable pens and debeaked the poults in there. Then he fed the poults, and now that they could no longer nip the crumbs between the tips of their beaks, they had to learn a new skill. So they bent lower and scooped up their feed all right, but they could no longer grip each other's feathers and pull them out.

By the time their beaks grew again, they would have been transferred to the release pen in the woods. They would have more space in there, they would be nearly ready to fly free, and they would have forgotten all about picking at each other's feathers.

Now that the poults were nearly old enough for the release pen, the gamekeeper worked hard to control the vermin on his beat. The poults were safe in their pens on the rearing field, but soon they would be out in the woods on their own; hundreds of young and vulnerable pheasants fending for themselves. They had to be protected. He had not worked every day for six months just to provide food for hungry predators.

He set his traps every day. He used his gun, he set snares, and he used poisoned eggs to kill corvids. He placed the eggs, which had been cracked and baited with alpha-cholerose on stumps in the woods where they could easily be seen from the air. Anything tasting those eggs was dead before it had moved ten yards from the stump. Anything. They were indiscriminate in their killing; but in the privacy of the woods only the game-keeper saw the incidental victims.

The gamekeeper was on his way to kill a fox. A farm worker had told him he had seen one sneaking out of the copse near the old bell pits. He thought he knew where it might be holed up, and he was on his way there now, with his shotgun and the terrier.

The bell pits had been sunk in the nineteenth century for the extraction of iron ore. When the shallow workings had been exhausted, the pits had been allowed to cave in, and they now formed a series of hillocks and craters on which trees had taken root.

Although the workings had been a mile away from the Big House, the raw dumps and the activity around them had been visible from the Terrace. So the 10th Duke had had a copse planted in front of them to restore the tranquillity of the view, and to repair the even skyline, which was so essential for the full appreciation of its character when enjoyed from that quarter of the House.

The old earthworks was now a labyrinth of tunnels which had been excavated through the years by rabbits, badgers and foxes. Foxes had not bred in them that year, the gamekeeper had dogged the holes in the spring, but a fox might be resting up in one of the holes during the day, then moving out in the evenings to go hunting.

Every summer, the gamekeeper was surprised how tall the vegetation grew, and as he waded chest-deep through the bracken in the copse, he picked the terrier up because the going was so hard for it. As soon as they were through the copse and on to the hillocks, the terrier had a beano. He kept running up and down the slopes, sniffing into the holes, sniffing at the trunks of the trees, and sniffing at the clusters of rabbit droppings deposited around the holes. The hillocks were composed mainly of shale, and on the bare patches where grass had not taken root the rabbits had beaten silvery tracks which marked the routes they took up and down the slopes.

At the bottom of one slope, the terrier stuck his head into a hole and started to dig in, sending out a spray of soil from between his back legs. The hole was too small, but there was something in there, and the terrier would have squeezed in after it if the gamekeeper had not called him off. The last thing he wanted was for the dog to get stuck down a rabbit burrow and then have to spend all afternoon digging him out.

He had once got stuck under a pile of rocks up on the moor. The gamekeeper had gone up there to take one of the high-ground keepers a young ferret. He had gone out on to the moor to meet him, and on their way back, the terrier had run up to an outcrop of rocks and started sniffing around the base; then growling, he had run into an aperture between two of the rocks.

The high-ground keeper released the safety catch on his gun in case he flushed out a fox. The terrier started to yelp. He had found something. He was struggling with something. Then he started to whine, drawn-out, frightened sounds. The keepers thought something had bitten him. But they could not hear anything snarling at the dog. They could not hear anything now. The gamekeeper called the terrier. It yapped. He called it again. But it did not answer, and it did not come.

'There's nowt in there. He's bloody fast, that's what's up with him.'

The gamekeeper got down on his hands and knees and looked into the opening where the dog had disappeared. It was too dark to see anything. He felt inside as far as his arm would go, even though he knew that the terrier was further inside than that. Then he stood up. The dog was fast. The keepers looked up at the jumble of rocks. They either had to start moving them to make a way down to the dog. Or they had to leave the dog underneath them. So they climbed up on to the rocks and started to tug them around and trundle them down the far side of the pile, away from the opening where the dog went in.

But some of the boulders were too heavy or securely wedged for the two men to shift. They needed more help. So the high-ground keeper walked back to his cottage and telephoned all the gamekeepers on the estate to come and help them, and to bring bars to lever the rocks free. If they were out, he left a message with their wives, and throughout the afternoon the keepers kept arriving, until by four o'clock they were all there, the five lowland keepers whose beats surrounded the Big House, and the three keepers who organized the grouse moors.

There was not enough room for them all to work on the crude pyramid together, so they worked in pairs and used the reserve labour for slabs that the two of them could not manage. They were trying to open up the tunnel from the top, hoping that George Purse could then climb down and locate his dog. The men who were not working sat in the heather offering conflicting advice as to the best way to shift each slab of stone.

But at seven o'clock they could see that the night was going to beat them. The lowland keepers had to go. They had their stock to feed and lock up. They said they would come back next morning. George Purse said that he would stay with the dog.

He left the dog to go for his supper at the moorland keeper's cottage, and afterwards, when he left the cottage carrying a blanket, he could hear the dog yapping as soon as he was past the outhouses. He called to the terrier as he walked back through the heather in the darkness, and when he reached the rock pile, he wrapped the blanket around his shoulders and sat down out of the wind to wait for the morning. Although the clouds concealed the moon and the stars, the night was never black, and he could make out the horizon, where the sky met the darker band of the moor. It was quiet up there in the night, just occasional sounds; the wind planing the rocks above him, a peewit calling somewhere in the dark, and a farm dog barking in the valley far below. The gamekeeper kept dozing, but he was always conscious enough to hear the terrier when it whimpered, and to wake up and let it know that it had not been abandoned.

He was shivering when he woke up. The blanket had fallen from his shoulders. His neck was stiff, and his head was sore where it had been resting against a rock. He remembered where he was and called the dog. No answer. He shouted. The terrier yapped back, and kept on yapping. The gamekeeper had woken it up, and it was now struggling to get back to him.

He stood up and stretched so hard that he went dizzy, and had to put his hand against a boulder to steady himself. The sky in front of him was becoming paler. He could see further now. He could make out individual rocks, and sheep resting, and the patches of bilberries, heather and peat were all coming up different shades of grey. He climbed up on to the rocks and looked back to where the moor sloped down to the valley, and gave way to farm lands and woods. The sky had not changed in that quarter. It was still night over there.

He started to work to keep warm, and because there was nothing else to do, and when all the sky had brightened, and it was really morning, the moorland keeper brought him a flask of tea and some bacon sandwiches for his breakfast. They started work again after the gamekeeper had finished eating, and they had shared the flask of tea, and throughout the morning, the other keepers arrived and took their turns on the rocks.

By one o'clock they had fashioned a rough chimney and they could see the floor of the tunnel where the terrier had run in. All the gamekeepers said that they would go down and get the dog, but they made their offers with the comforting knowledge that George Purse would insist on going down himself. Charlie Taylor offered to go down and set a few props for him if he liked.

All the others stood off the rocks when he squeezed down the chimney out of sight. It was easy going down and when he reached the bottom he knelt down and looked forward. The tunnel was too low to crawl along, but by lying on his stomach he was able to pull himself forward. It was cool in the stone tunnel and the light from the hole was soon behind him. He did not have to call the dog. It could smell him now, and was yapping somewhere ahead in the dark. The noise was shrill and piercing in the confined space. It was so loud that the gamekeeper thought it might cause a cave-in, like gunshots cause avalanches in canyons on cowboy films, and he shouted to the dog to shut up. But the sound of his voice only made the dog worse.

He reached the place where the racket was coming straight up at him and looked down. The terrier had fallen down a V-shaped cleft in the rock floor and was wedged at the bottom. He reached down, felt the dog's muzzle and tongue on his fingers, then edged forward so that he could reach over his head, and grasp his collar and ruff. He pulled gently, increasing the pressure until the dog came loose, and he was able to lift him out of the crack, then back off down the tunnel, using his elbows to push himself along. The dog would not leave him alone. It kept whining and butting and licking his face, and it pissed in ecstasy all over the rock floor.

The gamekeeper held the dog to his chest as he climbed out of the hole, and when he reached the top he held him up by the scruff of his neck to show to the others. 'He's here, look, the little bugger,' was all he said.

He called the dog away from the rabbit hole, but when they reached the series of larger holes in the bank where the badgers lived, he encouraged the dog into one of them. The hole had a well-trodden floor, and a tree root, which had been exposed by digging, formed a lintel over the entrance. The underside of the root had been polished smooth by the backs of generations of badgers moving in and out of the sett.

The gamekeeper crouched down on his haunches to wait for the terrier to come out. He did not have to wait long. The yapping turned to snarling. There was a deeper growl, warning him off, and then the terrier appeared, running hard out of the hole, hackles up, showing the whites of his eyes as he looked back where he had come from.

The gamekeeper stood up, laughing. It always amused him when he sent the dog in to have a growl at the badgers. The terrier would have gone back in. He stood at the mouth of the hole barking and snarling, but the gamekeeper placed his boot in front of him and pushed him away. Once was enough. He walked on, and whistled the dog after him.

George Purse left the badgers alone. It was unfortunate if one got caught in a snare, or swallowed a poisoned bait, but he never harmed them intentionally. He knew that a badger would eat pheasant eggs and leave behind a nestful of crunched shells if it found them, or kill a poult and eat it if it could catch one. But these were odd occurrences, chance encounters, and the gamekeeper was willing to tolerate these losses as long as they remained infrequent. But if a badger dug into one of his pens and killed all the chicks in there, his attitude would be different.

But some men kill badgers just for fun. They send a terrier into a sett, then lie with their ear to the ground while the terrier searches the tunnels below them. When the dog finds a badger, it nips at it to distract it from tunnelling an escape, while the men, guided by the barking, dig down with picks and shovels from above.

When they reach the badger, they haul it out with tongs, which they try to clamp around its neck and hind legs. But if the badger struggles too much they have to grip any part of its body they can get hold of, and the sharp edges of the tongs slash the badger's body and face, as they grapple for a hold. The injured badger is then either shot, or killed with a blow across the face with a shovel, or thrown down to be savaged by the terriers, there at the sett, or later, after being tipped from a sack, in somebody's back yard.

An adult badger fighting for its life is usually too danger-ous for a single terrier, so it is either matched against several at once, or handicapped first. There are several ways of doing this. It can be stunned by a blow across the head. It can have its head held down by a man's boot while the terrier bites at its body without hindrance. It can be held by the back legs by a wire snare pegged into the ground, or it can have its teeth knocked out first.

Badger cubs are useful for blooding young dogs, which oth-erwise could be severely mauled and spoiled for life if they were pitched in for their first fight against a sow or a boar.

George Purse never killed anything for fun. He only killed to protect his pheasants, which were then killed by other people for fun. And his terrier had to make do with cocking his leg over some badger shit, which had been dropped in a hollow scraped out by the badgers twenty yards from their sett.

The fox was using a disused badger sett in a hillock at the edge of the copse. While the gamekeeper inspected the holes leading into the sett, the terrier sniffed at the trunks of the birch trees growing on the bank. There were three holes in the bank, all in line like portholes on the side of a ship. George Purse knelt down at the middle hole and put his face close to the opening to smell at it. The air in the tunnel was rancid and made him pull a face and draw back. Just inside the hole a splinter of shale protruded from the tunnel wall, and several hairs from passing animals had rubbed off and stuck to it. The gamekeeper plucked out these hairs and examined them individually. Two were blonde, and three were ginger with white tips. He stood up and called the terrier to the hole.

Growling, it sniffed at the soil, at the air in the tunnel, then hurried into the darkness. The gamekeeper released the safety catch on his gun and stepped back to one side where he could cover all three holes should anything come out of them. The terrier started yapping and snarling. He was on to something. He yelped, then a fox came running out of the far hole. The gamekeeper mounted his gun, a right and a left, and the fox was knocked over before the dog appeared from the same hole. The fact that the fox was now dead did not deter the terrier from rushing straight at it and worrying the corpse. The gamekeeper let him bite and shake it for a minute before walking across and pushing him off with his boot. The terrier did not want to let go, and the gamekeeper had to make him stay back by stamping his foot and pretending he was going to hit him with the gun. The terrier stood back then, growling in its throat, hackles up, staring at the fox's head.

The gamekeeper prodded it with his boot. Its body was still supple. Its mouth and eyes were open and it looked as though it was grinning at the terrier. A handsome animal with its white bib and bushy tail, rather like a small ginger sheepdog. Such a pity it was not a vegetarian.

The gamekeeper picked it up by the tail and slung it into a bed of nettles. The terrier would have run after it again, but the gamekeeper ordered him to STAY in a tone of voice harsh enough to have halted the Hound of the Baskervilles.

George Purse never cut off a fox's brush, and there were no stuffed masks, mounted and snarling down from the walls in his house. He was not interested in trophies. He did not even have a gibbet along a fence to peg out all the vermin he killed, so that the Head keeper and the Duke could measure his effectiveness by the number of corpses twisting in the wind. George Purse was a conscientious killer of vermin, he could easily have proved this to his superiors by taking them on a tour of his beat, and showing them all the corpses scattered about. He was a functional killer, he was not proud of it, and he did not think that his work was anything to make an exhibition of.

The gamekeeper left the copse and walked across the fields towards the Duke's wood. He could walk unhindered across the meadows where the cattle were grazing, because they had left only clumps of ragwort and thistle standing, but in the other fields, where he would have had to wade through standing corn, or waist-high grasses, he made detours around their edges. But the new year's growth had fattened the hedgerows, and the dense growth along the banks kept forcing him back into the fields.

These were the banks where he worked his ferret in the winter. Where he could watch him go in, and come out of the holes. Now, the grasses grew up through the hedges, rosebays and nettles came up to his neck, and tangles of goose grass snagged his clothing and left their green seeds hooked on to his trouser legs. The stems of field bindweed which formed part of this dense fabric had threaded their way through, to point their pink horns at the sun. The hog-weed had forced its way through, to stand tallest of them all, a giant of a plant, with a grooved stalk like a garden hose, and umbels of white flowers as large as dinner plates.

For the gamekeeper, the flowering of the rosebay willow herbs signified the turning of the year. It meant that early summer, that vital, noisy time of life renewing, was over. Now, most of the birds had nested, their young had flown, and the woods were quiet. The leaves had settled to their size and colour, they were darker and coarser, and the leaves on the horse chestnut trees were already crozzled and ragged at their edges.

It was a dull, green, dense time of the year. There were other colours; rashes of poppies and rosebays, the rosettes of hogweed and ragwort in the pastures. But this detail was lost at a distance, and in certain directions, the landscape was composed of block after block of woodland and meadow, green upon green.

The gamekeeper was glad that the corn was ripening, just to relieve the sheer greenness of it all.

George Purse had a release pen in the Duke's wood. The poults which had been reared in the brooder house were ready to be transferred to it now, and he was on his way to check that it was in good repair.

The release pen was a wire-netting enclosure seven feet high. The rolls of netting had been nailed to stakes knocked into the ground at five-yard intervals, and the bottom six inches of the wire had been turned out and buried to prevent foxes from digging their way in. Thwarted in this direction, foxes were prevented from climbing into the pen by a floppy fringe of wire netting which stuck out at right-angles from the top of the wire-netting walls.

The gamekeeper had sited the pen across a ride in the wood, so that it included a clear wide strip where the poults could dry off and enjoy the sun, and also patches of nettles and tall grass, shrubs and trees, where they could shelter and hide, and flutter up into the low branches to roost at night.

The gamekeeper walked round the outside of the pen, checking that the wire netting had not rusted and snapped, making holes in the honeycomb pattern.

No, it was all intact, and the next morning he drove over to the Head keeper's house in his van to borrow a dozen hampers. It was an old van. He had traded it for two brace of pheasant and the right to shoot woodpigeon on his beat, from a man in the village. At first the van would not go. It had been parked up an entry for eighteen months without being moved. But the gamekeeper knew a lad who worked in a garage, and he made the van go for the promise of some rabbiting during the winter. The van had been blue when the gamekeeper had driven it out of the yard. It was black now. One of the painters had come across a couple of spare tins of paint after talking to the gamekeeper one evening in the Arms.

The gamekeeper stopped the van outside the cottage and called the boys out to help him unload the hampers from the back. The boys carried a hamper between them. The gamekeeper carried one on his own. They looked as though they were starting out on a picnic as they left the yard on their first journey through the trees to the rearing field.

The poults which had been reared under broodies in the movable pens had already been released earlier in the week. The gamekeeper had not taken them anywhere. They were to provide the shooting in his home wood, so all he had to do was to prop up one end of their pens with a brick and allow them to walk out with their mothers. To keep them there, the gamekeeper still fed them at the same time every day, and they spent the rest of their time foraging on the rearing field and in the edges of the wood.

They stacked the hampers outside the rearing pen, and on their last journey, the boys carried the landing net to catch the poults with. The gamekeeper had given it to John to carry, but Ian had immediately fallen to the ground, and in an imitation of someone having a seizure, complained that he wanted to carry the net. The gamekeeper got him back to his feet by threatening him with his boots, and now neither of the boys was handling the net directly; it was balanced across the lid of the basket between them.

When the gamekeeper entered the pen with the landing net, the poults still ran away from him in spite of his conciliatory whistling and reassuring tone. They now bore no resemblance to those fluffy pompoms which had stood amongst the cracked shells in the incubator. Those tiny cheeping toy-like creatures were now eight-weeks-old fully feathered young pheasants. They could run fast and take off and reach half-way up the wire-netting walls of the enclosure. They had also developed that characteristic way of standing up tall and stretching their necks, as though perpetually looking over long grass.

The gamekeeper had closed the pop hole into the brooder house, and for the last three weeks the poults had either been sleeping in the polythene tent or outside in the open air. But they were not yet fully grown. They all had short tails, and both cocks and hens had the same mottled fawn plumage. At the moment they looked more like the stubbly partridge than the larger, long-tailed pheasant.

The gamekeeper ushered the birds into the shelter pen, then popped the net over them and held them down until the boys had extricated them and placed them in the baskets; just as they had done earlier in the rearing season with the parents of these poults when they had caught them up in the laying pen and released them in the woods. Twenty-five birds to a basket, and when all the baskets were loaded they carried them down to the van to be driven to the release pen in the Duke's wood.

Some of the birds would travel in these hampers again, when they were dead, packed in layers, and on their way by rail to Smithfield market.

The gamekeeper turned off the road, and John got out of the van to open the gate into the Duke's wood. There was a no-trespassing board nailed to the gate. The board was painted black, the same colour as the van. John waited for the van to pass through, then he closed the gate and climbed back into the van. They drove slowly along the ride so as not to jolt and panic the poults in the back. Low branches scraped the sides of the van and as they passed over the green mane which grew up the centre of the track, tall grasses twanged upright behind them.

They drove right up to the gate of the release pen, then, while the gamekeeper opened the gate of the pen, the boys went round the back of the van and opened both doors. He would not let them start unloading the hampers until he was there. Then they slid the baskets carefully off the van floor and carried them into the pen. When they were all inside, the gamekeeper closed the gate behind them and knelt down at the first hamper. He told Ian to get hold of the other end, and gently they tilted the basket, at the same time opening the lid, so that the poults could walk quietly out of the darkness and into their new home.

The release pen had no roof, but the poults were not strong enough to fly out yet, and by the time they could launch themselves over the top of the wire from the low branches and shrubs growing inside the pen, they would be used to this new place, and they would stay in and around the wood because the gamekeeper would continue to come and feed them here every day. When the first few did fly out, they had to have a way of getting back if they wanted to. The gamekeeper dared not leave the gate open for them in case a fox or a dog came. That would also allow poults out into the wood which could not fly well enough to escape from their enemies. So he had cut for them two little doorways of their own on opposite sides of the pen. These square openings had been framed and fitted with a wire grid with holes large enough for a young pheasant to pass through but which would stop anything bigger. Once through the grid, the poults passed along a wire-netting funnel, which just allowed them to squeeze into the pen at the narrow end. This opening was so small that the poults inside the pen never thought of trying to get out that way. But even these custom-built entrances did not guarantee a bird finding its way back in. So the gamekeeper had fitted wire-netting baffles, which stuck out at right-angles from the centre of the entrance holes. These baffles diverted the poults back through the grids, and without them, they could run round the pen for hours and never realize that there was any way back in.

The gamekeeper let the boys empty the last basket. Then they took the baskets outside and the gamekeeper locked the gate. The boys got straight back into the van, but the gamekeeper watched the poults through the wire netting, exploring their new surroundings. They looked well. They were strong, well-feathered birds. It had taken him six months, working seven days most weeks, to produce them. All he had to do now was come and feed them every day, and when they could all fly, and were moving freely, in and out of the pen, just keep them in the wood until the pheasant-shooting season started in October.

Another rearing season over. A sense of relief, a sense of loss. He should have been pleased, but the sudden void upset him. He felt depressed, so he went back to the van and gave both boys a clip for winding the windows up and down as fast as they would go.

But there was no time for brooding, it was August, the grouse season began on the 12th, and on shooting days the lowland keepers had to go up to the moors and act as loaders for the shooting party. Another breeding season was over up on the moors as well. The young grouse, which develop faster than pheasants, were on the wing. The butts had been repaired, the beaters booked, and the luncheon huts scrubbed and dusted. All was ready.

Unlike the low-ground keepers, the moorland keepers did not breed their own birds and then release them. All the grouse on the moors were wild birds. The keepers' job was to maintain, and if possible, increase the numbers of the indigenous stock by judicious management of their habitat. They did this by erecting no-trespassing boards to deter walkers, by shooting and trapping predators, especially foxes, and by burning old heather in the months when the grouse were not nesting.

The shoots and flowers of heather are the main food of grouse. They do eat other plants like bilberries and cotton grass, heath rush and grass seeds, but heather forms their staple diet, and in winter they eat little else. But old heather grows rank and degenerates. It loses much of its food value and grows too tall for the grouse to reach up and pluck the green shoots. So, when the heather is dry, the keepers set fire to it, and using long-handled beaters, fashion scorched patches and strips. These fires do not kill the heather, they only destroy the scraggy branches. New buds soon grow on the charred bases of the stems, and new plants germinate from seeds lying dormant in the fertile soil.

This young, short heather provides nutritious accessible food for the grouse, but they still need patches of long heather for nesting and for cover. Especially for their broods, and during the vulnerable moulting time in high summer.

They were also ready at the Big House. A temporary band of women from the village had been recruited to prepare the House for the visit of the Duke and his party. Windows had been forced open, dust sheets removed. Furniture and floors had been polished, and picture frames and statues flicked with dusters. The whole house had hummed with vacuum cleaners as they quartered the acres of carpet and the exquisite oriental rugs.

The grounds were ready too. The lawns and hedges had been given a final trim, the flower beds weeded, and the gravel raked on the drive. The Head Gardener had selected the blooms which were to be cut for inside the house, and in the forecourt the fountain was working again, and the water was spouting from the mouth of the dolphin which the boy was holding in his arms.

But George Purse was not ready. After the effort of his own rearing season he was tired, he wanted a rest. He resented having to go and work up on the moor as well.

The Twelfth. The glorious Twelfth. 'What's fucking glorious about it?' the gamekeeper snarled as he struggled out of bed at half-past six in the morning. His wife pulled the covers round her shoulders and turned away from him.

'Your language is getting terrible, George.'

'Yours would be if you'd to get up at this time and go and stand up on that moor all day.'

He walked across to the window and parted the curtains slightly.

'At least it's not raining, that's one thing.'

His best keeper's suit and a clean shirt were arranged on a coat hanger, hooked on to the side of the wardrobe. He had taken it out of the wardrobe and hung it there before he went to bed because the wardrobe door squeaked, and he did not want to risk waking the boys up at such an early hour. If they did hear him, they would be up and wanting to help. But he had too much to do quickly to accept their help this morning. A new pair of green knee socks and his best knitted tie hung over the chair back at his side of the bed. He got dressed, pulled on his socks and carried his tie downstairs, carefully striding over all the steps which creaked.

His best brogues were standing by the kitchen door. But he left them there and stepped into a pair of wellingtons. He had polished his shoes the previous evening, and as he had some jobs to do before setting out for the moor, there was no point in spoiling them before the real day's work began.

He unlocked the kitchen door and went out into the yard. He had opened the door quietly, and he was wearing rubber soles, but the dogs had heard him, and they came stiffly out of their kennel, stretching and yawning and shaking themselves awake. There was a mist in the yard with no wind to shift it, and the gamekeeper felt cold in his shirt-sleeves as he unlocked the outhouse door. But above the yard the mist shaded into blue and the gamekeeper knew that it would soon disperse once the sun got through.

He scooped a bucket of grain from a sack, then started up the path through the trees to feed the pheasants which he had released on the rearing field. It was gloomy in the wood under the full leaf of the trees, with the mist blocking out the spaces between them. The mist had drenched the trees, and the moisture dripping from their leaves made it sound as though it was raining. The birds in the trees were quiet in the subdued light. The mist had retarded the morning.

As he approached the rearing field, he started to tap on the bucket and whistle the same notes that he had whistled at feeding time since the pheasants were only one day old. And they were soon there, scuttling about in the bracken and under the rhododendrons. When they showed themselves they were a darker shade of brown, because their plumage was saturated by the grass. The gamekeeper scattered some grain in the undergrowth as well as in the grass, so that the pheasants would have to search for their food, which would keep them occupied, and give them less time to wander.

Up on the moor the grouse were just starting their day as well. The coveys were moving out of the long heather where they had been roosting, into the shorter patches where they could pluck the shoots and flowers off the young plants. The cocks were standing on rocks and mounds surveying their territories, but they could not see very far because it was misty up here too. But on this high ground there was a breeze which kept the mist moving across the moor, and continually altered its consistency.

The grouse were accustomed to mists, and for them, this was a day just like any other day.

When the gamekeeper came out of the wood the mist was just as dense as when he had gone in. But the light appeared to be brighter because he had just come out from under the trees.

From the corner of their pen, the dogs watched him load two buckets of grain into the back of the van for the pheasants in the Duke's wood. They pursued him to the back of the pen when he drove out of the yard, and although he quickly faded from sight, they remained there, heads cocked, listening to the sound of the engine receding through the trees. Then they turned away; the terrier went back into the kennel, and the labrador and springer lay down on the platform in the centre of the pen.

But they were all up again at the sound of the van coming back, wagging their tails at the back of the pen, then at the gate, to watch the van drive into the yard, and the gamekeeper climb out and take the empty pails from the back. He walked across the yard and took off his wellingtons outside the kitchen door. They had dried during the drive back from the wood, but each boot was a collage of grass stalks and seed heads, tokens of his walk through the wet grass.

Mary Purse was in the kitchen, cutting sandwiches for his lunch. Bacon and fried tomatoes were cooking on the grill, and as soon as the gamekeeper walked into the room, she put down the bread knife and cracked two eggs into the frying pan, which was standing ready on a low flame.

'Nasty day for it, George.'

'It's not nasty enough.'

'What do you mean?'

'I wish it was that thick that you couldn't see a hand in front of your face. We might get a day off then.'

'It might get worse.'

'No chance. It'll be gone in an hour. They'll be shooting in their trunks this afternoon, it'll be that hot.'

'That'd be a sight wouldn't it?'

She flicked hot fat over the eggs with the spatula, until the yolks blistered and faded, like the sun being obscured by thin cloud.

'Do you want a hard-boiled egg packing up with your sandwiches?'

'No, I'm not bothered about them. They're too cloggy on a hot day.'

'I've done you some boiled ham, a pork pie, and packed you a couple of tomatoes. Is that enough?'

'Plenty. It makes me tired in the afternoon if I have too much snap. It's all right for the Duke and his team, they can scoff and sup as much as they like. If they feel dozy and miss a few shots nobody dare say a word, but we mustn't be slow when we're loading or they're soon on at us.'

Mary Purse arranged the bacon and tomatoes alongside the eggs and placed the plate in front of him.

'You'd better hurry up, George. What time do you have to be at the House?'

'Eight o'clock.'

'You'd better look sharp then, it's quarter to now.'

193

'That clock's fast isn't it.'

'Not that I know of.'

'Put the wireless on then to make sure.'

She did. This song came on:

> You load six-teen tons
> And what do you get?

'This used to be on the go when we were courting. Can you remember, George?'

'I bought it. My dad never stopped playing it.'

'Who sings it, Slim Whitfield?'

'Tennessee Ernie.'

'That's it. I haven't heard it for years. Perhaps it's coming back in.'

'It's never been out.'

He ate his breakfast quickly, and finished his tea standing up at the table.

Although he was in a hurry, he tied his tie carefully, making sure that there were no folds underneath the knot and that neither of the side pieces were showing between the wings of the collar. He knelt down to put on his shoes, and while he was tying the laces, Mary lifted his jacket off a chair back.

'I like this pattern better than last year's, don't you, George? The check's not as loud. You look like a bookie in your other one.'

'I wish I felt like one.'

He stood up, his face flushed from bending over, and took the jacket from her.

'It's not that bad. I wouldn't have chosen it myself, but beggars can't be choosers, can they?'

He put the jacket on, then his hat, adjusting it through the mirror above the fireplace, and when he turned round he looked like everybody's idea of a gamekeeper.

'All right?'

'Have you got your hankie?'

He patted his jacket pockets and nodded, then left the house and walked across the yard to the dog pen. All three were crowded at the door, hoping to come out. Before opening the door, he ordered them to SIT. But they were too excited, and he had to shout a second time before they slowly bent their hind legs and lowered their haunches to the ground. Then he opened the door a foot and called the labrador out. The other two half stood up and threatened to follow, but the tone of his reprimand would have intimidated King Kong. So they sat down again. He called the springer out, then closed the gate leaving the terrier sitting there. But not for long. Disappointment overcame fear, and it rushed at the gate barking and scratching at the crack between the door and the jamb.

The springer and the labrador ran about the yard sniffing and marking familiar objects. The gamekeeper waited to see if they wanted to shit. They did not, so he opened the back of the van and whistled them. Both dogs came immediately and jumped in. He closed the doors, and was on his way back to the house, when his wife came out carrying a polythene sandwich box with a rubber band around it to keep the lid on.

'I was just coming back for them.'

'Here then, catch.'

She swung her arm up as if to throw him the box. Surprised, he stepped back and prepared to catch it, but she had hooked her finger round the band and the box stayed in her hand.

'That tricked you.'

'Well done. I'll get you a job with the Duke. They tell me he's looking for a new jester.'

He took the box from her and walked back to the van.

'Don't forget to tell the kids to feed the hens and the ferrets.'

'I'll tell them. I'll leave a note about your dinner. I don't know what you're having yet 'til I've been to the shops.'

The gamekeeper started the engine. The dogs stood looking out of the back windows into the yard. With their tongues hanging out they appeared to be mocking the terrier which had been left behind in the pen. Like Popeye, the terrier had stood all he could stand, and when the van drove out of the yard, he started to run up and down the side of the pen howling and barking, scratching at the bottom of the chain-link mesh, then backing off and launching himself at the six-foot wire walls.

Mary Purse waited for a few minutes, until the van had gone and there was no danger of the terrier trying to follow it. Then she opened the gate of the dog pen, let the terrier out, and called him into the house with her.

George Purse drove his old black van down the drive of the Big House towards the line of estate cars parked on the forecourt. He drove straight past these vehicles, carried on down the side of the House, and parked his van behind a canvas-roofed lorry standing opposite an open door. There were two other cars parked there with dogs in them, and when the gamekeeper got out of his van, two yellow labradors walked over to meet him. He fondled their ears roughly, then walked up to the lorry where two other keepers were handing up boxes of cartridges and cartridge bags to a third keeper who was in the back.

George Purse was the last to arrive and he was greeted by a stutter of applause and a few sarcastic cheers. His reception would have been more raucous in other circumstances, but the message had come down from the Duke that the Head keeper must keep his men quiet, in case any of the guests were still sleeping. The shooting party needed all the sleep they could get. They had a hard day's work before them. But there was no chance of disturbing them. Their rooms were at the other side of the House. A band could have been playing outside that side door and none of them would have heard it.

'What's up with you lot anyway, I thought we were supposed to clock on at eight. Have you all been put on overtime or what?'

The Head keeper came out of the House carrying a gun case in one hand and two cartridge bags in the other.

'Morning, George. Looks like we're in for a scorcher.'

The mist was beginning to thin out now, and the sun was coming through strong enough to make the dew sparkle on the lawn at the side of the House. The Head keeper, like George Purse and the other keepers, was dressed in his suit of the year. Their accessories differed slightly, but only in shade, they were all dressed in green.

'You're loading for Lord Dronfield today, George.'

'Never heard of of him. Has he been here before?'

'No. It's his first visit. His estate's down in Suffolk somewhere.'

'Can he shoot?'

'I've no idea. The Duke asked me to pop in and see him on Thursday. He just gave me the list that's all.'

'I hope he's better than that last one I was loading for, what did they call him? The Earl of Cunningham's son. It was embarrassing. I was having to lean out of the butt and knock them down with a stick as they flew past.'

The Head keeper handed up the gun case to Charlie Taylor in the back of the lorry.

'You're a bigger liar than Tom Pepper, George. We don't see many bad shots up here.'

'We shouldn't see ANY bad shots. They've nowt else to do with their time but practise, have they?'

The Head keeper winked at Charlie Taylor as he passed him the cartridge bags.

'Anyway, the Duke asked special that you go with Dronfield today, George. He said he wanted him to go with a good man. He said he might need a bit of looking after.'

'Don't bullshit me, Henry.'

'I'm not. You know he thinks a lot about you, George.'

'He does that. The only time he thinks about me is when he sees me.'

He scuffed a hole in the gravel with one shoe.

'How's he going on anyway, the old bugger?'

'He said he was tired. They'd been driving up from Wiltshire most of the day.'

'Ar, it's a hard life for some.'

'He looks well though. He's got a tan on, and I think he's lost a bit of weight since last year.'

'He'll have been getting into training for this weekend.'

George Purse levelled off the gravel with his shoe then turned away to go into the House.

'He's a nice enough fella though, George, the old man. We could do a lot worse.'

George Purse turned round from the doorway.

'He should be a nice fella, Henry. He's no excuse for not being, has he?'

The door led into a square hallway with a black-and-white-checked marble floor. On the left were the stairs which led down to the kitchen block, straight ahead the panelled side of an oak staircase, with a banister as broad as a children's slide, and on the right, the open door of the gun room. The gamekeeper went in.

It was a small room. About as big as the gamekeeper's living-room and kitchen put together. A mere closet compared with most of the rooms in the House. The walls were half panelled, the broad floorboards polished oak. Standing against the far wall was a gun cabinet with glass doors, and cupboards underneath. The only other piece of furniture in the room was a large table with massive legs, which occupied most of the remaining floor space.

There were six guns standing behind glass in the cabinet, and on the table, the guns of the shooting party were packed up in their cases all ready to go. The table was also littered with boxes of cartridges, cartridge bags, gun covers, shooting sticks, cleaning rods, oily dusters, and cans of oil, and on one corner of the table lay a maroon vellum-bound game register with marbled edges, in which the bag was recorded after each day's shooting. The highest totals recorded in this book were,

> 902 brace of grouse,
>> shot on the 1st of September, 1912.
> 1,793 brace of pheasant,
>> shot on the 16th of November, 1902.

These are modest totals compared with the world records. On the 12th of August, 1915, at Littledale and Abbey Stead in Lancashire, 8 men shot 2,929 grouse. And on the 18th of December, 1913, at Hall Barn, Beaconsfield in Buckinghamshire, 7 men shot 3,937 pheasants.

Lord Walsingham holds the individual record with 1,070 grouse shot in one day, and the greatest lifetime bag is held by the 2nd Marquess of Ripon, who, altogether, shot a grand total of 557,000 birds, including 241,000 pheasants. The Marquess died the perfect sportsman's death. He dropped dead on a grouse moor after shooting his 52nd bird on the morning of the 22nd of September, 1923.

On one of the walls of the gun room there were matching prints showing gentlemen in frock coats and high hats shooting grouse with the aid of pointer dogs, and on the wall behind the door hung a large oil painting of a hunting scene, featuring the 10th Duke riding in the foreground, with hounds and horses chasing something not shown. The horses' action consisted of stretching both front and hind legs simultaneously. All they needed was a pole through them, and the huntsmen would have looked as though they were on a roundabout at the fair.

The gamekeeper walked round the table looking for Lord Dronfield's gun case amongst the others. The cases were made of leather, and looked like thin flat suitcases, with the owner's name or initials stamped somewhere on the lid. DRONFIELD, right in the centre, in gold letters. He unfastened the straps and flicked open the catches, then lifted the lid just far enough to see that all the pieces were lying in their baize moulds. Satisfied, he closed and fastened the case, then slid it off the table and carried it outside to be loaded on to the lorry.

'Going on holiday, George?'

'No, just coming back.'

'Where've you been?'

'Me and the wife's just had a couple of weeks at loggerheads.'

He passed the case up to Charlie Taylor, then went back into the House to fetch some more equipment from the gun room.

When the gamekeepers had loaded everything, and the tail-board of the lorry had been lifted and fastened, Henry Clay went back into the House to lock up. He locked up the glass cupboards from where he had taken the Duke's guns. He tested the windows, then, after a final glance back into the room just in case a burglar was lurking under the table, he locked the door and went outside to join the others.

'Right then, who's travelling in what? Will you ride shotgun today, George?'

The question was literal. A guard, with a shotgun on the floor of the cab, always accompanied the driver, because of the value of the load. There were sixteen guns in the back of the truck and each one was worth as much as a new car.

'What about my dogs?'

'I'll take them up with me.'

'Go on then, I'll keep Charlie company today.'

He transferred his dogs into the tailgate of Henry Clay's car. They jumped up without any fuss, and although the springer already in there stood up and sniffed them back and front, there was no animosity between them, and all three soon settled down. The other two labradors were whistled into the other car, George Purse climbed up beside Charlie Taylor, everybody looked out of windows at everybody else, and they were ready to go.

Henry Clay led the way, followed by the other car, with the lorry at the back. They drove slowly, in first gear, trying to be quiet. If the Duke had suddenly appeared on the steps of the portico, complaining about the noise they were making, Henry would have scrambled out of his car, apologized profusely and offered to push the vehicles up the drive until they were out of earshot.

But the Duke was awake. He was at his bedroom window inspecting the morning when the vehicles drove past below him. They passed the fountain, moved out of the shadow of the House, and drove slowly away up the centre of the drive in the silver sunlight.

They took the road through the village. Half a mile past the last house, they passed Charlie Taylor's cottage, which stood on its own by the side of the road. The cottage had recently been painted, Charlie had trimmed the front hedge the day before, and there was a nice show of flowers in the garden. George Purse looked out at it and shook his head.

'Is it true that they've set a painter on full time at your house, Charlie? They say as soon as he's finished, he starts again, like they do on the Forth Bridge.'

'Now, don't let jealousy creep in, George. I'm well in, that's all there is to it. He looks after me, does the Duke.'

'If they ever find another road up to the moors that bypasses your house, you'll see whether you're well in or not.'

The moors were fifteen miles away, on the other side of the City. Most of the land as far as the City boundary belonged to the Duke. To get to the moors, they had to pass through the industrial area of the City, down roads flanked by steel mills.

Through their open doorways, they glimpsed piles of steel rods, furnace fires, and men working in the dim interiors. George Purse looked in every entrance that they passed.

'I'll bet the Duke makes his guests shut their eyes when they go through here, in case it offends their senses.'

They crossed a bridge over a river, and followed the road which ran parallel to the river. The water was opaque, the colour of khaki. On the far bank there was a long brick building which looked like the back of a football stand. It had window holes high up on the walls and a sloping black, corrugated-iron roof, on which the name of the firm was painted in giant white letters. George Purse nodded across at the building.

'Look, that's where I used to work, Charlie, in there.'

'I know, George, you tell me every time we come past.'

'On a clear day you can see it from up on the moors. In fact you can read the name on that roof through a good pair of binoculars.'

'That's where you want to be reading it from an'all. As far away from the bloody place as possible.'

They left the factories behind and began a long drag uphill, through council estates, and past the council tower blocks which surrounded the industrial area of the City.

And then they were out in the countryside again, still climbing, with hedges and dry stone walls and fields on either side. They saw the river again, cutting between alders and ash trees, making a natural boundary between the fields. Here, the water was as clear as tap water, and all the pebbles and large stones were visible on the bottom. The river passed diagonally underneath the road, and at this intersection, a notice board had been planted in the bank. It read:

They were back on the Duke's land again. The road became steeper and narrower. Arable land gave way to pasture, and they started to meet sheep, which ran up the road before them until they found a way back into the fields.

One sheep turned off the road past a notice board nailed to a birch tree. It read:

PRIVATE ROAD
NO ENTRY

The lorry followed it, up a steep stony track through a birch copse, then between high banks overflowing with heather and bracken. The sheep scrambled up the bank and ran off into the heather. The lorry kept to the track, crawling in first gear because the surface was so steep and rocky. The track was so narrow now, that if they had met a cyclist coming down, he would have had to dismount and climb the bank to let them pass. Bracken scraped the sides of the lorry and they left a trail of broken fronds right up to the top.

At the top of the rise, the two cars which had left the Big House with them were parked at the side of the track. The three lowland keepers, and the three moorland keepers who had arranged to meet them here, were standing in a group waiting for them. This was as far as these vehicles went. After this point, the track was too narrow for the lorry and the other keepers did not want to risk damaging their cars. They would unload the lorry here, and carry the equipment the rest of the way.

George Purse looked out through the windscreen. The moor stretched before him. A purple sheen as far as the next rise, then no more, because the sun had not yet burned away the mist.

He jumped down from the cab and walked round to the back of the lorry. His dogs walked up to him and he scuffed the tops of their heads briefly, before extracting the chained peg which held up one side of the tailboard. Charlie Taylor released the other peg, then climbed into the back of the lorry and started to pass down the shooting equipment to the other keepers. They slung the cartridge bags and gun slips over their shoulders, then, carrying the gun cases and the boxes of cartridges, they set off with their dogs up the track towards the two luncheon huts, whose roofs became visible as they walked, over the top of the next ridge.

The beaters were assembled at the huts, standing around in groups, waiting to be told to move off to take up their positions in time to bring in the first drive, which began at half past ten. The beaters were farm workers, men on shift work, men on the dole and teenage schoolboys. All of them either knew one of the gamekeepers personally, or had been recommended by someone who knew a gamekeeper. Some of the beaters had brought dogs with them to assist them with their work, and when the keepers' dogs walked over the rise and mingled with these dogs, there were one or two exploratory skirmishes, but they never developed because so many men turned on them, shouting and raising sticks, that they quickly separated, and had to assert themselves by marking rocks and the corners of the luncheon huts.

The huts had been built one on each side of the track. The gamekeepers walked straight into one of them and unloaded their tackle on to the trestle tables, which had been set up in a line down the centre of the room. There was a row of odd chairs along the two long walls, and the only other fixture in the room was an iron stove at the far end, with a chimney pipe projecting up through the apex of the roof.

The gamekeepers started to unbuckle the straps round the gun cases and flick open the catches. The gunmaker's labels were stuck on the underside of the lids, Holland and Holland, Thomas Bland, Churchill, James Purdey, BY APPOINTMENT TO HER MAJESTY QUEEN ELIZABETH II CARTRIDGE MAKERS, BY APPOINTMENT TO HRH THE DUKE OF EDINBURGH GUN MAKERS. Every one a London Best, built by the finest London gunmakers. Above the maker's name on Lord Dronfield's case, there was a brass plate inscribed with the following legend:

TO LORD DRONFIELD
FROM HIS TENANTS
TO CELEBRATE HIS 21ST BIRTHDAY
JUNE 1ST 1936

1936. The year of the Jarrow Crusade. Over one and a half million men still unemployed, and the agricultural workers on Lord Dronfield's estate clubbed together and bought their young master a pair of best London double-barrelled shotguns.

George Purse lifted the first pair of barrels from the case, unclipped the fore-end from underneath them and placed it on the table. He took out the stock, hooked the lumps of the barrels into the action, then clamped the fore-end back on. He squinted up the barrels, then closed the gun and placed it carefully on the table. He assembled the second gun in the same way, laid it beside the first one, then closed the gun case and placed it on the floor against the wall.

Before slipping the guns into their canvas slips in which they would be carried to the butts, George Purse picked up the first gun and mounted it to his shoulder a few times, aiming out through a window. It came up smoothly, well balanced in the hands. It came up even better in Lord Dronfield's hands, because it had been fitted to his own requirements as meticulously as his tailor fitted his suits. Before deciding on the length and design of the stock the gunmaker had measured the length of Lord Dronfield's arms, the breadth of his body and the length of his neck; then he had taken into consideration his stance, the position of his left hand and the weight of the gun.

George Purse smoothed his hand over the oiled walnut stock with its dark, well-figured grain. He examined the tiny bouquets and exquisite scroll work engraved on the silver action and trigger guard; the italic letters of the maker's name, and the screw heads disguised as flowers on the lock plates, all of which contrasted nicely with the functional plainness of the smooth dark barrels. Yes, it was a fine weapon. He could not have traded this for a couple of rabbits, or a young ferret. He could not have traded it for a year's wages.

When the keepers had assembled the guns, they slipped them into the leather and canvas gun slings, loaded the cartridge bags from the boxes, then went outside to wait for the shooting party to arrive. Some of the keepers and beaters had brought flasks with them, and they stood in groups or sat on rocks, drinking tea or coffee while they waited.

It was a sunny morning now, a fuzzy sun, but the men were making shadows now, and they could see over the line of butts in the hollow as far as the next ridge. The moor looked empty. There were no grouse flying about. But they were there in the heather, cackling and chortling, and feeding off the flowers and young shoots.

George Purse sat down with a group of beaters and nodded out at the moor before them.

'I don't think I've ever seen the heather looking as good. Just look at it on that far ridge. What do they say, plenty of bloom, plenty of grouse?'

One of the beaters winked, and inclined his head in the direction of Sam Dobie, who kept the moor, and who was walking towards them.

'Ask Sam, see what he says.'

George Purse waited for him to approach. He knew why they wanted him to ask.

'I was just saying, Sam, everybody reckons we ought to see a lot of grouse today.'

Sam Dobie glanced out across the moor, fearful that any hint of optimism would immediately put the ju-ju on his birds and cause something dreadful to happen. But when the sun continued to shine, and the grouse did not rise in packs and wing their way into the far distance, he grew bold.

'There might be a few. Then there might not. It all depends what happens.'

The beaters were delighted with his answer. Moorland keepers are notoriously non-committal with their estimates, and it was just the sort of cautious reply they had anticipated. One of the beaters was so appreciative, that he beat a tuft of cotton grass to pieces with the stick of his white flag.

'Talk about state secrets. You ought to get a job in the secret service, Sam.'

Sam Dobie hauled his hunter out of the breast pocket of his jacket and snapped open the guard.

'Come on you buggers, it's time you were on your way. You'll not be laughing when you're tramping through that tall heather and bracken on your way back.'

The beaters stood up and moved off. They had a two-and-a-half mile walk back round the edge of the moor to reach their places in time for the start of the first drive.

George Purse lay back against a rock, linked his hands behind his head to make a pillow, and tilted his face to the sun.

'I don't know, Sam, you've got a right job up here you blokes. Nobody to bother you, no birds to rear, just a bit of heather to burn now and again. Let's face it, you've nowt to do have you?'

'Stop moaning. You're all the same down there, you're not happy unless you can find something to grumble about. If it was raining five-pound notes you'd grumble because you'd to bend down and pick the buggers up.'

'If it was raining five-pound notes Lord Dronfield would be loading for himself this morning, I can tell you.'

Sam Dobie pointed down the slope towards the line of butts half a mile away at the bottom of the shallow depression in the moor.

'I don't know about nowt to do. I'd all them butts to rebuild the other week.'

George Purse lifted his head with his hands to have a look.

'It's about time an'all, they were a bloody disgrace. I heard the Duke say so the last time we were up here.'

'You're a liar. They were in perfect condition.'

'What did you rebuild them for then?'

'Because some kids knocked them down.'

'How do you know?'

'I saw them. One Saturday morning about a month back. I came over that far ridge and there were about a dozen of them pulling them to pieces.'

'Did you catch any?'

'No, they could see me a mile off. As soon as they saw me they were off. I never got near them. I wish I had have done; at least they'd have taken a couple of barrels of shot home with them.'

He looked out over the moor again, replaying the incident, but this time adding the fictional ending.

'It'd be a gang of cowboys from the City, Sam, getting a bit of practice in for the start of the new football season.'

'It'd have been me that'd got some practice in if I'd have got anywhere near them.'

'Were the butts destroyed altogether?'

'Nearly, except for the far one. They hadn't got round to that.'

'Bloody hooligans. It's a pity they've nowt else to do.'

'Vandalism, sheer mindless vandalism, that's what it is. I can't understand their mentality at all. I mean, why would anybody want to go and do a thing like that?'

The boys belonged to a party of fifth-form students who had been walking about the moors on an environmental studies course, which had been devised to keep them as far away from the school premises for as many days as possible, until it was time for them to leave school. They had missed the no-trespassing signs, and come across the butts. A few of them knew vaguely what they were for, the others had no idea, so they asked the teacher. He told them that men, or Guns, as they were called in shooting circles, stood in them and shot grouse, which were driven towards the butts by a line of beaters walking forward waving white flags. Some of the boys said this was cruel. The teacher said it was a matter of opinion. Some people were for it, some against, and everybody had a right to their own point of view. They walked on. Sam Dobie had been checking his snares and traps on another part of the moor, and he never knew they had been.

The following Saturday, eight of the boys caught a bus from the City, walked across the moor, and started to pull the butts to pieces. They left the end one intact because there was a meadow pipit's nest with five young in it, built into one of the turf walls. Before they had finished their work, the gamekeeper had appeared over the ridge, shouting and brandishing his gun. They immediately ran away. But the gamekeeper did not chase them. He had no chance of catching a gang of sixteen-year-old boys with half-a-mile start.

'It's been a right summer so far, what with one thing and another. All that fine weather we've had's brought them out here in droves. There's families wandering about picking bilberries. I told one bloke I'd get the buggers sprayed next year so there'd be no fruit on them. Then there's hikers tramping about all over the place. They're a bloody menace, they are. And some of them, you can't talk to them. You try to be reasonable, you try to direct them to places where they CAN walk legally, and what do you get for your trouble? Dirty looks and a mouthful of foul language. The way they carry on, anybody'd think the moors belong to THEM. We'll be lucky to see any grouse, I can tell you. It's been just like Piccadilly Circus up here.'

And he went away, to tell the rest of the beaters that it was time to move off. Piccadilly Circus. It was the 12th of August. A sunny morning in the middle of the holiday season. There were acres of spectacular moorland, which, apart from the people involved in the day's private event, no one else was allowed to enjoy.

They were ready now. The beaters had gone to their places, the guns were in their slips, and the cartridges had been transferred from the boxes to the leather satchels. All they were waiting for was the shooting party.

Mr Friar, the brewery owner, was the first to arrive. He lived close to the moors and had travelled from home. His estate car came bumping down the track at walking pace, driven by his chauffeur, with his black labrador Toby standing up in the back. The car turned off the track and pulled up at the back of the other luncheon hut. The chauffeur got out. He was dressed in a belted, navy blue mackintosh and peaked cap. With his knee socks and brogues on, he looked like a naval officer who had travelled straight to the moors from his ship. He was in such a hurry to get round the front of the car to open the back door for Mr Friar, that he slipped on a sheep turd and had to clutch the bonnet to stop himself falling. The gamekeepers laughed at him.

He opened the door and helped out Mr Friar, then he opened the door of the boot and let out the dog. Fully trained to retrieve, it had cost Mr Friar two hundred guineas. The chauffeur took off his hat and coat, and underneath he was wearing a three-piece shooting suit, the same style as his boss, but cut from a coarser, cheaper tweed, like the gamekeepers'. He slid Mr Friar's guncase off the front seat, and put it down on the grass to unfasten it. Besides being chauffeur, he was Mr Friar's loader as well. The other loaders did not greet him, or shout anything across to him; they just watched from the front of their own hut, at the other side of the track.

The rest of the shooting party arrived in two Land Rovers, the first driven by the Duke's chauffeur, the second by one of the workers on the estate. They parked the Land Rovers at the side of Mr Friar's car, then got out and opened the doors for the Guns.

There were eight Guns in the party. Five of them were regular members of the shoot, the other three occupied the floating places which were reserved for occasional guests of the Duke. Just as they were all climbing down from the Land Rovers, Henry Clay's spaniel crouched and shat on the track between the two huts. Cursing the dog quietly, he swiftly ripped up two handfuls of grass, scooped up the offending heap and threw it into the heather before any of the gentlemen should see it.

George Purse stood up and moved towards the vehicles, where the Guns were limbering up by flexing their legs and inhaling deep breaths of the sharp moorland air. He did not approach the Duke directly, and ask him straight out which one of the gentlemen was Lord Dronfield. He just had to linger there until the Duke noticed him. Then he would be summoned, and the proper introductions made. He had worked out who Lord Dronfield was. He knew the five regular members of the party; the Earl of Harley and Brigadier Stanton had been guests before, so the tall stout man wearing the bow tie and brown trilby must be Lord Dronfield.

But the Duke was too busy to notice George Purse, he was standing beside his Land Rover shaking eight wooden balls inside a cloth bag. When he had rattled the balls around for several seconds, he loosened the draw string, and invited each Gun to dip in and choose one. Each ball was numbered, this was the number of the butt they had to occupy for the first drive. After each drive, the Guns moved up the line two places, which meant that after the fifth and final drive of the day they had experienced a fair span of the line.

The Duke took the last ball, rolled it between forefinger and thumb to read the number, then dropped it back into the bag. The others did the same, and the Duke handed the complete bag to his chauffeur to return to the Land Rover.

The other keepers, who knew which Guns they were loading for, had gone into the luncheon hut to collect their tackle, ready for the walk to the butts. George Purse waited. Rather than just stand there, he called his spaniel, and started to disentangle goose grass seeds from the matted hair behind its ears. Then the Duke noticed him. Why was he crouching there grooming his dog when everyone else was preparing to move off? Curious. Ah!

'Ah, George!'

The gamekeeper walked forward smartly and touched the peak of his hat.

'Good morning, your Grace.'

'Good morning, George, nice to see you again.'

He extended his hand, the gamekeeper accepted it and shook it.

'Nice to see you, Sir. I trust you are keeping well?'

214

'Very well indeed, George, thank you. Very well indeed. I had a spot of back trouble out in Kenya earlier in the year, but it's cleared up now I'm glad to say.'

'I'm glad to hear it, Sir.'

'Good, jolly good.'

He said this, just to fill in the time while he looked around for Lord Dronfield.

'Ah! Edward!'

Lord Dronfield looked round, excused himself from his conversation with Mr Friar and Lord Cannock, then walked across to the Duke and the gamekeeper.

'Ah, Edward. This is George Purse, one of my lowground keepers. George will be loading for you today.'

The gamekeeper touched his cap again.

'Good morning, My Lord.'

Lord Dronfield nodded.

'Good morning.'

'George is a good man, I hear he's extremely fast. In fact, as soon as Henry shows any sign of faltering I shall put him out to grass and nab George for myself.'

He laughed, a real Ho! Ho! Ho! George Purse laughed. He had to. Lord Dronfield just took a folded sheet of paper from his jacket pocket on which were typed the details of the day's programme.

'Does the first drive begin at ten forty-five, or ten thirty?'

'Ten thirty, My Lord.'

Lord Dronfield would not take his word for it. He unfolded the timetable and looked for himself. It took him so long that finally the Duke leaned forward to have a look, convinced that there must be additional information on Lord Dronfield's sheet

215

that had been omitted from his own. But it was just the same; the time of each drive, with luncheon at 1.15 p.m. Without a word, Lord Dronfield slowly refolded the paper and replaced it in his pocket. The Duke glanced at his wrist watch and started to move away.

'That's right, ten thirty. We'd better get a move on or they'll be starting without us.'

He laughed, and looked round to see if anyone else thought it was funny.

George Purse looked as though he did. Lord Dronfield looked as though he had not even heard.

'Purse, would you get my shooting stick from the Land Rover?'

The Land Rover was ten yards away from where they were standing.

'Certainly, Sir.'

Lord Dronfield did not say which Land Rover, and George Purse did not ask him. He just waited until the gamekeeper chose the wrong one, then told him that it was the other.

'There you are, Sir. I'll just get your guns and then we'll be off.'

Lord Dronfield was off without him. Using his shooting stick as a walking stick, he tagged on to the procession of Guns and loaders heading down the path towards the butts. George Purse went back into the luncheon hut to fetch the tackle. He slung the two cartridge bags over one shoulder, one gun over the other, and carried the second gun in his hand. The gun slings were identical, made of canvas and reinforced with leather at both ends, with Lord Dronfield's initials stamped on the flap. They were supplied with both a leather sling for carrying over the shoulder, and a handle to carry by hand. Carried either way, they appeared to take on different functions. The one over the gamekeeper's shoulder looked as though it contained a fishing rod, the one in his hand, a musical instrument. Loaded up, he went outside, called his dogs to heel, and started down the path after the rest of the party.

The keepers had to keep their dogs in now. They could not let them run wild in the heather because there might be grouse in there, and there was no point in flushing them until the Guns were ready. The path leading to the butts was so narrow that they had to walk single file, the Guns strolling untramelled, the loaders humping their gear.

Brigadier Stanton had drawn butt number 1. The path linked the butts which were sixty yards apart, and when Lord Dronfield reached number 5, he went in. By the time George Purse arrived, he had already settled himself on his shooting stick. The butts were like roofless huts, just big enough to hold four people. The walls were built of peat turfs on a stone foundation, and came as high as the men's chests. The turfs were still growing, and the heather and the bilberry provided the walls with living decoration which blended with the vegetation of the surrounding moor. The butts had slatted floors. There was a bench across one end, and at the opposite end, a gate in the wall with a metal number plate screwed to the outside.

George Purse ordered his dogs to lie down under the bench so that they would not get trodden on. Then he placed the cartridge bags on the bench and unsheathed the guns from their covers. He did not load directly from the cartridge bags, but transferred a handful of cartridges into his jacket pockets. He could load quicker that way. While he worked, Lord Dronfield sat on his shooting stick, looking over the top of the butt in the direction from which the grouse would fly. George Purse loaded both guns, and placed them behind him on top of the wall, with the breeches open and the barrels pointing down and out of the butt. They were ready. They were ready all along the line now, with the Guns either resting on shooting sticks, or leaning on the wall looking out over the moor. Their loaders stood behind them, ready to pass them their guns as soon as any grouse were sighted.

George Purse looked to see who was in the adjacent butts. On their right, butt number 4 was occupied by Count Mauriac, a regular member of the party who flew over from France for every shoot. And on their left, in butt number 6, Charlie Taylor was loading for Senhor Aveiro, a retired Portuguese Ambassador who had settled in England after his term of office.

10.30 a.m. Two and a half miles away, behind the folds of the hills and out of sight of the butts, the beaters started to bring in the first drive. The Guns were ready for them. The grouse on the moor between them continued to feed and preen and call. They were not alarmed yet. It was still a morning, just like any other morning. A warm, fine morning now, with familiar sights and familiar sounds. Meadow pipits sprang continually from the heather, their flight as jerky as the Large Heath butterflies, which flitted on the breeze, seeking nectar in the heather bells. Swallows swept the moor with shallow stoops, and above them all hung skylarks, showering them with song.

Sounds travelled far on this high and lonely place, and the bleating of sheep, huddled, and uncertain of the approaching beaters, could be heard two miles away by the men in the butts.

The line advanced. Twenty-five men spread out across the moor waving white flags, some hollering, some whistling, some

218

with dogs to sniff out any grouse which might be sitting tight, waiting for the danger to pass.

The cocks saw them first from their rocky perches, then the birds in the heather heard them and stretched their necks and peered towards the unfamiliar sounds. When to go? Some, if they were midway between two beaters, so that the men or their dogs did not come too close, crouched hidden in the long heather, until they had passed. Some waited until they were almost trodden on before exploding into flight, and a few flew back over the line of the beaters in spite of the flags which were raised and waved in order to turn them in the opposite direction. But most of them flew early, before the beaters reached them; singly, in pairs and in coveys. They cackled as they rose, auburn, solid birds flying fast and low, tracing the contours of the land. They did not fly far, just a flurry of wingbeats, then a long glide with down-swept wings, to land a few hundred yards away from the dogs and the men and the flapping and waving of their flags.

But the beaters came on, and as they drew closer to the butts the line gradually shortened until they were only fifty yards apart. The grouse were concentrated before them now; it was more difficult for them to sit still and avoid detection, and all the time they were being flushed and driven on.

In the butts all conversation had stopped. No orders had been given, and no grouse had arrived yet, but they were due, and it was time to be quiet now and to concentrate. The shooting party reached for their shotguns off the butt walls, or held out their hands to receive them from behind. Lord Dronfield stood up. George Purse placed his shooting stick on the bench, handed him his first gun, then stepped behind him and picked up the other.

Looking hard at the distance, George Purse saw the first covey come sweeping over the ridge, a few feet above the heather. He glanced at Lord Dronfield, but he had seen them at the same time. He stiffened slightly, stood a little straighter and leaned forward. At the first sight of the game that aloof, slightly ponderous elderly gentleman had suddenly focused into a harder, sharper man.

In case any of the grouse decided to sheer off at any sudden movement in the butts, or looked like missing the butts altogether and escaping down the sides, a line of men had been positioned at an angle on both flanks. Their job was to pop up from the heather and wave their flags, in an attempt to scare the deviants back into the line of fire.

But there were no deviants in this covey, which formed the vanguard of the birds in flight from the beaters. They were heading straight towards the middle of the line of butts, trying to escape over the top of the butts, where eight double-barrelled shotguns were waiting to receive them, with another eight in reserve when those had discharged. Straight forward, head on; it was now possible to see the downward-curved silhouette of their wings as they glided, the way their bodies rocked from side to side when they flew.

Forty yards out, thirty, Lord Dronfield mounted his gun and fired. He missed, the bird jinked, second barrel, same bird, a puff of feathers and the grouse collapsed in front of the butt. He passed the gun back, the gamekeeper took it, pushed forward the second gun and rapidly reloaded the first. Guns to the right and guns to the left were also firing. Grouse which remained untouched by the swarms of lead pellets zinging out towards them were still not safe. The Guns waited until they had passed between the butts, then shot at them as they flew away.

Grouse were arriving frequently now, not in great flocks which darkened the sky and allowed all the Guns to blaze away simultaneously, but in families, and pairs and odd penny numbers, presenting themselves at different places along the line so that the Guns were kept busy, but not overworked.

George Purse was bristling with cartridges. They were stuck between his fingers and there were two clenched in his teeth. He had to be quick now, the birds were coming in fast. Right barrel, left barrel, pass back, hand forward. He broke the breech, the cartridge cases ejected automatically and there was the reek of powder from the barrels. He inserted two fresh cartridges and closed the gun to reload and pass it back. They handled the guns smoothly, there was no fumbling between them, and when they exchanged guns, their barrels were always pointing skywards for safety. In the confined space of that hot little fortress, George Purse served his Gun expertly. Lord Dronfield never had to think about him. All he did was pull both triggers, hand back the gun and another took its place. Sometimes a quiet voice said, 'on your left, sir', and there it was, on his left, or, 'a brace on your right, sir', and there was a brace on his right. When Lord Dronfield swivelled to take a bird behind, George Purse always anticipated the move and ducked early, to give him an unobstructed shot. Besides loading, and looking for the grouse, he also had to remember where they fell so that he would know where to direct his dogs when the drive was over.

Shooting etiquette between the Guns was strict. They only shot the birds in the area before or behind their own butts. If there was any doubt whose bird it was, they called to establish rights, and they never shot at birds passing between the butts in case they hit someone in a butt further up the line.

Then they were all gone. The last gunshot reverberated around the hills, and the line of beaters came walking over the ridge, waving their white flags. The shooting party watched them, guns ready, should anything get up between them. But nothing flew, all the grouse were either dead, wounded, or had temporarily escaped to the other side of the moor. Two hundred yards from the butts the beaters stopped and lowered their flags, and for a few seconds the Guns and the beaters faced each other in silence. The moor was quiet again, and larks and meadow pipits started to reassert themselves in the temporary peace.

The Guns and the loaders made sure that the shotguns were empty before placing them on the butt walls and opening the gates to go out and pick up the fallen birds. George Purse whistled his dogs out from under the bench, and they rushed through the gateway together, glad to be released from their noisy confinement. The beaters and their dogs moved forward to help and all along the line Guns, loaders, beaters and dogs searched the heather for dead grouse. The heather around the butts had been burned, so that any birds lying on the charred earth were obvious. But the ones that had fallen into the dense heather were well hidden, and the dogs were needed to find those.

Both Guns and loaders knew approximately where the grouse had fallen, and the dogs were directed to these areas to scent them out. Some of the men worked their dogs with a whistle. George Purse just used his voice. 'Hi look! Hi look! Hi look!' he kept telling them, and if they were not far enough out, he made a series of overarm throwing movements accompanied by the order to get out! Out! Out! It was hard work for the dogs, scouring the dense heather. It was a hot morning, the pollen from the heather flowers clogged their nostrils and deadened the scent of the birds, and sometimes they had to work the same patch over and over again before they found them.

When they did nose one out, they picked it up and carried it back to the gamekeeper, who took it from their mouths. They did not bite the birds; not even when the birds were still alive. They just carried them softly between their jaws, blinking but unruffled by the flapping wing, and let the gamekeeper do the killing. He did this by twisting its head to one side and jerking it back over its body. Some of the handlers used a different method. They just held the bird by the head and swung it round, using the weight and momentum of its own body to break its neck.

One beater standing a hundred yards out from Mr Friar's butt, chased a pricked bird which had fallen and run back. When he caught it and picked it up Mr Friar shouted, 'Put the bloody thing down man, and let the dog do its work! What do you think I paid two hundred guineas for the damned thing for?'

Everybody working around the adjacent butts stopped and looked. The beater did not say anything. He just dropped the bird and moved away.

But walking back to his mark on the other side of the moor, for the start of the second drive, and waving his white flag all the way back, he was thinking what he ought to have said, and what he would have liked to have said. This was his favourite. After Mr Friar had shouted at him, and everybody was looking, he walked deliberately and menacingly up to Mr Friar with the bird in his hand, then, loud enough for everybody to hear, said,

'Just who do you think you're talking to? You speak to me like that again, and I will put it down, I'll put it straight down your fucking throat,' and he brandished the limp body in Mr Friar's face. Then, looking round, satisfied, the beater flung the grouse down, turned his back and walked away across the moor.

At the end of the drive, when he had rolled his stick round his flag and the battle was over, he avoided Mr Friar's patch, and moved further down the line to help pick up, where he hoped the Gun would be more civil. He could not afford to row with Mr Friar. Mr Friar was the Duke's guest. The beater worked on one of the Duke's farms. He had a wife and three children and he lived in a tied cottage. What he wanted just then was his wife to come running across the moors waving a telegram, and shouting, 'You've won the pools, Dan! You've hit the jackpot!' Things would be different with that telegram in his pocket.

While they were picking up, the Ladies arrived from the Big House to join their husbands for the last drive before lunch. They strolled up the path between the butts, chatting, and asking each Gun in turn how he had fared so far that morning. The older ladies were dressed plainly in tweed skirts and twin sets in colours which blended with the surroundings, but the three younger ladies were concerned much more with style regardless of the environment. Lady Harley was wearing a black velvet suit. It had been modelled on the traditional knicker-bocker design but hers had less material in the leg, and a waisted jacket. She wore a matching black velvet cap with a peak, which contrasted nicely with her white blouse and plum-coloured silk scarf.

As he was changing butts for the next drive, George Purse stepped off the narrow path into the heather to let her pass.

224

She walked near enough for him to smell her. He did not know whether it was scent or soap or talcum powder, but it made him want to follow her and keep smelling. He touched his cap. She smiled and said, 'Good morning'. Her face was lightly tanned and lightly decorated on the lips and around the eyes. George Purse made the excuse of calling his dogs so that he could turn round and look at her for a bit longer. She was the same age as his wife. She had had two children like his wife. He knew all this because he had loaded for Lord Harley several times, and once, when Lady Harley had shared the butt with them, they had talked about their families. Her boys were away at school now. She looked ten years younger than Mary Purse, and in ten more years the difference would be even more significant. She would still be an attractive woman, Mary Purse would just be another mother. George Purse hitched up the gun slings on his shoulder and carried on down the path towards butt number 1.

Lady Dronfield was already waiting for them inside the butt. She took off her cardigan, and when she turned round to place it on the bench, George Purse noticed that there was a little hole in one of the heels of the ankle socks that she was wearing over the top of her stockings. She sat down on the bench so that she could reach down to pat the dogs, which were both lying on their sides, still panting after picking up from the last drive.

'They appear to have been working very hard, Mr Purse.'

'Yes, Mi'Lady. It's a bit too warm for them really. It's the pollen as well, it kills all the scent and makes the birds harder to find.'

'Yes, yes, it really is an extremely warm morning for working.'

And she stood up again and looked out over the front of the butt where Lord Dronfield was watching for the arrival of the

225

grouse. The moors were visible for miles now that the sun had burnt away the mist. But the skyline was hazy, the light was soft, and the landscape was all pastel slabs of purple, browns and greens. Above the first ridge, the pale wall of the sky appeared to be shimmering behind the heat haze which was rising from the moor.

'I think this calls for shirt-sleeve order.'

And Lord Dronfield took off his jacket and loosened his tie.

'That's a good idea, Sir, I'll do the same if you don't mind.'

And the gamekeeper took off his jacket and loosened his tie. They both kept their hats on. When the first covey of grouse arrived, Lord Dronfield performed a right and a left with his first two shots, both birds crumpling and falling in front of the butt.

'Good shot, Sir.'

'Splendid, Darling.'

Next, a single bird flew diagonally across the line. Number 3 butt missed it, number 2 jolted it, and Lord Dronfield killed it with his first barrel.

There was a smattering of shooting all the way up the line, but the action was more frequent at the bottom end. George Purse was loading continually, and the barrels of both guns grew hot from the frequent explosions inside them. One bird jinked away from a covey which was flying directly towards the butt, and flew for the unguarded area at the end of the line. Lord Dronfield missed it with his first barrel and killed it with his second. When the pellets penetrated its body, all energy and tension left it. One second, flying forcefully with purpose, the next, a bundle of feathers flopping to the ground.

Not all the grouse died in the air like this. Some were only wounded. The impact checked their flight, they staggered on, but then, too weak to fly any further, they planed down into the heather. The loaders marked these birds carefully, as they usually landed further away from the butts than the dead birds, and could easily get lost and stay unrecovered.

By the time the drive was over, most of these birds were already dead. A few still had sufficient strength to flutter and drag themselves away, to die quietly during the night concealed in thick heather. And the rest just lay there, too weak to run, listening to the voices and the footsteps and the snuffling and the swishing of the heather as the dog came closer. Closer. Sometimes, terror lent them explosive strength when the dog's face appeared above them; they fluttered up and flew a few yards, but the dog was on them again, and again, until, exhausted, the bird had no choice but to allow itself to be picked up and carried on its side, still alive, still looking, to the dog's handler.

George Purse broke the bird's neck and carried it back to the butt where Lord and Lady Dronfield were surveying the morning's work. Lord Dronfield's contribution to the carnage had been placed separately for counting.

'A nice drive I think, Purse?'

The gamekeeper threw the last bird down with the others and counted them.

'Sixteen, Sir. Very good.'

'Yes, that was a jolly good drive. And that brings us nicely up to lunch I think.'

And he turned away, followed by his wife, leaving George Purse to pack up all his gear and lug it back up the path to the luncheon huts.

One hut was for the use of the shooting party, the other for the loaders and beaters. Each group kept strictly to its own hut.

The Guns and their Ladies refreshed themselves with whisky and tall iced glasses of gin and tonic, then sat down to a cold buffet luncheon. White cloths had been laid on the trestle tables, and the light reflecting from these cloths brightened the room, which was dim after the sunlight outside. On cold days, hot meals were prepared at the Big House and driven up to the moor in containers. But whatever the weather, there was no variation for the loaders and beaters, it was always sandwiches and beer. They brought their own sandwiches, but the Duke stood them a few crates of beer.

As it was warm, the stove in the loaders' and beaters' hut had not been lit, and most of them were picnicking outside on the grass. Some of the dogs were resting in the shadow of the hut, some were scrounging around for fallen food, and some were sitting with their owners watching them eat, hoping that they would save them a crust. George Purse separated his last crust into two pieces, gave them to his dogs, then stood up and went into the hut to fetch another bottle of beer. The crates were on the table with the shotguns and guncases, cartridge boxes and bags, and a selection of jackets and water-proofed overcoats. In the crates, there was only one bottle left with a cap on. George Purse lifted it out and picked up the opener from the table. The cap came off too easily, the bottle was empty. Two beaters, who had been watching him from their chairs by the wall, started to laugh.

'Don't tell me all the beer's gone, George.'

George Purse turned round on them.

'I don't have to tell you, you two buggers have got it all. Come on, let's have a bottle.'

One of the beaters held up the bottle he was drinking from. The light from the window showed that it was nearly empty.

'You can have this if you like, George. But it's my last drop.'

'Last drop my arse. I'll tell you what, if I've to search them two haversacks under your seats I'm keeping everything I find in them.'

They laughed and picked up their haversacks together.

'Don't be like that, George, you need a few bottles when you've been tramping around that moor all morning.'

They opened their bags and gave him a bottle each. They did not let him see how many they had left inside.

'You greedy buggers. You'd better get them supped, because if anybody asks me if there's any left I'll tell them.'

'It's all right for you lot, standing in them butts all day. It's better than being on holiday.'

'Holiday! I don't know the meaning of the word.'

He opened both bottles and left the beaters sitting there in the gloom with their diminished cache. They immediately finished the bottles they were drinking and dropped them back into the crate. It was time to get cracking before anybody else came in wanting a drink.

George Purse went back to the place where he had left his dogs and sat down next to Sam Dobie.

'Is one of them for me, George?'

'It is if you want one.'

'Is there any left inside?'

'No, these are the last two.'

'In that case, as I've only had one. I'll have one then if you don't mind.'

George Purse gave him one, and licked the froth off the top of his own.

'I can't understand it, George. There must be somebody getting more than their share.'

'It's simple, Sam, there isn't enough beer. If there was a few more crates, and everybody knew there was enough to go round, they wouldn't go making pigs of themselves, or storing it away in their knapsacks, would they?'

'You know why that is, don't you?'

''Course I do. He thinks we'd all get drunk.'

'He's right an'all.'

'No, he's not. Would you, Sam?'

Surprised at the question, Sam Dobie looked at him, then had a drink to give himself time to answer.

'No, come to think of it, I don't suppose I would. Not while I was working.'

'No, and neither would I. Them who want to get drunk get drunk anyway. The rest wouldn't have any more than they do now.'

'Well, what's the point in having any more then?'

'Because you'd be able to make up your own mind, instead of him making it up for you.'

He had a drink, just enough to empty the neck of the bottle, then put it down on a rock. Sam Dobie's springer walked across and had a sniff at it. Sam pushed it off.

'Hey, don't piss in that. It's weak enough as it is.'

'What gets me though, Sam, is nobody can say owt when They get drunk. It's all good fun then. They can just please themselves what they do.'

'Ar, well, there's nowt we can do about that, George.'

George Purse picked up the bottle and had another drink, then he sat there, revolving the bottle in his hands, alternately looking at it, then looking up across the moors. But he was not seeing either.

230

After they had eaten all their sandwiches and drunk all the beer, the beaters and loaders lazed on the grass, talking and snoozing. Across the track, the shooting party began to emerge from their hut. They sat down on their own part, talking and snoozing, until it was time to walk back to the butts for the first drive of the afternoon.

Sam Dobie helped himself up by gripping George Purse's knee.

'Well, I suppose somebody had better show willing.'

'I reckon we might as well pack up and go home, Sam. They'll be sitting that tight in this heat, the beaters'll have to kick them up into the air.'

'Never mind, George. What doesn't show today will still be there tomorrow.'

And he walked away to sort out several brace of young grouse for the chauffeur to take back to the Big House so that they could be prepared in time for the evening meal.

When he had finished, he watched the Land Rover move away up the track, then got the beaters on to their feet to start their trek back across the moor.

The beaters suffered on that first drive. They had walked the moor three times already. Over lunch, their aching legs had stiffened, and the food and the beer and the rest in the sun had made them more tired than they were before they had eaten. Now the sun was hotter, and they had to walk in it. They were fed up with walking. They wanted to lie down in the heather. But they had to keep on, to maintain the line, and the pace was just as fast as the morning's drives because there was the timetable to keep to. Most of the beaters had lost interest in the grouse by now, they did not care if they rose in ones or twos or flew in blizzards like locusts. They were more interested in the land ahead, its rise and fall, and the density of vegetation growing on it. It was not like walking across a cricket field waving a white flag. The land undulated. There were gullies where the streams had cut through the peat as far as the rocky bed, and the men had to slither down steep banks, then clamber up the sticky peat banks at the other side. There were stretches of old heather which came up to their knees, and had the same effect on their thighs and calves as walking through water.

Different areas of colour meant different vegetation. But, just now, the beaters were not interested in colours, or the subtle patchwork they created on the moor. They were only interested in what the colours were made of, and what effect they would have on their legs when they walked through them. The vivid green patches were sphagnum bogs. If these bogs were too large to detour, the beaters walked straight through them and sank up to the ankles in brown water.

There were also holes in the ground, which were so well concealed by overlapping heather and grasses, that the only way the beaters found them was by stepping into them. They always contained water. Sometimes it only came up to the knee, sometimes the whole leg was wet through.

The short heather and the strips of scorched heather were the easiest to walk on, the acres of bracken the worst. It was chest high, and they had to beat individual paths through it with their flags. And when they were through it they were in the heather again, and there was the pollen again, puffing up from the flowers and settling on their clothes, making them look like workers from a flour mill.

At the end of the drive they sat down in the heather and let the Guns and the loaders do all the picking up. One to go. Although they were tired, they needed no telling to get back to their marks for this one. The last drive was always the fastest drive of the day.

Lord Dronfield was back in butt number 5 for the fifth and final drive. Lady Dronfield entered the butt first and sat down on the bench at the far end. The wall behind her made a shadow, and it was cooler down there. Lord Dronfield decided to sit down as well. But not on the bench, because it was too low to see over the wall. So he set his shooting stick. Looking straight from the glare of the sun and the bright sky down into the dim well of the butt, he did not notice that he had placed the point of the stick on the edge of one of the slats and not in the centre. Lady Dronfield did not notice either because she was dabbing her brow with a handkerchief. George Purse noticed, but did not say anything.

As soon as Lord Dronfield settled on to the seat his weight drove the metal point into the wood, the slat splintered, and the point disappeared into the gap between the slats. Lord Dronfield's arms and legs shot out simultaneously in an effort to keep balance, but there was nothing to grab hold of. The butt wall was too far in front, and George Purse was out of reach behind. The shooting stick toppled sideways and Lord Dronfield fell heavily on to the boards.

George Purse had anticipated the accident and watched it happen, even though he could have prevented it. He was all mock concern as he helped Lord Dronfield to his feet, his face a parody of anxiety, with lowered brows and clenched lips. He had to consciously hold this manufactured expression or he would have started laughing.

'Are you all right, Sir?'

'Yes, yes, I think so. It was just the shock of it that's all.'

Groaning, he kneaded his buttocks, while George Purse held one arm and Lady Dronfield held the other.

'There doesn't appear to be any bones broken, that's the main thing. What the devil happened anyway?'

George Purse released him and picked up the shooting stick.

'The point of the shooting stick must have slipped between the boards, Sir.'

'Damned careless of me that. It's a good job I wasn't holding a gun at the time or there could have been a nasty accident.'

'Yes, Sir. It just goes to show how easily accidents can happen.'

But he would not have let it happen if Lord Dronfield had been holding a gun. There was no telling where the barrels would have pointed when his arms went up into the air.

'Do you want to sit this drive out, Sir?'

Drops of sweat were standing on Lord Dronfield's face like water on lard.

'Good Lord, no. I'll be all right now.'

But he was not, and when the grouse were disturbed and driven over the butts for the fifth and final time that day, Lord Dronfield only killed two birds. His reactions were slower, his mounting was jerky, and his hand trembled when he passed the guns back for reloading. At the end of the drive, when the last bird had hurried by, he sat down on the bench with Lady Dronfield and let George Purse and the dogs go out to retrieve the fallen brace.

In the north of England, in Scotland and in Ireland, on millions of acres of moorland owned by the old aristocracy of landowners, and rented by the new aristocracy of businessmen, the shooting was being concluded for the day, the bag collected, and the day's sport being discussed over drinks.

The grouse were carried from the butts up to the luncheon huts in sacks, or in bunches, by hand. The tarpaulin sheet which had been placed over the morning's kill was peeled off and the afternoon's effort thrown down with them. When they had all been brought in, Sam Dobie knelt down and arranged them into rows, eleven neat rows of twenty, and a short line of seven at the bottom. The Duke came across with Lady Harley to ask what the bag was. They were both holding glasses of whisky and soda.

'A hundred and twenty-three and a half brace, Sir, with the ones I sent off at lunchtime.'

'Jolly good. That's a jolly good total considering the heat.'

'Yes, Sir, I reckon if it hadn't been so hot we could have topped two hundred brace today.'

'I'm certain we could. It's a pity those clouds which are collecting over the tops there didn't arrive earlier.'

Lady Harley bent down and picked up the last bird from the bottom row. She had taken off her jacket, and as she reached for the grouse her white blouse stretched smoothly across her back revealing its contours. She was wearing nothing underneath it. She stood up and weighed the bird in her hand. It had white feathered legs which seemed incongruous against its rich chestnut plumage. They looked more like the legs of an owl than a gamebird.

'Nice young bird that, Mi'Lady.'

'How can you tell it's a young one?'

Sam Dobie took it from her and spread one wing like a hand of cards.

'Look how pointed the two outer primary feathers are.'

He put the bird back in its place, and sorted through the others until he found an old one.

'This is an old one look. Can you see how much rounder the first two primaries are?'

'Well, yes, now that you've pointed it out, I suppose I can. There doesn't appear to be all that much difference though. I imagine you have to be an expert to spot it.'

'I'm no expert Mi'Lady. I've only been at it for thirty-five years.'

Before he packed the birds into the hampers, he paid the beaters. £2.50 they received for their day's work. With part of their wages some of the beaters bought a brace of grouse. The price was £1.30 for a brace of young birds, 75p for a brace of old birds. George Purse would not buy them, if they were not free he would not have them.

Sam Dobie packed a hamper of young grouse for the Big House, then the keepers helped him to sort the others and tie them up in pairs according to age. These birds were destined for a game and poultry dealer in Smithfield Market in London. Some estates had contracts with exclusive London restaurants to provide a few brace for the evening of the 12th. Before the advent of express trains and fast roads, this tradition of dining in the capital on grouse which had only been shot a few hours previously, hundreds of miles away in remote parts of the North, called for all kinds of ingenious transport arrangements to ensure that the birds arrived in time. Much energy and expenditure went into the hiring and timetabling of vehicles, and some restaurants used to charter light aeroplanes in which to carry the birds from the moors. It's there on film, with the keepers throwing the birds into the back seat, and the pilot in front, in goggles and moustache, turning round to face the

236

camera. But this was all part of the fun. The cost was passed on to the customers, and they could afford to pay for it anyway.

And during the same period there was the General Strike, when the miners stayed out for six months and were eventually starved back to work, and the Depression, with millions of people unemployed throughout the country.

The gamekeepers were in a hurry now. They wanted to get home. The beaters had gone, so they were the only ones working. After they had packed and locked the hampers, they went into the luncheon hut, slid the shotguns out of their slips, dismantled them and fitted them into their cases. While they worked, the shooting party and their ladies stood around in groups drinking and chatting. The Duke's chauffeur was acting as barman. He had produced the bottles and glasses from a small military chest, fitted with brass corners and inset brass handles on each end. Mr Friar was sitting on a rock drinking whisky, while his man pulled off his heavy shoes and re-shod him in a pair of slippers for the drive home. The gamekeepers had nothing to drink. They had finished all their beer at lunchtime.

Charlie Taylor picked up Senhor Aveiro's guncase and invited George Purse to share the carrying of one of the hampers back to the lorry. George Purse declined the invitation. He said he wasn't ready. But he was, he was waiting for something. The other gamekeepers were all ready now, and were deciding who should share the carrying of which baskets. George Purser had to be included. He was just picking up a hamper with Henry Clay, when Lord Dronfield detached himself from a group and called him over. He did not say anything. He just nodded sharply and shoved a folded five-pound note in George Purse's palm. George Purse touched his cap.

'Thank you very much, Sir, much obliged.'

When he got back to Henry Clay, who was waiting to lift the hamper, he said, 'I thought the bugger had forgot.'

Mr Friar was the first of the shooting party to leave. He passed the procession of gamekeepers just over the ridge, on their way down to the lorry, and they had to step off the path and call their dogs to heel until his shooting brake had passed. The rest of the party stayed a little longer to savour the day. The sun was still out, but a pile of dark and puce-coloured clouds was tumbling towards it from the east. The thunder which accompanied these clouds seemed to be the noise of their movement, and as the party turned towards these gathering sounds, a sudden chill wind crossed the moor and whipped up the dust on the track. They turned away. It was time to go. They drank up and put on their jackets and cardigans. The chauffeur locked up the bottles and glasses in the chest, and they all climbed into the Land Rovers.

As the Land Rovers moved slowly up the track, the moor was still bright, and the sun picked out the glossy plastic cartridge cases which littered the ground around the butts. But the clouds were catching the sun. The hills to the east had taken on their dark hues, and the wind that ruffled the heather was drawing their shadow closer. And with the cloud came the thunder. Nearer. Louder. Sonorous noises, which lasted longer and travelled further than the harsh cracks of the shotguns which had been fired there earlier in the day. The moor would be a different place when the storm arrived.

The lorry and the keepers' cars kept together on the way back, and they arrived at the Big House in convoy. Henry Clay went into the House and unlocked the gun room door, then, while the other gamekeepers unloaded the shooting tackle from the back of the lorry, he unloaded the hampers of grouse with Charlie Taylor. They stacked the hampers which were destined for London outside the door, from where they would later be picked up and taken to the station in one of the Land Rovers. Then they carried the hamper of selected young birds into the House and started down the staircase which led to the kitchens. The stairs were so wide that they could walk down together with the hamper between them. Charlie Taylor tested his nostrils as the smell of hot food became stronger.

'That smells good, Henry. What is it?'

'I don't know. Some kind of soup I suppose.'

'Well it's not fish and chips. That is a certainty.'

They reached the bottom of the stairs and carried the basket along a high wide corridor with a red tiled floor. Doors led off either side of the corridor, and through one open doorway they saw the Duke's valet, dressed in pinstriped trousers and a white shirt with armbands, pressing the Duke's evening clothes. Through another door they saw another man polishing a table-ful of black shoes.

The kitchen was at the end of the corridor. Even though the door and the top windows had been opened to create a draught, the lower windows were still steamed up, and the room was so hot that it was like walking into another climate. All the ovens were lit and there was a huge pan on every ring. The chef had six women to help him to prepare the dinner. They were all wearing white overalls, the women were wearing white caps, and the chef wore a tall white hat. Two of the women were scraping potatoes at a sink; two were slicing kidney beans and podding peas at a large scrubbed table in the centre of the room, and the other two were transferring pans from ring to ring under the direction of the chef, who was ladling and teeming soup in a large aluminium pan. The gamekeepers lifted the basket on to the table and went out.

'Smells good enough to eat,' Charlie Taylor said.

The gamekeepers cleaned the guns quickly. The smell of food which permeated the hallway at the top of the stairs had followed them into the gun room. It made them feel hungry, and they wanted to get home and eat.

George Purse wrapped a soft patch of material around the end of a cleaning rod and inserted it into one of the barrels. He pushed the rod up until it appeared out of the far end like a sweep's brush out of a chimney, then withdrew it and pushed it up the other one. He squinted up the barrels to make sure they were clean, wiped the barrels and stock with an oily rag, then replaced them in their baize moulds. He cleaned the other gun in the same way, then closed the case and pushed it a bit further on to the table so that it would not get knocked off.

'Right, that's it. I'm off. Same time tomorrow, Henry?'

'Same time, eight o'clock. And don't be late.'

George Purse turned back from the doorway.

'Late, I'm never late. As Alf Clark said when he came in one Monday morning at seven o'clock, and the foreman stormed up to him and said, "Hey up! What time do you call this? Do you know you're an hour late?" "An hour late," Alf said. "No I'm not, I'm seven hours early. I should never have bleeding come in the first place."'

The boys were playing cricket in the yard when he got home. They were using a rusty milk churn as a wicket. John was batting.

George Purse let the dogs out of the back of the van and the labrador immediately ran across to the pitch and picked up the ball. He told them to put the dogs away and feed them before it started to rain. Then he went in. There was no one in the house. His wife was up at the Big House working in the kitchen. Before she had gone she had cut him some chips and left them in a basin of water on the draining board. At the side of the basin there was a tin of peas with a note underneath it.

Pie in fridge. Do it at number 5 for 20 mins.

George Purse lit the oven and left the door open. The day had been so fine that no fire had been made in the kitchen. Yesterday's ashes were still in the grate, and now that the sun had gone, the room was chill and gloomy. He took off his jacket and washed his hands. It was grouse for dinner at the Big House, and grouse for dinner at the Savoy Grill. For George Purse, it was chips and peas and a meat pie in a tin-foil tray from the supermarket on the council estate.

The Duke shot grouse on his three moors on alternate weeks, Friday, Saturday and Monday, and when he was not shooting on his own moors, he was touring the north of England and Scotland shooting on somebody else's. It was a full-time job, travelling and shooting, through August, September and for the first two weeks in October. He had a change for one week in September when he went over to France to shoot partridge on Count Mauriac's estate, and after the last shoot in October, he took a fortnight's holiday on his estate in Ireland to recuperate in time for the pheasant shooting in November.

George Purse was busy too. His main jobs, when he was not loading on the moors, were trying to prevent his pheasants from straying, and patrolling his beat to protect them from poachers. He had not spent the best part of a year raising them for anybody to shoot. The Duke would expect maximum returns when the season started, and there would be no excuses.

He fed the birds at the same time each morning, on the rearing field in his home wood, and on the ride near the release pen in the Duke's wood. When he approached them and broadcast the grain, he whistled the same staccato notes that they had heard from their first feed as chicks.

The pheasant shooting season started on 1st October. But the Duke never started shooting until the leaves were down in November. The pheasants were bigger and stronger then. They flew higher and faster, and provided more sporting shooting with that extra month behind them.

The pheasants really looked like pheasants now; they had grown their long pointed tails, and the cocks were darkening into their adult plumage. And as their plumage changed, growing richer, and more varied in pattern and colour, the countryside around them changed too.

Through September the changes in the woods were subtle. Most of the trees were still green, the undergrowth still rank, and on sunny days it was as warm as in summer. But in amongst the leaves, acorns, beechmast, conkers and sweet-chestnuts were maturing. Birds were singing again after their summer moult, and the sun took longer to dry the dew in the mornings. The horse chestnuts lost their leaves early, but from the fields, the woods looked as green and as dense as they had done in July, when George Purse had taken the pheasant poults to the release pen.

After the pheasants had fed in the woods in the mornings, they wandered out into the fields, where the signs of the changing seasons were more obvious. They gleaned the stubbles, and when the farmers ploughed the stubbles under, they walked along the furrows seeking roots and insects. Some birds followed the plough, and in one field, pied wagtails landed on the upturned soil even as it curled from the shining blade.

And when the sun shone on those September days, and the slabs of turned earth gleamed like armour in the fields, there was a softness in the light, and a stillness across the land that meant that summer was spent. Those quiet days were summer's embers, a respite, a last warming before the harder days to come. The robin seemed to say it in the tone of its song; and the swallows in their twittering, as they ganged up around the farms in preparation for their long flight south.

And as the sap fell in the trees, their leaves dried up, changed colour and began to fall. Sporadically at first, through the misty mornings and the hazy sunshine of the still afternoons, until, by mid October, enough leaves had fallen to reveal the span of the branches through the sketchy foliage. The farmers sowed the winter wheat. The swallows left, and in their place came redwings and fieldfares, travelling and calling through the cold clear nights, across the sea from Scandinavia. In hungry flocks they stripped the hedgerows of their late blackberries and elderberries, of their haws and rosehips, and the strings of woody nightshade berries which hung along the hedges like discarded swag.

And then the weather changed. The wind strengthened from the north-west and brought rain, and the wind and the rain accelerated the stripping of the trees. For three days and three nights the leaves slanted down in a second rain. Then the wind bated, and shifted to the north-east, and there was frost in the night, and the frost brought down leaves which the wind had not removed.

And when George Purse trod through the leaves after that week of wind and rain and frost, the woods were a different place. There was more light between the trees, he could see further, and the grassy paths and rides had been overlaid with brown. He was glad the leaves were down. He was not interested in the aesthetics of their changing tints. It meant that the first shoot was near. There was room now for the pheasants to get up between the trees, and for the guns to see them clearly from their stands in the rides.

It meant that the poachers could see them clearly as well. At night men came from the mining villages and the council estate and roamed the woods armed with .22 rifles fitted with silencers. They shot the roosting pheasants from the branches; they were so close, and the birds were so clearly silhouetted, that all the poachers had to do was blank them out with the end of their rifles and pull the trigger. It was harder to miss. They had no intention of giving the birds a sporting chance. The nearer the better for them. If they could have plucked them from the branches, that would have been better still. They were interested in the money. They could not afford the sport.

So George Purse and the other keepers worked nights as well, to make sure that there were plenty of pheasants for the Duke and his party to shoot when the season started. George Purse hated poachers taking his birds. It's like working for nowt, he always said.

He did not go out into the woods every night. If it was raining hard or foggy, he went to bed. He guessed that the poachers would stay home those nights as well. But if the nights were dry, especially in mid-week, when wages and dole money were running low, and a few brace of pheasants sold in the pubs, or in the City market, might tide a man over until pay day, then he had to work.

He left the house around eleven o'clock, when his wife went to bed. Sometimes he worked on his own and sometimes he worked with Charlie Taylor, and they covered both beats. In the two woods where most of his pheasants were, he had hollowed out little dens in the bracken, and when the air was still, and it was quiet in the wood, he would settle down in one of these dens and listen.

On windy nights when the gusts boomed through the tree tops, and it sounded as though express trains were rushing through the woods, he walked about more, visiting his dens for short periods then moving on. It was all guesswork really. He could be guarding one wood, while poachers were at work in another. He just had to keep awake, listen hard and hope he was in the right wood at the right time.

It was not pleasant in the woods at night. He was not afraid of the natural sounds of the night, like the barking of a fox, or the wavering call of the tawny owl. He knew that the little ghost sitting on the fence post was really a barn owl, and those grotesque figures with the clawing hands were only trees. But he was afraid of a natural figure stepping out from behind those monsters with a raised gun. The supernatural held no terrors compared with that.

Because he could not see well in the dark, he heard more, and certain sounds that he would have barely noticed in the daylight scared him; like the breeze rattling the dead leaves on an oak sapling, or rubbing a dried thistle head against a stone. He never learned with sounds like these, his heart lurched every time, and he swung his gun with his finger on the trigger.

He had confronted poachers several times in the woods at night. One time, he had been with Charlie Taylor, when they surprised three men who immediately ran away. The game-keepers chased them to the edge of the wood, and as the last one placed his hand on a fence post to vault over, George Purse hit it with a stick. This stopped the man and they caught him. Three of his fingers were broken. The other two poachers got away. In court, the injured poacher swore blind that he had been on his own all the time, and that the gamekeepers had attacked him when all he'd been doing was taking his dog for a walk. At two o'clock in the morning and in possession of a rifle? The magistrate said. You can't be too careful, the poacher replied. You never know who you might come across at that time of night. The magistrate commended him on his prudence, fined him fifty pounds, and added a six-month suspended sentence as a further deterrent.

Another time, he walked up behind a man who was just bend-ing down to pick up a pheasant off the floor. The man jumped when George Purse shouted at him, but when he saw that the gamekeeper was on his own, he relaxed and answered George Purse's questions readily, admitting all. He was just describing where he lived, a street somewhere at the far side of the estate, which the gamekeeper had never heard of, when somebody hit George Purse on the back of the head with the butt of a gun.

When he woke up they had taken his gun. He never got it back, and he never saw the pleasant poacher again. He remem-bered where he said he lived, Black Street, and how to get there; you keep going 'til you reach that row of shops, turn right at the

Co-op butchers, then it's the first on your left . . . But he knew better than to go and try and find it.

Now he never confronted poachers, unless they surprised each other, and he had no choice. Armed men startled in the dark were too dangerous. Justifying his policy, he always said he was defending pheasants, not Fort Knox. Now, when he heard poachers shouting in whispers through the trees, or heard the splat of a rifle, or a dog scuffling in the undergrowth trying to scent a fallen bird, he stayed still until he had worked out which way they were going. He stalked them to within twenty yards, then hidden behind a tree he fired both barrels of his gun into the air, shouted all the names of the keepers he could think of, plus the names of anybody else who came to mind, and ran around kicking leaves and thrashing bushes. Surrounded by the posse of keepers, the poachers ran away. It worked every time. He dreaded the night coming when a gang of them might decide to stay and fight.

He stayed out all night. From high places in the fields and the edges of the woods he could see the street lights of the village, and the council estate, and the lights of the mining villages which surrounded the Duke's estate. He could see the head-lamps of vehicles crawling along distant roads, and he could see the silhouettes of prominent buildings in the district, like the Big House and the tower of the village church.

Sometimes he could not stay awake all night, and he snoozed in one of his dens; jerking awake stiff and cold, wondering where he was, whether he had slept minutes or hours, and convinced that teams of poachers had been at work while he slept, and were, at that very moment, staggering from the woods with sackloads of pheasants slung across their backs.

Then, when the light began to seep into the eastern rim of the sky, and the objects in the wood became themselves again, when perspective returned to the wood, and distant trees stayed darker than the spaces between them, George Purse went home and went to bed for a few hours, before the real morning came, when he had to get up and feed the pheasants again.

The first day's shooting was on George Purse's beat, so it was his job to organize it. On the morning before the shoot, he worked out all the drives, and in the afternoon went round the fields and fixed up the markers where the Guns would stand. In each field he planted a line of sticks, twenty yards apart, with plastic cards numbered 1 to 8 slotted into the split end of each stick. Each line of stands was about forty yards from the edge of the wood (he paced it) so that the pheasants had time to gain height as they flew out of the trees and passed over the guns. The shooting party believed in giving the pheasants a sporting chance. Unlike the poachers, they were sportsmen. Unlike the the poachers, they could afford to be.

George Purse went to bed that night. It was Friday, pay day, and the poachers would have wages to spend.

Next morning it was fine. It had rained during the night, but a strong wind from the north had blown away the clouds, and the sky was blue all over. The air was clear, and the sun seemed to be just above the fields behind the gamekeeper's house. The light was so bright in the direction of the sun, that it made George Purse sneeze just to look at the dazzle on the plough-land beneath it.

'It's a very fine morning, said Mr Drake Puddle-Duck,' Mary Purse said, as she wiped a floor cloth along a plastic clothes line which hung across the yard from the cottage to the outhouses.

'Not for long though,' George Purse said, twanging the line and making her drop the cloth. 'It's too bright to stop fine.'

The loaders and the beaters had arranged to meet in a field at the side of the Duke's wood at nine o'clock. When George Purse arrived at a quarter to, most of them were already there. He could see there was something up as soon as he walked through the gate. They looked as though they were holding a meeting in the middle of the field. He could not hear what they were saying, but he could tell it was serious by the set of the men's faces, and the way they leaned into each other as they spoke. As he walked towards the gathering, Henry Clay saw him and came forward to meet him.

'What's up, Henry, has there been a fight?'

'No, but there will be when the Duke gets here.'

'Why, what's going off?'

'It's the beaters, they've gone on strike.'

George Purse scrutinized him for a few moments to make sure that he was serious, then he laughed.

'Gone on strike!'

And he said it so loudly that everybody turned round and looked at him. Henry Clay was offended by the laugh.

'I can't see owt funny about it. Go and have a word with them will you, George, and see if you can talk any sense into them?'

George Purse walked past him and approached the group of beaters and keepers in the middle of the field.

'Hey up, what's all this then? How long have the beaters had a union?'

Because the beaters could not determine his attitude, no one answered him.

'A beaters' strike, eh? That really is one for the *Guinness Book of Records*.' And he laughed and started to shake his head.

'What you lot got to strike about anyroad? Fifty bob a day and all the free conkers you want. You don't know when you're well off.'

George Purse and the other keepers laughed at this, but none of the beaters did. One of them, angered by George Purse's flippancy and apparent opposition to the strike, moved to the front of the crowd to confront him before his scorn destroyed the tenuous militancy of the beaters.

'Trust you to be against it.'

'How much are you after, anyroad?'

'Three pounds a day.'

'Three pounds!'

'Why, don't you think we're worth that much?'

'No.'

'Why not?'

'You're worth more. You should be asking for a fiver at least.'

Henry Clay came from behind him to look at his face, to see whether he was serious or not.

'Don't tell me you agree with them, George?'

'They've no choice have they? They've been promised a rise for years now, but they're always fobbed off with some lame excuse that the estate can't afford it. It's ridiculous. What's two pound fifty for a day's work these days?'

'But that kind of thing's never been done here before, George.'

'Well it's about time it was then. They'll let you talk until you're blue in the face, but a time comes when you've got to

250

stop talking and show them that you mean business. They'll keep you talking for ever if you let them.'

George Purse was the first gamekeeper to speak out openly on the side of the beaters. Some of the others agreed with him, but not publicly when Henry Clay was there. It was too dangerous. Henry Clay was the Duke's man, and word travelled. Charlie Taylor was the second to speak out.

'They'll never get five though, George. Only management get one hundred per cent increases.'

'I know, but if they ask for five they might get four. If they only ask for three they've no room to negotiate, have they?'

'You should have been a union man, George.'

'I used to be, didn't I?'

Henry Clay was disgusted with both of them.

'I know what they will get when the Duke gets here. They'll get the bloody sack, all of them. You two an'all if you're not careful.'

He could not understand their attitude. Strikes were not part of his world. He had been born and brought up on the estate. So had his family before him. He had worked all his life on the estate. So had his family before him. Henry Clay's family were loyal servants of the Duke and his family, and Henry felt privileged just to work for them. Even if the Duke did pay him the minimum wage laid down by the National Union of Agricultural Workers (plus an extra five pounds per week for his position as Head keeper). Even if he did work seven days most weeks, and was only allowed the minimum number of holidays laid down by law. And even if it did take an epic of perseverance and a succession of minor bribes to get repairs done to his house. But Henry accepted all this exploitation and the subservience which it bred, because he had been brought up to it. He had been educated from birth to think that paternalism and social inequality were the natural order of things, and therefore immutable.

George Purse and Charlie Taylor did not know how to bring about a social revolution either. But they did know how to win higher wages. They had been born in the mining villages which surrounded the estate. They were both from mining families. Charlie had worked in the pits and George in the steel industry. They had poached the Duke's land before they had become gamekeepers, and now, even though they were employed by the Duke, their early experiences and loyalties reasserted themselves. They knew whose side they were on.

And they also knew that if the energy, solidarity and determination to win that went into industrial confrontations was ever harnessed and used for political ends, then even the Duke would not be immune from the repercussions that would follow major trade union victories.

George Purse shook his head.

'Of course they'll not get the sack. They've timed it just right. Where's he going to get another team of beaters from this late? If he sacks these lads he'll have to cancel the day's shooting, and he'll not do that when they've travelled from all over the country for it. They've got him over a barrel, Henry. They could ask for a tenner this morning and they'd get it.'

But the beaters decided to stick at three pounds. They did not want to look greedy, they said. Another fifty pence would be enough.

'You'll learn,' George Purse said.

'It's all right for you,' Henry Clay said. 'It's me that's got to tell the Duke when he comes.'

252

'And I'm going to tell him that it was all your idea in the first place, Henry, and you said that if they don't get what they want, you're going to bring all the keepers out in support.'

Henry Clay coloured up, and George Purse had to slap him on the back to keep things right between them.

When the two Land Rovers drove into the field, and the Duke climbed out with the rest of the shooting party, the keepers who were acting as loaders walked across to the lorry to unload the tackle and the guns. George Purse stayed where he was. He was not loading today. Because the shooting was taking place on his beat, it was his job to organize and supervise the beaters through each drive.

At that moment, when the shooting party arrived, and the loaders walked away from the beaters, if one of them had said, let's call it off, he might have received enough support to retract their demand. But it was too late, Henry Clay was already walking across the field to the Land Rovers.

'Good morning, Henry. Things are rather slack aren't they? Look at the beaters; shouldn't they be in position for the first drive by this time?'

The loaders assembling the guns at the back of the lorry, and the beaters standing together in the middle of the field, watched the conversation between Henry Clay and the Duke. As Henry Clay talked, he kept flicking his head back and jerking his thumb over one shoulder in the direction of the beaters. The Duke watched them over his other shoulder, and when Henry had finished speaking, the Duke moved away from him, turned a slow, complete circle, then stepped close to Henry and started to harangue him. As he railed on, he kept jabbing his forefinger at the ground. Henry just stood there, looking down, nodding his head; and watching the scene, it looked as though what was in contention was the dollop of cowshit on the grass between them.

When the Duke had finished his invective, he turned round abruptly and strode back to the Land Rovers. Henry turned round slowly and walked back to the beaters. The loaders were assembling the guns automatically. They had done it so many times that they could do it without looking. They watched the beaters surround Henry, listen for a few moments, and then it was obvious by the way they stepped apart, looking at each other and smiling, that they had won that one.

George Purse clapped his hands like the captain of a football team encouraging his men.

'Come on now lads, let's go and get some work done. We've lost one drive already.' He led them out of the field, and up the lane at the side of the wood, to take them to their positions for the start of the first drive. The beaters were still excited about their success, and some of them started to lag behind as they talked about it. George Purse noticed how they were beginning to straggle, and he stopped and let the leaders pass him.

'Come on now, you've got your money. Let's see you do some work for it.'

He had planned two drives for the Duke's wood. Working from the feed ride which divided the wood in two, they were going to drive the pheasants through the top half of the wood over the line of Guns waiting in the field they had just left. Then walk back to the ride, and drive the bottom half towards the Guns, who would be at their new stands in the field at the opposite end of the wood.

When they reached the ride, the beaters climbed over the wall into the wood, and their dogs scrambled over after them. George Purse walked up the ride with them, stopping them at ten-yard intervals, and as he left each man in his place, he told him to walk nice and steady when he heard the whistle, and keep in line. All the beaters were carrying thick sticks, and while they waited for the whistle, some of them thrashed the grass, or knocked the twigs off the trees and bushes. The swishing of the sticks made the dogs wince when they came too near.

When he had sent the flank man to his position at the edge of the wood, George Purse walked back to the centre of the line, looked along the ride in both directions, then blew his whistle. The line of beaters moved forward, and the wood was immediately filled with wild and unnatural sounds. They whistled and made herding noises, Hi Yi Yi! and Ya Ya! They knocked on the trees as they passed them, and they beat the undergrowth to flush any pheasants sitting tight in there.

They put the creatures in front of them in a tizzy. Rabbits sat up, still and tense, listening. They crouched like stones until they could no longer stand the strain, and had to run for it. Little birds zig-zagged between the trees across the face of the advancing line, and blackbirds streaked out of bushes and skimmed the floor of the wood chattering with alarm. But it was the pheasants that made the most row when they got up. They crashed out of the undergrowth, wings whirring like something clockwork; rising steeply, clumsily, banging into branches and snapping twigs as they laboured for the sky. Clear of the branches, most of them flew on over the tree tops in the direction of the Guns. George Purse did not worry about the ones which flew back over the beaters' heads. They would land in the bottom half of the wood and be there for the next drive. And on the second drive, and succeeding drives, there would be a Gun walking behind the beaters to shoot any birds which decided to break back.

No shots had been fired yet. Pheasants are not strong fliers, and the ones which had flown forward had pitched down in the wood a bit further on. None of them had cleared the end of the wood yet. Some of the pheasants did not get up at all. They just waited until the beaters and the dogs sounded too near, then ran forward from one patch of cover to the next.

George Purse walked along the line of beaters, shouting instructions and trying to keep them in line. He stopped them on a path to allow the stragglers to catch up, and while they were waiting, he told the standing beaters to tap their sticks on the trees. They filled the wood with a tense, urgent noise, which kept the pheasants running forward and got the Guns up from their shooting sticks in the fields. From outside the wood, the muffled shouting and the tapping sounded like someone building amongst the trees. 'Right now! Nice and steady! You'll walk over them and leave them sitting there if you walk too fast!'

And the beaters were off again. The Guns stood waiting for them with their forefingers touching the trigger guards, ready for the smooth mount and fire. Their loaders stood behind them, barrels pointing to the sky; ready to pass the second gun forward when the first one had been fired. They could hear the pheasants bursting upwards now in the wood, and they could hear what the beaters were shouting when the pheasants took off before them, 'Over!' 'Over on your right!' 'Over straight ahead!'

The pheasants were now too near the edge of the wood to land back amongst the trees. Once they had cleared the tree tops they were quickly out of the wood and over a freshly ploughed field, where a line of men were spaced out along one furrow forty yards out. Most of the pheasants never crossed that line. They were shot in front of it, and those that were missed in front were shot going over, or just behind.

The pheasants flew higher and slower than the grouse which most of the shooting party had been shooting so far that autumn. They came over singly, just above the height of the trees, preceded by the beaters' calls. The Guns saw them coming all the way, and they did not have to hurry the guns to their shoulders and snatch at the triggers when they fired. After the sporadic shooting at the early fliers, the shooting became continuous as the beaters neared the end of the wood. All the pheasants which had not already flown were now concentrated into a band of woodland between the beaters and the hedge. After the hedge there was open ploughland with men and no cover in there. They could see the men through the struts of the hedge and hear the banging they were making. They could see the men and the dogs in the wood behind them. They could hear the men shouting and whistling and slashing the undergrowth with their sticks. They could hear the dogs snuffling and panting as they came closer. They had to fly now, and all along the line of beaters, pheasants whirred up before them, making for the tree tops, and the open sky above the branches.

George Purse was now close enough to the edge of the wood to see the pheasants flying over the Guns. When he had been further back in the wood and seen that there were plenty of pheasants and heard plenty of shooting, he was glad. It meant that he had done his job well. But now that he could see them being shot he felt differently. He had spent ten months rearing those birds. He had organized the production of the eggs. He had turned them daily, regulated the humidity and temperature of the incubators and watched some of them hatch from their shells. He had clipped their beaks, kept them clean and administered medicines to keep them healthy. He had shot and trapped hundreds of birds and animals to keep them alive. He had walked miles in the day and sat up at nights risking serious injury to protect them from poachers. He had watched them grow from pompoms into lanky poults and finally into strong young birds.

And now, he stood by the hedgerow at the edge of the wood and watched them tumbling out of the sky. This was what he was paid for, but at times like this he sometimes wondered what it was all about. When he saw one young cock missed by two barrels in front, then by two behind from the next gun, he could not help punching it on its way with a clenched fist.

'Go on, you bugger,' he said, as he watched it fly on unharmed, and carry on right over into the next field.

The rabbits trapped in that narrow strip of woodland had no choice, they had to run for it. One dashed back and escaped between the beaters, the others were driven forward into the field. They had no chance in there. One ran along the end furrow parallel with the hedgerow, and two ran diagonally across the field, making for the end of the line of Guns. None of them made it. The force of the shot sent them cartwheeling and left them dead, draped across the crests of the furrows.

While all this shooting was taking place, the dogs at the stands had to sit still until the drive was over. They watched the pheasants falling around them, and the rabbits sprinting, then just lying there, but they could not pick them up yet. They had been trained not to move until they were given permission. Although none of them ran for the game, they could not help whining occasionally, and although they were all sitting down, they kept brushing the earth with their tails in anticipation.

The beaters reached the hedgerow, but the drive was not over yet. George Purse told them to walk along the hedge and thrash the thick grass and brambles beneath it. He was right. A hen and then a cock got up, exploding from the brambles like rockets from the sea. The hen tried to fly up the face of the wood and escape back over the tops of trees, but the Duke killed it before it reached that height, and it fell back on to the hedge. The cock was killed overhead by Lord Cannock. It was so straight that it nearly fell on his dog. The labrador just looked at it and blinked. It was used to being rained on by pheasants.

That was the last bird. The dogs could get to work now and pick them all up. The old cock pheasants were big for their mouths, and sometimes they had to take several gulps at them, before they could grip enough to hold on to without biting. Small feathers came off the birds and stuck to the dogs' noses and mouths, and after the pheasants had been taken from them, they spluttered and snuffled until they had blown all the feathers away.

The beaters kept their dogs out of it. They could have done the job just as well as the dogs working in the field, but they did not have time. They had to get back to their positions on the middle ride ready to drive the bottom half of the wood. As soon as all the pheasants and the three rabbits had been picked up and thrown into the back of the lorry, the loaders climbed in after them, the Guns got into the Land Rovers, and they all drove round to the other end of the wood to take their stands.

Colonel Garmonsway got out at the end of the middle ride where George Purse was lining up the beaters. The Colonel was the walking Gun on this drive. He would follow the line of beaters and try to shoot any pheasants which broke back over their heads.

The drive had only just started when George Purse found a greenfinch fluttering in the leaves underneath a beech tree. It had made a hole in the leaves, and the flattened grass was showing through like lino through a hole in a carpet. He picked it up, still fluttering. Its little green body was fluffy and warm, and its eyes were bright and wide open. He touched its toes with his little finger and it gripped the finger with both feet. He lifted the feathers on its chest and gently felt its wings at the shoulders, and while he was examining it, it died in his hand. Its wings stiffened, its head lolled and its tiny eyes became glazed. Two beaters on his left were walking together and he could hear them talking about cars. He told them to spread out, then he walked down the line and shouted to the beaters on the left flank to steady up and stop racing. He was so busy organizing the drive that at the end of it, when the last shot had been fired, and he had stopped walking, he realized that he was still holding the dead greenfinch. It looked thinner and darker now because its feathers were slicked together with the sweat from his palm.

There was a fence dividing the wood from the field where the Guns were standing. George Purse climbed over the fence, and while the dogs and the loaders and the Guns were picking up the dead pheasants, he walked across the field until he was in front of Mr Friar's stand, then he bent down and pretended to do something to his wellingtons. When Toby, Mr Friar's labrador, was hunting close by him, he quietly called it over, let him sniff the greenfinch, then pushed it into the dog's mouth. He stood up and walked back towards the fence while Toby trotted back to the brewer, swishing his tail. Mr Friar saw the little head and blunt beak protruding from the side of the dog's mouth. The dog gave him the bird, and when he held it up by the tip of one wing, the weight of its body made it unfold, and it hung like a fan from his fingers.

'What the devil's this you've brought?'

The Duke, who had been shooting at the next stand, heard him and looked across.

'What's that you're holding, Jack?'

'I'm not sure. It looks like a damned finch of some kind.'

'A finch! What in heaven's name did you shoot that for? Did you mistake it for a snipe or something?'

'I didn't shoot the bloody thing. It must have been lying in the field. But why the devil Toby had to pick this when there's all those pheasants lying around, God only knows.'

And George Purse; who was leading the beaters along the side of the fence to the next drive, which was in Duck Wood by Duck Lake. The stands had been fixed in a field of barley stubble midway between the lake and the wood. When the beaters walked across the field, they flushed a flock of Canada geese, which was feeding amongst the stubbles. There were so many of them that they made a single shadow which moved across the land towards the lake, where they landed on the water with a sound like a deep sigh.

The beaters stopped to watch them, and after they had landed, and the ducks and other swimming birds were bobbing around in the wash they had made, George Purse said, 'A grand sight that. There's summat majestic about geese when they're flying.'

'There's summat majestic about them when they're in the oven with roast taties all round them,' one of the beaters said.

It was a dirty field they were in. The farmer had been burning straw and the ground was scarred with black stripes and patches. When the beaters walked across these charred areas, their wellingtons disturbed the ashes, and the smell of burning was revived in their nostrils.

So far the beaters had enjoyed a good morning. They had won a pay rise and one drive had been cancelled. The sun was shining and it was dry in the woods. They had completed two drives, just seen the geese, and now it was a quarter to one, and there was only one more drive before lunch.

George Purse could not hold them on this last drive. He kept shouting to them to steady up. They kept relaying his messages along the line, kept on ignoring them, and kept on walking just as fast. Then a rabbit with myxomatosis stopped three of the beaters in the middle of the line. They could tell that it was infected by its attitude. It did not sit up straight with its ears pointed, then show them its scut and back paws like a healthy rabbit. It just cringed there in the middle of the clearing, occasionally creeping a few yards, then doubling back, as though it was confined in a low wire-netting enclosure.

The rabbit knew there was something wrong. It could hear all the noise, and it could smell the men and the dogs, but because it was nearly blind, it could not see to run away from them. One of the spaniels just ran up to it, picked it up, and carried it squealing and struggling like a baby back to its owner. The beater took it from the dog's jaws, and the other two beaters closed in to look at it. They could only just see its eyes, they were so far back inside the swollen lids. The men shook their heads and curled their lips, registering sorrow and disgust at the same time.

'Poor bugger.'

And the beater swung it by the back legs and knocked its head against a tree. He did this two more times, made sure that it was dead, then threw it into some brambles.

'Leave it!' He had to tell his dog, and the three men moved on. But they had fallen well behind by this time. There was a hole in the middle of the line, and when a cock pheasant flew up in the gap where they should have been, and flew back over their heads, they were not near enough to tell the walking Gun that it was coming until it had cleared the tree tops. He snatched two shots at it, but the pheasant kept on flying.

'Damn! I wish someone would tell me what's happening up there!'

George Purse heard him and shouted for the beaters to stop. Stop! Stop! Stop! All the way along the line, sometimes one man to the next, sometimes just an indiscriminate shout, which leapfrogged several men and was taken up again by someone several stations down the line.

When the three centre men had caught up, and the line was nicely spaced again, George Purse started them off again.

'And let's have no racing this time! We're supposed to be driving pheasants, not chasing them!'

But there was a level bare stretch between the trees on the right, where all the beaters had to walk through were leaves. Instead of slowing down and waiting for the others, who were having to work undulating land matted with rhododendrons, brambles and beds of old nettles, they strolled on, tapping the trees as they passed them.

George Purse saw that the line was becoming dog-legged and stopped to give them a shout.

'Steady on the right!'

Perhaps they had not heard.

'*Steady on the right!*'

They must have heard that. He made a megaphone with his hands.

'HEY UP! ARE YOU DEAF OVER THERE? I SAID STEADY UP ON THAT FUCKING RIGHT!' His amplified exhortation carried through the wood and out into the field where the Guns were waiting. They had been joined by the Ladies for the last drive before lunch. The loaders set their faces to stop themselves from laughing. Some of the shooting party pretended they had heard nothing and concentrated their gaze on the wood, willing the pheasants out so that they could start shooting and ease their embarrassment with some noise and action. The Duke turned to Henry Clay, who was loading for him.

'I say, that was a bit much, wasn't it, Henry?'

'Yes, Sir.'

'Who was it?'

Volume and distance had distorted George Purse's voice, and made it unrecognizable to anyone who did not know him well.

'I think it was George, your Grace.'

'Well, have a word with him at the end of the drive will you, Henry? It's most embarrassing, especially when the Ladies are present.'

'Yes, Sir. I'll tell him.'

The first pheasant flew out of the wood. Lord Cannock shot it. The shot echoed across the lake as though he had fired his second barrel as well, and most of the birds were off the water before the dead pheasant had reached the ground. They flew in all directions, and the mass beating of their wings sounded like a coming wind. Geese, gulls, coots, waterhens and miscellaneous ducks; hundreds of them, some flying away, and some recovering and circling the water, wanting to land again. The only birds which did not panic at the lingering crack were two swans, which stayed where they were, sitting in a parched bed of bulrushes.

Two mallard, sweeping out wide and twisting their necks as they looked back at the lake, came within range of the Guns. Four triggers released four hails of lead shot at them. One bird crumpled in the air and plumbed down like a Christmas treat dropped from an aeroplane. The other one had a spray of feathers knocked off it. It staggered as though buffeted by an air current, lost height, then started to fly again. But its wings could not keep it up, so it stopped using them and glided towards the lake. The glide weakened into a fall and it crashed out of control into the water.

Then a teal copped it. Then the pheasants started to come over from the wood. The gunfire became frequent, and each shot sent an echo barking across the lake and kept the wildfowl off the water. All except the two swans, which looked as though they were making a deliberate show of their indifference by preening their backs and wings in the rushes.

A woodcock sprang up from a tuft of grass at George Purse's feet. It rose in a sitting position for the first few yards, its beak sticking out like chopsticks, its expression surprised but not angry, like a long-suffering cartoon character being blown through the roof of his house. Again.

'Woodcock over!'

It would have been if the Guns had allowed it to get that far, but it was shot coming out of the trees by the Right Hon. R. Spencer-Davies. The lead pellets which did not pierce the woodcock rattled the branches of the trees behind it and scared a woodpigeon out of a beech tree. The Duke of Leicester shot it, and it fell down trailing white feathers like a vapour trail. Two rabbits sat up in a gap in the hedge bottom. They split and dashed in opposite directions, running parallel with the hedge as though executing a predetermined tactic to confuse the guns. They confused nobody. Lord Cannock shot one of them. Sir Patrick Fitzpatrick Q.C. shot the other. A hare immediately sprinted through the hedge, and judging by the speed it was coming at, it looked as though it had started its run way back in the woods. The Earl of Harley stopped it with his first barrel, but he did not kill it. It got up and started to gallop around in small circles, screaming. His second shot knocked it down again, and it stayed down this time, half on, half off a burnt strip of straw.

A spaniel filled the hole in the hedge bottom where the hare had come through. It was panting and its tongue kept slithering in and out of its mouth. From the wood behind it, voices were shouting Tally Ho! and laughing, and another voice was shouting, 'Meg! Meg! Come here! Meg!' But the Guns had no time to bother about the dog now; there was shooting all the way along the line now and pheasants were falling all over the field. One cock came over high. It had carried on rising once it had cleared the tree tops and was nearly forty yards up when it passed over the guns. It was the tallest bird of the day; flying directly over the Duke. He leaned well back, his weight on his right leg, his gun pointing straight up. He heard the pellets from his first cartridge snick the bird's primaries as they flew by. His second shot visibly checked the bird as though it had suddenly met a strong headwind. It stopped flying, spread its wings and started to lose height in a long, slow, shallow dive. It cleared the rest of the field, cleared the narrow end of the lake, and swooped towards a copse growing on the slope at the other side of the water. It looked under perfect control, like a flying fox gliding between trees, but when it reached the trees, it just crashed into the top of an oak and bounced all the way down the branches.

The Duke marked it. It was an easy tree to mark because it still had plenty of brown leaves on it. But it was not under the tree when the Duke sent one of the beaters to look for it with his dog at the end of the drive. It had run away through the copse and worked its way into a patch of brambles when it was too weak to run any further. It just sat there, blinking and listening, tucked up and comfortable-looking, as though it was on a nest. It died like that early next morning, as the grey sky turned blue, and the moon became thin and transparent.

The next pheasant that the Duke shot was also a runner. It fell behind the line, got up, and set off down the field at such a rate that it was hard to understand how the pellets had brought it down in the first place. It started to trail one wing, but this did not slow it down, and it approached the lake so fast that it looked determined to run across the surface like some avian Messiah. Twenty yards from the bank, and without slowing down, it tipped forward on to its face and lay there, flapping its wings, as though it had been struck down for its pretensions.

That was the last bird of the morning. The Duke passed his hot gun to Henry Clay.

'A jolly good drive in the end, George!'

'Thank you, Sir!' George Purse shouted back, as he crawled through the hedge into the field. There were two yelps from the edge of the wood which made everybody look. Meg's owner had just caught up with her.

George Purse picked up a rabbit and carried it forward to Lord Cannock's stand.

'Is this one of yours, Sir?'

'That's right. Thank you very much.'

George Purse threw it down at the side of the pheasants that Lord Cannock had killed.

'Seeing as you're such a keen sportsman, Sir, I'm surprised you've never named any of your cars after game.'

'We've thought about it. But it's not a new idea of course. There were the old Humbers, the Hawk and the Super Snipe. And there's the Singer Gazelle and the Stag. But we have seriously thought about it.'

He reached down to take a hen pheasant from the mouth of his labrador. Its plumage was so pale that it looked as though the rain had washed some colour out of it at some time.

'The obvious ones, the pheasant, the partridge, the grouse are out of course. They don't conjure up the right image. They're a bit stuffy, a bit plump, a bit slow for today's market.'

'There's some good 'uns left though, Sir. What about the . . . Wild Goose?'

'Too long, too dreamy, needs more snap. You need alliteration when you use two words.'

'What do you mean?'

'Well, like Super Snipe. Or, Grey Goose. Both words beginning with the same letter.'

'Grey Goose. That sounds good.'

'It's not bad. But you would never sell anything using the word grey, especially a motor car. It sounds like a very dull performance.'

'Yes, I see what you mean, Sir.'

Lord Cannock pulled his shooting stick out of the ground, and closed the seat to make it into a handle again.

'We've considered them all; the curlew, the quail, the teal, the mallard. In fact we're designing a little two-seater at the moment. But that's a trade secret. I'd better say no more about that.'

He turned round to his loader, and asked him if there were any more birds to be picked. George Purse started to pick up some of the pheasants at his feet to carry back to the lorry.

'If I was naming a sports car, I'd call it the Hare.'

Lord Cannock looked round at him sharply and stared at him just to see how serious he was.

'Why?'

'Because it's fast.'

Then, with his wellington, he nudged the rabbit that he had thrown down with the pheasants.

'No, I wouldn't, I'd call it the Rabbit!'

'The Rabbit!'

Lord Cannock frowned and looked disappointed at the change.

'The rabbit's not fast.'

'It is in some ways. In fact, better still, why not call it the Buck? That's a right name for a sports car.'

Lord Cannock just looked at him. Then he started to nod, slowly. 'Yes.' Vigorously. 'Yes,' and he laughed.

'Yes. I like it. You could be on to a winner there, George.'

The hare which had been shot by the Earl of Harley was nearly as big as the spaniel that retrieved it. She had to drop it twice to get a better grip and balance, and when she did pick it up, her neck was tense with the weight, and she carried it back across the field with a slow stylized action, like a horse doing dressage.

Henry Clay's spaniel fetched the fake Messiah which had just failed to reach the water. It was still alive, and kept trying to move its wings in the dog's mouth. When Henry Clay took it and held it by the neck, it clapped its wings together so hard, that they sounded like flags snapping in a high wind. He killed it by holding its head and whirling it round like a football rattle. George Purse watched him, and shook his head.

'Look at that. That's the worst thing you can do to game. It'll have a neck like a bloody giraffe when he's finished.'

The Right Hon. R. Spencer-Davies walked down to the lake with his labrador, Pip, to retrieve the mallard he had shot. It was drifting on its side ten yards from the bank, like a toy yacht with its sails wet. It was trying to dive, and it kept slapping the water with one wing. But it was too weak now, its other wing was broken, and all it could manage when it saw the man and the dog, was to duck its head under the water.

As the dog was swimming back with the duck in its mouth, cloud covered the sun. The water went black, and suddenly looked colder. The Right Hon. R. Spencer-Davies looked up. The sky was in two halves, one blue, the other an even shade of grey. It looked as though someone was cutting out the sun and the sky with a Big Top.

By the time all the game had been picked, and everyone was moving towards the lorry and the Land Rovers which were parked on the cart track at the side of the field, the tent was up, and darker bulkier clouds were arriving to fill the space underneath it. These clouds seemed to be travelling faster than the high cloud because they were lower in the sky.

George Purse threw four pheasants and a rabbit into the back of the lorry, then wiped his hands on his trousers and walked forward to the Land Rovers to speak to the Duke.

'Ah, George, well done. It's been a good morning in the end.'

'Thank you, Sir.'

'What's the half-time score?'

'I couldn't tell you, Sir. I haven't had time to count them yet.'

'We've done pretty well, I would say.'

'Yes, Sir. Are we having an hour for lunch?'

'What time is it?'

'I don't know, Sir. I haven't got a watch.'

So the Duke looked at his own.

'An hour. Yes. Mm. No. I think we'll make it forty-five minutes so that we can all be ready for a two o'clock start.'

'Right, Sir.'

'If we don't waste any more time this afternoon, I think we could make up the drive we lost this morning.'

'We'll try, Sir, but I wouldn't bank on it. It'll be tough going this afternoon for the beaters.'

'Well, do your best George.'

'I always do, Sir.'

'Yes, yes, of course you do.'

The shooting party drove off in the Land Rovers to the Big House for a hot lunch. The loaders and beaters stood around the lorry debating the best place to eat their sandwiches.

'We might as well stop here and have ours. There's no time to go anywhere else.'

George Purse climbed into the back of the lorry to fetch out his sandwiches and flask.

'You can please yourselves what you do, but I'm going up to the farm. I've seen old Alec. He says we can use his barn if it's raining.'

'It isn't raining.'

'No, but it will be before long.'

This made them all look at the sky; nobody dissented and what he had said now seemed like a good idea.

'Is he charging us to go in, George?'

'No, but I'd my shotgun at his head when I asked him.'

The farm was at the other side of the lake, behind the copse where the wounded pheasant was sitting. It was only a five minutes' walk up the lane. A bumpy minute's ride in the lorry. Some walked, some rode. There were no arguments. It was not far enough to bother about.

George Purse walked it with Sam Dobie and a gang of beaters. Now that the Duke had stopped shooting grouse, it was the turn of Sam Dobie and the other high-ground keepers to come down off the moors, to beat and load for the Duke and his guests while they shot pheasants.

'Colonel Garmonsway was on form this morning, George.'

'What with, the gun or the flask?'

'Both.'

'He'll be all right this afternoon then, when he's had a few more over lunch.'

Without stopping, he looked back over his shoulder to talk to the beaters.

'I'm warning you, if you're anywhere near him try to keep behind a tree, 'cos he's likely to let fly anywhere when he's been on the bottle.'

He fastened the top button of his jacket and turned the collar up.

'Christ, that wind's cold now the sun's gone.'

He rubbed his lips together and wet them with his tongue.

'I wouldn't mind a couple of tilts from that little silver flask of his, come to think of it.'

Sam Dobie nudged him and started to grin at a thought.

'Perhaps old Alec'll have a bottle waiting for us when we get up to the farm.'

They all laughed. They were just passing the end of the lake, but after all the shooting, their laughter did not distress any of the birds which had settled back on the water. The geese and the gulls had gone. But there were some ducks left, and some coots and waterhens. When the men passed, they just swam away, leaving widening V's behind them on the water.

'A bottle of water perhaps! And even then he'd want the bottle back afterwards. Me and Charlie settled him once though, didn't we, Charlie?'

He looked round for Charlie's confirmation. But Charlie was not with them. He had gone ahead in the lorry.

'We'd been rabbiting over in the Gypsy Wood and we'd left my van in Alec's yard. Anyroad, just as we were coming back they were bagging taties. So Charlie goes up to them, opens one of the sacks and says, "Are a couple of these sacks for us, Alec? Go and fetch your van round, George, we've just come right." "They're bloody well not," he says, wheezing and puffing on his cig and looking at everybody but who he's talking to, like he always does.'

And George Purse did a shrugging, puffing impersonation of him that was accurate enough to make everyone laugh. He looked a bit like a boxer limbering up in training.

'"Come on," Charlie says. "Let's have a couple of bags. We'll see you right, Alec, you know that." "There's some over there you can have," he says. And he pointed to some bags stood up against a wall. Ar, there were. They must have been some that he'd sorted out to feed his pigs on. They were terrible, all gashed and manky. So I kicked one of the bags and says, "We're not having these buggers Alec." "You can please your sens," he says. "But you can't have none of these, they're all weighed and counted." And off he goes for his dinner, cig ash dropping all down the front of his jacket.

'So I says to Charlie, "Right, we'll settle his hash." There was that little corgi in the yard that his wife keeps, so we started to gut all the rabbits we'd killed and throw it all the innards. It didn't half gobble them down I can tell you. There must have been a dozen.

'Anyroad, a couple of days later, I saw old Alec in the Arms and as soon as he sees me he comes across. I knew there was summat up. "Hey up," he says. "Did you two buggers give my missus's dog owt when I saw you the other day?" "How do you mean, give it owt?" I says. "What do we want to give it owt for?" "Well it's funny," he says. "It wouldn't eat its supper and that was unusual for a start. And then, just as we were sitting down to watch the tele, it was sick under the table, all over the living room carpet. It was a grand mess I can tell you. God knows what he'd been eating."

'Well, I'd a job to keep my face straight, I can tell you. "It probably ate some of them bad taties that you tried to give me and Charlie," I said. He just looked at me and walked away. He knew we'd done summat, but he never knew what it was.'

Charlie Taylor and the other riders had started their sandwiches when George Purse's gang arrived at the farm. They were sitting on bales of straw inside a barn, which stood on its own, outside the quadrangle of farm buildings. The bales were stacked nearly to the ceiling, and at the front of the barn they went up in tall steps like a steeply raked auditorium. Some of the men had climbed the steps, and they were all sitting on different levels facing outwards as though waiting for a show to start.

Crates of beer had been lifted from the lorry and placed on the bottom row of bales. There were still plenty of unopened bottles left in the crates. George Purse picked up two bottles simultaneously like a pair of binoculars, and offered one of them to Sam Dobie. He shook his head and went to sit down next to Henry Clay.

'No thanks, George. It's too cold for beer sat here. I'd sooner have summat a bit warmer.'

George Purse replaced one bottle. He let it drop the last two inches and when it hit the bottom of the crate, it made the other bottles rattle against the sides of their narrow compartments.

'I think I'll treat myself today, and go and sit in the one and nines.'

He climbed up the bales and sat down near the top of the stack next to Doug Westerman, who made his labrador get up from between them and sit at his other side, just in case it started to sniff at George Purse's sandwiches when he opened his box.

'Now then, stranger, how's it going? I haven't had chance to talk to you yet, I've been that busy.'

'Steady you know, George. I keep going. That's as much as you can do isn't it?'

George Purse stretched the elastic band to take it off his lunch box.

'Let's have a look what she's packed up for me today. If it's caviar sandwiches again I'll kill her when I get home.'

'How's Mary going on, George? I haven't seen her for, O . . . ages now.'

'She's all right. She's always grumbling about summat though. She's never right for two minutes at a time these days.'

'She's perhaps ready for a change, George.'

'We're all ready for a change, Doug.'

'You want to try and get yourself transferred down Wiltshire, like I did. Bob Blower retires at Christmas. Why don't you apply for his job?'

'Old Bob retiring? Never. He's been there longer than the Hall, hasn't he?'

'He's been keepering down there for forty years. He's sixty-eight you know, George, and he still doesn't want to retire. He's kept putting it off. Anyway, the Duke threatened to have him put down if he didn't pack up at the end of the year. Mind you, he thinks the world of old Bob does the Duke.'

'I should think he does an'all, all that work he's had out of him for the money he's been paid.'

George Purse took an onion out of his sandwich box, opened his penknife and cut off the ends against the tough skin of his thumb.

'It's a right busman's holiday this you've come on isn't it, Doug? What's up, haven't you any work to do down there?' Charlie Taylor, sitting two rows further down the stack, heard the question and turned round.

'They don't know they're born down there. Life's that bloody slow they're all walking about backwards.'

Doug Westerman kicked some loose straw on to him and Charlie Taylor stood up, shaking a sandwich.

'Hey up! Gi'o'er then, all over my bloody snap! I reckon this fella's nowt but a trouble causer, George. In fact I wouldn't be surprised if it was him that put the beaters up to it this morning. He's nowt but an agitator, he was the same when he worked at the pit.'

'I'd like to see it. They don't know what strike means down Wiltshire. They think it's summat that only happens to matches.'

Charlie Taylor sat down again, but he stayed half round this time so that he could stay in the conversation.

'Are you stopping at your dad's, Doug?'

'Yes. He hasn't been too good with his chest again, so I thought I'd pop up and see him. I might not get chance again for a bit, 'cos we'll be busy now 'til after Christmas.'

'When's your first shoot?'

'Next week. I knew you were shooting today so I thought it'd be a good chance to kill two birds with one stone, see the old fella, and see how you lads were going on.'

'I hope you got the Duke's permission before you took a day off and came gallivanting up here.'

'I got Wilf's. It's hardly a day off though is it, a day's beating? And anyway it is Saturday you know, Charlie.'

'Saturday! What's that got to do with it? I told you he was dangerous didn't I, George? He'll be wanting a forty-hour week next, like everybody else.'

George Purse swigged half a cup of tea to wash down the food in his mouth, then he opened his next sandwich to see if it contained cheese like the first. It did. In a state of mild panic he looked at the other two to see what was in them. Boiled ham.

'Thank God.'

'What?'

'You wouldn't want many cheese sandwiches packing up if you were walking across the Sahara would you?'

He cut a slice of onion, and when all the rings fell out of each other into his sandwich box, it looked like a baby's educational toy.

'Have you got plenty of pheasants down there this year, Doug?'

'Well, I can't grumble. I lost a few chicks in that terrible week in June, but apart from that it's been a good year for breeding.'

'You're lucky down there though, aren't you? You don't get poached to the same extent as we do up here.'

'No, but we get a lot more trouble with foxes, I can tell you.'

"Course. You've got the Hunt to cope with, haven't you?'

'And don't we know it. It's a right battle, I can tell you. We're at loggerheads all the time with the huntsmen. There's them trying to keep foxes alive for hunting, and there's us trying to keep them down for shooting. You can't win, George.'

He was so absorbed in the telling of the conflict that he did not notice the ramshackle state of the sandwich in his hand, and how precariously the slice of bacon was balanced on the bread. When he paused for a bite and carried the sandwich to his mouth, the sudden movement dislodged the bacon and it fell on to his knee. Before he could pick it up, his dog reared up, ate it, and lay back on its side again. Doug Westerman relieved some of his frustration by giving the dog a thump. Then, as there was nothing left between the bread he fed that to the dog as well.

278

'Here, you greedy bugger. You might as well have it all.'

'What does the Duke say, Doug?'

'He don't say owt. How can he? He hunts and he shoots. He just tries to keep the cart on the wheels that's all. But it's bloody ridiculous. I'd seventy-six poults killed in one of my release pens one night by a fox. Luckily they were well developed and a lot of them flew away over the wire. But imagine if it had killed them all, and it had been a bad year for wild birds. What would he have said if he'd come to that wood next week and about three birds had have shown? I'd have looked a right cunt wouldn't I?'

He stroked his dog to show that all was forgiven.

'So what do you do?'

'We do the same as you. We snare them, we shoot them, and we poison them. We're not supposed to, yet the estate buys the snares, the cartridges and the poison. The Duke knows what's going on, but as long as it's done on the quiet, and nothing's brought to his notice, he turns a blind eye. Every fox that we kill we've to bury to make sure that nobody finds it.'

He picked up a bottle of beer from the bale beside him and looked round.

'Who's got that bottle opener?'

Without a word being spoken, a bottle opener was relayed up the stack to him, then, when he had opened the bottle, it was relayed back down. He slotted the cap between two bales and had a drink of beer.

'I thought I was going to be taking my suitcase down off the top of the wardrobe though, a few weeks back.'

'Why, what happened?'

'Well, I'd set this snare in a little copse and a vixen got in it. I'd fastened the snare to a log so that it could drag it about a bit and not break the wire by pulling against owt rigid. It seemed heavy enough. It made me sweat just dragging it a few yards into position and hiding it amongst some bracken. Anyway, next morning when I'm out on my rounds and I come to that wood it had gone. The log, the snare, the lot. It was easy to see where it had gone to, it looked as though somebody had dragged a garden roller through the wood the way everything was flattened. It had dragged it right out of the wood, God knows how it didn't choke first with all that weight round its neck, and finally collapsed on some stubble amongst some bales of straw. Unlucky for me, one of the farm lads who'd come to pick the bales up, found it first, drives off to fetch his boss, and then there's hell on.

'The fox was in a right mess as you can imagine. It was still alive when he found it. The wire had cut right into its neck and there was blood everywhere. When Major Miles arrived he went crackers. He took the fox straight down to the Hunt kennels to show the Hunt servants. He phoned Wilf Bunch. He said he was going to phone the R.S.P.C.A. And then he phoned the Duke. It was a right carry-on I can tell you.'

George Purse watched him have a long drink from the bottle. However much he tilted it the surface of the beer always stayed horizontal. When he took the bottle away from his mouth, George Purse said, 'Bit of bad luck that, dragging it out of the wood into the field.'

'Not half! And then Major Miles finding it. It couldn't have been worse. He's joint Master of Fox Hounds with the Duke!'

He finished off his beer and put the bottle down. Now that it was empty and lighter, it would not stand up on the straw as easily. It fell over and started to roll towards the edge of the bale. Doug Westerman stopped it.

'You wouldn't have believed it though, George, if you'd have seen that log. You wouldn't have thought a dray horse could have shifted it.'

'I know. It's amazing the strength an animal has when it's in pain or it's frightened.'

He poured the rest of his tea, then made a mould with his hands around the flask top.

'You didn't get your cards then, Doug?'

'No, it seems to be blowing over. The Duke had a word with Wilf, then Wilf had a word with me, telling me to be more careful next time. But Wilf knew that it wasn't my fault, it could have happened to any of us. I was just unlucky that's all. It's crazy. You don't get into trouble for killing foxes, you only get into trouble when you get found out.'

Without turning round, one of the beaters shouted, 'You were right, George!' As if the gamekeeper was somewhere in front of him, outside the barn.

'What about?'

'The weather. It's raining.'

'Good. I hope it chucks it down. We might get home a bit earlier then.'

He slid further down the bales to remove his head from the draught blowing across the top of the stack.

'It's an idle wind this, an'all. It goes through you, instead of going round.'

He touched Charlie Taylor on the shoulder with his boot.

'Ask Henry to pass his bottle opener up, Charlie.'

When the message reached the bottom of the stack Henry felt for the bottle opener. Then, with his hand still in his jacket pocket he turned round.

'Who's it for?'

'George.'

'George hasn't to drink any beer. Duke's orders.'

George Purse crushed his sandwich papers around the remains of the onion and threw the weighted ball down the stack. Henry Clay had to duck.

'What orders?'

'The Duke says your language is bad enough when you're sober. He says he daren't think what obscenities might come flying out of the trees if you get a few bottles inside you.'

'Bugger my language. Let's have that opener.'

The opener travelled up the stack. George Purse angled it against the cap to lever it off, stopped, then looked at the bottle as though he was seeing it for the first time.

'Do you know, I don't want this bottle. I'm cold enough as it is without cold beer going down my gullet.'

He offered the beer to the men sitting around him. But nobody wanted it, so he passed the bottle opener back to Charlie Taylor.

'Somebody run up to the Big House and see if they've a drop of port or brandy left over from lunch, that they don't want.'

And he sat there, high up on the straw bales, twisting the cold bottle around in his fingers; listening to the wind humming through the iron rafters, and watching the low fast cloud travel over the farm buildings, and the driving rain putting a shine on their slate roofs.

'I don't know. It makes you wonder what it's all about sometimes doesn't it?' He stood up and knocked straws off the seat of his trousers and the backs of his legs.

'Come on lads, we'd better make a move.'

Charlie Taylor looked up at him.

'Nay! Bloody Hell, George! We've only just sat down. I'm only on my cheese and biscuits. I've my brandy to sup, and my cigar to smoke yet.'

'You're not at the pit now you know, Charlie. You don't get travelling time on this job. Anyway, there's no pleasure in sitting here freezing in this draughty hole is there?'

'No, and there's no pleasure in getting wet through out there either.'

The men started to pick up their sandwich papers and pack them into their boxes. Charlie Taylor threw an apple core at some hens which were scavenging for crumbs amongst the loose straw at the bottom of the bales. They kept scratching the straw aside and revealing the ground, which was still dry where the straw had been on it. One of the hens picked up the core and ran away, the others followed in earnest pursuit.

'I could just get ligged down for an hour, I don't know about owt else.'

George Purse stepped past him.

'We'd better get down to that wood or the Guns are going to be there before us.'

'No chance. They'll have taken one look at the weather and decided that another glass of port's a better idea.'

'You're probably right, Charlie. But you never know. We'll have to be there on time even if they don't show up 'til half past three.'

George Purse was first down off the stack of bales. When he reached the bottom he turned round to the others who were ranged above him like students in a lecture theatre.

'Listen lads, it's going to be a lot harder this afternoon. The cover's a lot thicker, and in some places you're not even going to be able to see the next man to you. So just listen to instructions, or we're going to be walking about anywhere. All right?'

Nobody said anything, so he assumed that they were.

'Right, come on. Let's go and make a good job of it.'

He dropped his unopened bottle of beer back into a crate and turned round again.

'And I hope you've brought your waterproofs, 'cos everything's going to be sopping this afternoon.'

Henry Clay came up to him and dropped two empty bottles into another crate.

'Watch your language this afternoon, George. The Duke didn't like it when you shouted out down at Duck Wood.'

'I'm surprised he heard me. I thought we were too far back in the wood.'

'Heard you! I bet they heard you in the village.'

'What did he say?'

'He said, was that George? Just tell him to curb his language will you, Henry? It's most embarrassing for the guests, especially when there's ladies present.'

'Fuck the ladies, Henry. Let him get in that wood and see if he can do any better.'

He walked away to the lorry to replace his sandwich box and flask, and take out his waterproof coat and leggings.

The beaters and the loaders climbed down off the bales and came out of the barn looking up at the sky and holding out their hands to test the rain. Just out of the barn it did not seem to be raining fast, but as soon as they walked out into the open it was siling it down. And there were no breaks in the cloud, or lighter sky in the distance, so that they could tell each other that it was only a shower.

The quickest way to George Purse's home wood was straight through the farmyard and back into the lane which ran past the farm. The front of the farmhouse, which faced into the yard, had a little flagged yard of its own, surrounded by a low wall, to keep the animals and muck away from the front door. At the side of the wall there was a kennel with a sheepdog fastened to it on a long chain. As soon as the men and their dogs started to cross the yard, the sheepdog ran to the end of its tether and back, jumped on the wall, jumped down, then ran out and back again. Round and round its narrow track, running with the same tense, lowslung action that it used when it chivvied the cattle in from the fields. The sight of the crowd had started it working again. Its reaction was instinctive.

A cow poked its head over a barn door and went moo at the men. So much vapour came out of its mouth and nostrils that it looked as though it had eaten fire. A ginger cat watched them from a window sill. It crouched so still that none of the dogs saw it. Three geese shuffled out of their way, and from underneath a cart they stretched their necks and shook their wings to show the men that they were afraid of nobody. And on the hayloft roof a flock of fantail pigeons ignored them all. They seemed to be too busy playing cards with their own cocked tails.

The men walked through the gateway at the back of the yard and Charlie Taylor closed the gate behind them. Behind the hayloft there was a long wooden hut with plastic fertilizer sacks nailed over the window frames. At one side of the hut stood a rusty trailer up to the axles in a sludge of hen droppings, and at the other side, the cold ashes of a bonfire, surrounded by a fringe of partly burnt feed sacks, egg trays, collapsed charred skeletons, and odd wings and heads of hens. The door of the hut was partly open, and there was a low throaty clamour from inside. George Purse went across to have a look in.

The hut was lit by a single bare bulb which hung by a long flex above the central aisle. On both sides of the aisle four tiers of wire cages covered the walls. There were three hens in each cage, and there were heads poking out of each one. As soon as one head withdrew another took its place. There was not enough room for them all to look out together, and sometimes one hen clawed its way on to the backs of the others and they formed a brief raucous pyramid. Their necks were bare from rubbing against the wire and some of the birds were nearly bald. They had no room to flap their wings. They spent all their lives in a crowd.

Charlie Taylor came and looked over George Purse's shoulder.

'They ought to debeak them. At least it'd stop that feather-picking.'

'Why don't you get a petition up, Charlie, and write to the R.S.P.B.?'

Charlie Taylor was right; the shooting party was late back from lunch. The beaters had to wait in line twenty minutes at the top end of the wood before they heard Henry Clay's whistle telling them that the Guns were at their stands, and they could start. They were glad to get moving again; it was cold standing there in the wind and the rain.

It was raining twice amongst the trees. There was the ordinary rain which missed the trees, and an irregular heavier fall which accumulated in the trees and leaked off the elbows of the branches. George Purse was protected from the rain by his waterproof jacket and leggings. Some of the beaters had brought leggings as well, but many of them had trusted the sunny morning and had only brought jackets and anoraks, to protect themselves from the wind. They were all wearing wellingtons, but by the time they had walked a hundred yards into the wood the ground cover was so dense that their trousers were saturated, and sticking to their thighs.

George Purse was right; the beaters really had to work to get through this wood. It was a jungle in parts, the beaters could not see each other, and they had to keep calling to keep contact with the next man in line. They had to bash through dead rosebay stems which were as tall as they were, struggle through beds of nettles and tangles of rusty bracken which dragged at their waists and legs, climb over fallen trees and branches festooned with brambles. The briars caught on their clothes, screeched against their wellingtons and scratched the backs of their hands. Twigs poked their faces and knocked off their hats, and one beater had his glasses removed and a lens smashed when a twig hooked under the side piece, and they fell against a log. They were faced by clusters of rhododendrons which had grown together, and formed such massive barriers that it was quicker to tunnel through them than to try and find a way round. The beaters ducked into them and moved in a crouching position through the dim dripping caves.

Everything they touched dripped, and the water went down their necks and wellingtons and up their sleeves. They had been cold when they started the drive, but the heavy work had soon warmed them up and they were starting to sweat and feel sticky. The men were wet, the dogs were wet and the pheasants were wet and reluctant to fly. They ran forward, or sat still in cover until they were nearly trodden on, and when they did fly, they had to work their bedraggled wings hard to get themselves over the trees.

Mary Purse and the boys could hear the beaters from the house. As the line passed by, it sounded like a riot with all the thrashing and knocking and shouting. Ian ran to the door to have a look. He just saw the man on the right flank amongst the trees before he disappeared behind the outhouses. His mother and John just looked up at the noise when he opened the door, then resumed what they were doing. As the noise faded into the bottom half of the wood, a gun fired, and the single shot was louder but further away than the shouting of the men. More shots were fired, until the cartridges were exploding with the frequent but unpredictable timing of jumping crackers. Then there was so much shooting, that the noise of it drowned all trace of the men.

In spite of their reluctance, the pheasants were having to fly now. Either that, or walk out of the wood into the field. They were trapped in the last fifty yards of the wood, and there were so many going over at once that George Purse stopped the line to give the loaders chance to reload. These were the birds that George Purse had reared under broodies. Their foster mothers were sitting in the hen house listening to the noise.

At the end of the drive, he did not wait to count how many pheasants had been shot. His job was to show the birds to the Guns, and he knew from the number of shots that he had heard that he had done his work well. He shouted to the beaters not to hang about and move straight on to Boundary Wood. One of the beaters stood and watched the dogs running about the field, and touched George Purse's sleeve as he walked past.

'Hang on, George. He might call it a day after they've picked these birds.'

'No chance, not after one drive. They're not wet enough yet, and the fortifications they had at lunch haven't had time to wear off either. Anyway, look at all the birds they're picking. They'll whet their appetite for another drive at least.'

'Go and ask him. You never know. I'm wet through.'

'I'm not asking him. I wouldn't ask him if I was drowning.'

He walked away and the other man followed.

'What's Boundary Wood like, George? Is it as bad as this?'

George Purse turned round and grinned at him.

'Bad. It makes this wood look like a billiards table.'

The quickest way to Boundary Wood was straight across the fields. The loaders threw the freshly killed pheasants into the back of the lorry, which was parked at the side of the field with the Land Rovers, and started to walk with the shooting party. When they came to a fence the loaders held their guns for them while they climbed over, then handed them back when they were at the other side. The shooting party was walking up game on their way to the next drive. There was no danger of shooting the beaters because they were too far ahead. George Purse had kept them close to the hedgerows and fences, because he knew that the Duke usually shot this strip of land between the two woods.

The Duke had organized his party and the loaders into a line, ten yards apart, so that they were beating for themselves as they walked. A covey of partridges sprang up from the grass and hurtled away, wings whirring across the field. They flew low, and when Sir Patrick Fitzpatrick Q.C. killed a brace with a right and a left, they only had to fall a few feet to the ground. They hit the ground hard at an acute angle and bounced forward. The impact

289

knocked some feathers off them, which mingled with the feathers which were still drifting down. The other partridge hurried on, fixed their wings and glided out of sight over a hedgerow. Two dogs retrieved the birds, and the line was nearly up to them by the time they had picked them up and were on their way back.

They waded through a field of kale which came up to their knees, and slapped against their wellingtons. A rabbit ran away from them, and although they only saw it once, they were able to follow its progress across the field by the shaking of the leaves as it rushed through the kale. The Duke of Leicester, walking on the right flank, shot it when it broke cover and set off across a meadow.

A cock pheasant struggled up from the same field with water spraying off its wings. Its bronze plumage had been stained a deeper shade by the rain, and its glossy head was almost black. It looked as though it had just been surprised in the bath. The Duke gave it a sporting chance. He let it clear the dark background of Boundary Wood, then, when it was clearly silhouetted against the lighter sky, its barred tail shaking like a rope ladder, he shot it. It was dead in the air, and fell close to the place where it had been crouching and listening a few seconds earlier. Henry Clay told his dog to fetch it, and the spaniel plunged through the kale like a dog in the sea.

This was the last bird before they reached the ploughed field where the stands were spaced out in front of Boundary Wood. The 9th Duke had won this wood and five hundred acres around it in a game of cards in the nineteenth century.

By the time the Guns and the loaders reached the stands, their wellingtons were heavy with mud, and they were all standing several inches taller on compressed platforms of soil.

The beaters' wellingtons had been in the same state when they had climbed over the fence into the other side of the wood; but as soon as the drive started, the long wet grass wiped them clean and their footwear was soon shiny black. Boundary Wood was a soggy place even in a drought, and an afternoon's rain turned it into a swamp. The beaters paddled through puddles and shallow ponds with clumps of willows growing round their edges. Branches had fallen across the water to make extra obstacles, and all the land above the water was choked with saplings and bushes, nettles, brambles and reeds. With twigs and branches brushing them all the time, it was like walking through a car wash. The brisk morning's walk through crisp leaves had deteriorated into a slog through a dripping bog.

In spite of the tough going and the rain, the beaters were working well, and George Purse had not had to shout all afternoon. They kept spaced out, passing his instructions quickly along the line, and in places where they could not see the next man, they called out to each other, so that they could make the necessary adjustments in distance or pace. In places where the undergrowth was impenetrable, and they had to come together, they sent the dogs in and lashed at the tangled foliage to frighten out any pheasants that even the dogs might miss.

It was dusk already in the wood. It was lighter out in the field where the Guns were shooting the pheasants, but there was nothing in the sky to suggest that the light would improve, or the rain would ease in time for the next drive. The Duke would decide that after the birds from this wood had been shot. But not many were showing. Cover was so dense, and the pheasants were so wet and reluctant to fly, that most of them found hiding places and sat it out until the line passed them by.

George Purse did not worry because they were only sending odd birds over the Guns. They had enjoyed good shooting up to now. He knew why the pheasants were not rising and he knew that the Duke would know. Even the Duke did not expect his keepers to control the weather as well. Twelve birds had been killed when the Guns saw the beaters coming through the trees towards the fence. It looked to be all over, then a woodcock flicked out of a tuft of common rush at George Purse's feet.

'Woodcock over!'

The woodcock jinked between the trees until it reached the edge of the wood, then started to climb as though it meant to clear the line of guns. The Duke raised his gun but the woodcock sheered away and it was no longer his bird.

'Yours, Colonel!'

But even as he shouted, the woodcock dipped and flew low across the face of the wood. Excited by this late bonus, after standing cold and wet on sticky soil for four shots (all missed) Colonel Garmonsway pointed his gun at the bird and kept on swinging even when it was flying just above the fence. He missed with both barrels, and two loads of lead pellets zipped into the woods, snapping off twigs and smacking against trunks and branches. The beaters ducked and turned their backs and shouted angrily under their arms. The other Guns turned round wincing and placing their hands across their eyes when they saw what the Colonel had done. Colonel Garmonsway passed his gun back to Sam Dobie and stepped forward.

'I say! I'm dreadfully sorry about that! Is everyone all right?'

No one answered him. No one moved. The beaters just stood in a line twenty yards inside the wood, facing the line of Guns at the other side of the fence.

George Purse was the first to move.

'All right lads, that's it. There's nowt else in here now.'

He climbed over the fence and walked across the field to the Duke.

'Nearly a nasty accident there, Sir.'

'Yes. Yes. That was most unfortunate. Tends to get carried away, the Colonel, you know.'

'Somebody nearly got carried away on a stretcher, I know that much.'

'Yes. I think the light's not too good now, George.'

They both looked up, with their backs against the rain so that it would not get into their eyes.

'The rain doesn't appear to be easing at all either, George.'

'No Sir, it's set in for the day now. The wind'll have to change before this lot stops.'

The beaters and the loaders and the Guns were all watching them, waiting for the Duke's decision.

'Do you want us to move down to the Willowgarth now, Sir?'

Still looking up, the Duke scratched his chin, and George Purse could hear his nails on the stubble.

'Will there be pheasant in there, George?'

'There will if the crocodiles don't get to them first, Sir.'

'I think you're trying to tell me something, George.'

'Not at all, Sir.'

'Right. Now give me your real opinion.'

'My real opinion. Well, as you've already said, it doesn't look as though it's going to stop raining, and the light's definitely getting worse. I reckon by the time we've walked down there and all got in position it'll be nearly dark. There doesn't seem a lot of point to it, especially as the pheasants are that wet that a good part of them won't show anyway.'

The Duke fingered his nostrils, then stroked the lobes of both ears. George Purse watched him. He looked as though he was considering having them pierced.

'You're right, George. We've had plenty of shooting in spite of the weather. Let's not be greedy. We'll call it a day.'

'Right, Sir. Anyway, what you don't shoot today'll be there for the next time.'

'Exactly, George. That is unless poachers don't get to them first.'

'Yes, Sir.'

George Purse turned away and walked back to the beaters, who were waiting by the fence at the edge of the wood.

'Is that it then, George?'

'It isn't it! We've the Willowgarth to do, and then if we hurry up we might just manage that little spinney near the Newt Pond before it gets dark.'

'Jesus Christ, George! What's he want, blood?'

Then they saw that he was grinning, and they knew it was all over.

'You lying bugger.'

'What's up with you? You've done nowt yet. If it was up to me I'd have you working by torchlight.'

The beaters climbed the fence and followed the Guns and the loaders back across the fields to the lorry and the Land Rovers, which had been left outside George Purse's home wood.

The birds and the rabbit from the last drive were placed in a line on the ground, and then George Purse and the other keepers took the rest of the bag from the lorry and matched them up into three lines on the grass. The total dead was 158, consisting of 137 pheasants, 2 partridges, 2 mallard, 1 teal, 3 woodcock, 1 snipe, 5 woodpigeon, 2 hares and 5 rabbits.

Charlie Taylor's spaniel walked across to the display, picked up a hare and carried it back to his owner. Charlie Taylor took it from the dog's mouth and fitted it back into its place in the top line.

'Leave it,' he said, 'dead, dead.'

George Purse walked across to a group of beaters who were standing at the back of the lorry waiting to climb in. He spoke to them for a few seconds, then went across to the Duke, who was using the bottom bar of the fence as a boot scraper.

'Have you seen the bag, Sir?'

'No, what is it, George?'

'One hundred and fifty-eight, Sir. One hundred and thirty-seven pheasant, and twenty-one assorted.'

'One hundred and thirty-seven. That's pretty good, considering.'

'Yes, Sir. I reckon we'd have topped two hundred today if everything had gone to plan.'

They walked past the Land Rovers and round the back of the lorry to where the keepers had set out the game. Two beaters were lying with the furred and feathered dead, their arms crossed over their chests, their caps pulled over their eyes. It took the Duke a few seconds to realize what they were doing there, and then he twigged it and started to laugh.

'Ho! Ho! Ho!' he bellowed, shaking all over.

The other Guns hurried round the back of the lorry to see what he was laughing at. Then they started to laugh. Even

Colonel Garmonsway, against whom the joke was directed, had to laugh, although he almost became a genuine corpse when he had a drink from his silver flask and nearly choked because he was laughing at the same time. It was only when his face started to turn purple and his eyes stand out that the others realized it was serious, and nearly broke his back pounding breath back into his body.

When they saw that he was going to survive, it turned into a joke, especially amongst the beaters, who laughed at the Colonel's discomfort much more than they had at the fake corpses stretched out on the grass. The two beaters sat up and pushed their caps back from their faces. The shooting party drifted across to the Land Rovers, and some of the beaters started to pick up the pheasants ready to throw into the back of the lorry. George Purse stopped them and walked after the Duke.

'Excuse me, Sir. Do you want any birds picking out for the Guns?'

'Just a brace each, George. Pop them into the Land Rover, please.'

'Right, Sir.'

He turned away to go and do the job himself.

'George.'

'Yes, Sir.'

'I thought it went very well today, in spite of that nonsense this morning, and the atrocious weather this afternoon. Thank you very much.'

And he pushed a five-pound note into the breast pocket of George Purse's coat.

The gamekeeper touched his hat.

'Thank you very much, Sir. I'm glad you enjoyed it.'

He selected a cock and hen pheasant for each Gun, feeling at their breasts to make sure that they had plenty of meat on them, and choosing fully feathered birds that had not been mutilated by shot. The rest of the bag was thrown into the back of the lorry, and the space around the pile was filled by beaters and loaders and dogs. Those unable to get in started to walk it. The lorry would come back for them after it had dropped off the first load at the Big House.

George Purse lifted the tailboard of the lorry and checked that none of the dogs' paws or tails were trapped in the crack before he slammed it shut and slotted home the chained pins. He was not riding anywhere. He only had to walk up through the wood and he would be home. As he looked over the tail-board into the damp and steaming crowd sitting around the pile of game, one of the dogs reared up to lick his face. He pushed its face away and stepped back.

'Gi'o'er you mucky sod. I'm wet enough as it is!'

The Land Rovers started up and drove slowly out of the field. George Purse stayed back from the lorry until it started moving, then he followed it for a few yards while it was still going slow.

'I'll see you then, lads. I know it hasn't been very nice for you, but I think you've done bloody well.'

They waved and shouted to him as the lorry accelerated and left him behind. He stopped and watched it turn into the lane, and he could hear the men shouting and cursing the driver as the lorry bumped along the unmade track. He watched the progress of the convoy through the hawthorn hedge, and when the lorry followed the Land Rovers round a bend in the lane, and he could only hear their receding engines, he turned away, and walked back across the field to the gateway that led into the wood.

It was still raining. The sky was too dark to see it now, but he could hear it on his clothes, and he could feel it on his face and hands. But the weather did not matter now, he was nearly home, and he started to whistle as he closed the gate behind him, and walked towards the light amongst the trees.

That was the first day over. In another month it would be Christmas, and the season would be almost over. His work would be easier then, for a few weeks; until February, when it would be time to catch up the pheasants again.

ACKNOWLEDGEMENTS

I would like to acknowledge the use of the following material in the writing of this book:

The Game Conservancy booklets, an article in *The Guardian* entitled 'Grouse Groan' by Martin Woollacott, *The Case Against Badger Digging* published by the League Against Cruel Sports, and *Churchill's Game Shooting* by Macdonald Hastings.

I have quoted directly from an article in the magazine *Birds* published by the R.S.P.B., and also *The Guinness Book of Records*.

'I Wish I Were In Love Again' (from *Babes in Arms*) by Richard Rodgers and Lorenz Hart is reproduced by permission of Chappell & Co. Ltd. © Copyright 1937.

I would like to thank the Yorkshire Arts Association and the English Literature Department of Sheffield University for providing me with the Fellowship which made the writing of this book easier.

I would also like to thank Roy Walker, Macdonald Hastings, Anthea Joseph, and above all, Trevor Jones, without whom this book would not have been possible.

Dear readers,

As well as relying on bookshop sales, And Other Stories relies on subscriptions from people like you for many of our books, whose stories other publishers often consider too risky to take on.

Our subscribers don't just make the books physically happen. They also help us approach booksellers, because we can demonstrate that our books already have readers and fans. And they give us the security to publish in line with our values, which are collaborative, imaginative and 'shamelessly literary'.

All of our subscribers:

- receive a first-edition copy of each of the books they subscribe to
- are thanked by name at the end of our subscriber-supported books
- receive little extras from us by way of thank you, for example: postcards created by our authors

BECOME A SUBSCRIBER,
OR GIVE A SUBSCRIPTION TO A FRIEND

Visit andotherstories.org/subscriptions to help make our books happen. You can subscribe to books we're in the process of making. To purchase books we have already published, we urge you to support your local or favourite bookshop and order directly from them – the often unsung heroes of publishing.

OTHER WAYS TO GET INVOLVED

If you'd like to know about upcoming events and reading groups (our foreign-language reading groups help us choose books to publish, for example) you can:

- join our mailing list at: andotherstories.org
- follow us on Twitter: @andothertweets
- join us on Facebook: facebook.com/AndOtherStoriesBooks
- admire our books on Instagram: @andotherpics
- follow our blog: andotherstories.org/ampersand

The son and grandson of miners, BARRY HINES (1939–2016) was born in the mining village of Hoyland Common, near Barnsley, in what is now South Yorkshire. He attended Ecclesfield Grammar School, on the edge of nearby Sheffield, where he played football so well that he was offered trials for Manchester United, played in the reserves at Barnsley, and represented England in a School Week XI (effectively a national Grammar School Boys team) in a 3–0 loss to Scotland, an experience which enabled him to see 'the class system close up', and 'to place football into some kind of social perspective'. Despite attending a grammar school, he worked first as an apprentice mining surveyor for the National Coal Board, before a miner neighbour's admonishment to 'use his brains' led him to go to college to study Physical Education. He worked as a PE teacher for several years, first in London and later in South Yorkshire, where he wrote novels in the school library after the children had gone home.

He would go on to become a full-time writer, publishing nine novels and writing screenplays for film and television. Hines is often considered to be part of the generation of celebrated Northern writers that included Alan Sillitoe, Stan Barstow, John Braine and Keith Waterhouse, though he was a decade younger than most of them. His debut book, *The Blinder* (1966), was one of the first novels about football. He followed it with a series of novels reflecting the lives of the proletariat: *A Kestrel for a Knave* (1968), an immediate bestseller when published in Great Britain in 1968; *First Signs* (1972); *The Gamekeeper* (1975); *The Price of Coal* (1979); *Looks and Smiles* (1981); *Unfinished Business* (1983); *The Heart of It* (1994); and *Elvis Over England* (1998). By 2002, he had finished the manuscript of a final novel, *Springwood Stars*, a story of a football team in a mining village during a 1920s miners' strike. Never published, And Other Stories will publish *Springwood Stars* in 2024, as well as bringing other Hines classics back into print over the coming years.

Four of his books – *A Kestrel for a Knave*, *The Gamekeeper*, *The Price of Coal* and *Looks and Smiles* – were adapted for the screen by Hines and filmed by Ken Loach. Hines is still best known for *A Kestrel for a Knave*, which became the film *Kes*, regarded as one of the great classics of British cinema. Hines also wrote other successful television and radio plays, including the script to the BAFTA award-winning film *Threads* (1984), a speculative television drama examining the effects of nuclear war on Sheffield that remains a terrifying and beloved example of its genre.